Best wishes
[signature]

MARIO

MARIO

R. G. David

Published by Alderman Publications
6, Northampton Road,
West Haddon
Northamptonshire NN6 7AR
Tel. 01788 510656

Contents © R. G. David 2006

A CIP record for this book is available from
The British Cataloguing in Publication Data Office

ISBN 978 0 9554042 0 7

All rights reserved. No part of this publication may be reproduced,
Stored in a retrieval system, or transmitted at any time or by any means
electronic, mechanical, photocopying, recording or otherwise, without
the prior permission of the publisher.

Printed in Times New Roman by Printondemandworldwide.com

For an old friend, Brian Lane of Briton Ferry.
Who died.

1

I smiled and lowered the binoculars, replacing them in the carrying case slung around my neck. The manoeuvres had been well rehearsed that was obvious, probably out of sight of land or near some isolated coastline and I had watched it all from my vantage point high upon the New Fort.

The boat had come spanking in from the southeast with all canvass set. About a mile out she changed course to avoid an outgoing ferry before turning north past Vidos Island. She was travelling fast, heeled over with a creaming bow wave, her wake boiling astern. Through the glasses I could see Mario's rotund figure at the helm, there were only two other crew on deck, one man crouching at the bow and the other, a woman, standing near the mainmast.

The red ensign streamed out from the stern. It was faded enough to have seen some sea miles but new enough to be picked out by the rays of the afternoon sun before it dipped behind the ramparts whose shadows were already beginning to creep across the port.

Mario had surely planned it this way. Always the showman he was obviously savouring his flamboyant arrival for there were many eyes other than mine to witness it. The masters of the ferries and cargo carriers lined up along the commercial quays, weekend sailors, port officials, customs and immigration officers, they could all have been watching. I'm sure Mario hoped they were for this was no millionaire's luxury yacht, no sleek steel or glassfibre ocean racer. This was a boat from another century and another world, a Bristol Channel pilot cutter, built of timber and painted black and dark green with brass and iron fittings instead of stainless steel.

She passed the anchorage before going about. As the bows came round and the sails began to flap, the staysail came down smartly into a heap at the base of the bowsprit where the crewman tied it into a loose bundle against the port bulwark. She was head on to me then, close hauled and coming for the anchorage at high speed in spite of the reduced canvass. As she turned into the wind Mario threw something over the stern, there was a line paying out after it and she lost way very quickly. I saw the man at the bows kick at something on the foredeck and the anchor dropped with a splash followed by the chain, there was no sound, the stiff offshore breeze taking it away from me.

While the anchor chain was still running out, Mario left the helm and lifted a trestle like contraption near the stern, at the same time the female crew was lowering the mainsail, both gaff and boom coming to rest in the cruck of the trestle. Simultaneously the man at the bow struck the foresail.

The finale to these proceedings was what had brought the smile to my lips. I saw the woman move to the base of the mainmast. She appeared to be tugging at a rope and the small black blob I had noticed at the end of the starboard crosstree broke out into a courtesy flag which streamed out in the wind. It was the familiar blue and white cross and stripes of Greece.

The woman moved to the other side of the mast and began hauling on a halyard. Up to the port crosstree went the European Union flag with its circle of gold stars on the azure blue ground and a little below it the red dragon with white and green background. The flag of Wales.

The timing had been perfect. The sun caught the fluttering colours for several minutes before the creeping rampart shadows dulled them. Mario Franzoni, the Italian Welshman, had arrived in Corfu in spectacular style.

2

All this time Spiro had been sitting beside me on the bench high above the harbour silently chainsmoking. Out of the corner of my eye I saw him take a small vacuum flask from the pocket of his anorak, saw him unscrew the cup, remove the stopper, heard the clink of ice as the liquid poured. Our eyes met as he raised the cup.

"Yammas," he grinned.

"You shouldn't be drinking ouzo, you're supposed to be driving me," I said.

"Only little ouzo. Plenty lemonade. Mario say okay," he replied.

"Mario won't be sitting in your car."

"Mario pay me. You not," he countered taking a drink. He had a point but even so I was about to argue when the sound of a mobile phone interrupted me. I looked around at the general area but we were alone. Spiro pulled the instrument from an inside pocket and placed it to his ear. "Nai?" He listened nodding from time to time and after a moment or two he handed it to me, "is Mario," he said, "for you."

I took the phone and spoke into it, "Mario?"

"Jim. You made it then. Look I've booked a table for tonight. Spiro knows where, he'll drive you. Be about nine thirty."

"How did you manage to fix up a package deal for me this late in the season?" I asked.

"I've got friends in the travel business," he replied.

I said nothing, wondering what had prompted him to contact me with his mysterious proposition in the first place. It wasn't as if we knew each other all that well. We had both been apprentices at the same Midlands company in the days when the UK still had an engineering industry and we had both lived in the same apprentice hostel for a time but his crowd were not my crowd. We called him the Welsh Wop. Not to his face of course for he was a fiery little devil at times and he knocked around with some pretty tough rugby players from his neck of the woods.

No, the time we really met was years later at a reunion dinner. I had been standing at the bar getting drinks for Jean and me when the dumpy balding figure beside me said: "I know you don't I?" It was Mario. He was unaccompanied, having travelled up from Wales by train and booked into a B & B for the weekend. I had introduced him to Jean and they hit it off straightaway, the mutual interest? Sailing.

I did manage to prise them apart and have a chat with him during the evening and we exchanged youthful memories and chewed the fat about the old days. That's the trouble with reunions, all there is to talk about is the past, still it was an enjoyable night and I met others there with whom I had much more in common and to be honest I didn't expect to see or hear of Mario again.

That must have been all of four years ago now, for Jean and I have been apart at least two. In fact that was how Mario had managed to contact me, through Jean at our old address. She had given him a list of the agencies I worked through and eventually he tracked me down. At that time I was coming to the end of a pipework design contract at an office off Euston Square. He had telephoned me there.

"So listen," Mario went on, "you get Spiro to show you around Corfu Town this evening. Do some shopping, drink some ouzo, chill out a bit but remember, the table's booked for nine thirty. See you."

I offered the phone back to Spiro but he waved it aside. "No, Mario say you keep," he said and passed me the charging unit that went with it, I stuffed them into the pockets of my fleece. "Mario say I gotta show you Old Town, OK?"

"Lead on," I replied.

Looking back, that initial contact by phone in London was as bizarre as all that followed. He had asked me how I was, what I was doing these days, if I still enjoyed engineering. When I said yes he just laughed before going off into a coughing bout. "Engineering is finished man," he said breathlessly, "didn't you hear those Whitehall pundits say we could live without a manufacturing industry in this country?"

"Well . . .."

"Listen boyo, I took them at their word, OK there was money in the family and I got more than my share I suppose, just in time as it happened. Remember the Welsh coal industry?" Before I could answer he went on, "another of their expendable items. Mind you we were lucky, we'd made a lot of money in the halcyon days before that so a lot of it filtered down to me. You ever heard of a place called . . . . . ," the phone clicked and went dead for an instant then he was back on the line, "it's on the coast about . . . What was that clicking?"

8

"Just the phone lines I think," I said defensively. "Look Mario I am at work you know and I'm getting some dirty looks from my snotty boss."

"They're probably monitoring your calls, recording them even. The swines are up to anything to grind you down. So when does this contract of yours finish?"

"About three weeks."

"Right, well how do you fancy a paid holiday in the sun?"

"For how long?"

"What does that matter if you're being paid?"

"I don't suppose it does when you put it like that."

"You tied up with a woman or something?"

"No, it's just . . ."

"Not with a man?"

"Christ no."

"Just checking. There are those who've got me pegged for a nancy boy just because I've always been single. Look, it'll be four to six weeks in the Med. Just pencil in the first week in October, I'll get back to you. You got a mobile number?"

"No," I said, "I don't own a mobile."

"No mobile phone? The whole bloody world and his dog's got a mobile. How come you haven't?"

"Anyone wants me they write or phone me on the landline and leave a message. I can access my voicemail from anywhere."

"No email?"

"No computer except the one at work and I don't use that for private emails, too easily monitored by the management." In the end I gave him the phone number of the boarding house I was staying at in Cambden Town.

The contract ran on for another five weeks in fact, taking me close to Mario's pencilled in date and as I was packing my things together in the office on that last Friday afternoon he phoned me again: "That bloody contract finished yet?"

"Today," I answered.

"We're cutting it fine mind. Now listen, you got somewhere I can send your travel docs to?" I gave him my permanent address in Coventry, the small terraced house backing onto the railway that I had bought with the proceeds of the separation. It still had a mortgage on it so without Mario's offer of payment this trip would have been out. "I'll get everything sent to you over the weekend," he continued, "you got a passport I presume?" I told him I had and then I asked him about pay. "I'll put it all in with the docs," he said.

"But what if . . ."

"If it's not acceptable?"

"Well, yes."

"Just phone me and tell me and we'll call the whole thing off OK?"

"OK," I said weakly, feeling a little small to be haggling over pay when what I should actually have been asking about was the real reason behind all this. Mario had said holiday but it was clear to me even then that there was more to it. He had never mentioned the fact of our marriage break up although Jean must obviously have told him.

I wondered what else she had told him.

3

The place was just coming back to life after the midday 'siesta' as Spiro led me around the narrow streets of the Old Town. We passed the shoe shops, the leathergoods shops and the clothes shops. We looked in at the woodcarving shops, the antique shops and the cheapy tourist shops. We stopped at a small bar and drank some ouzo as Mario had instructed and later I bought a new leather wallet for myself. And so the time passed.

I remembered the last time I visited Corfu with Jean. We were celebrating our wedding anniversary, the second or third I think, I'm not sure now. We had stayed at . . . .

Spiro had stopped some way ahead, he glanced back pointing to his wristwatch. I caught up with him. "Time to go soon," he said.

"Where did you say we were eating?" I asked.

"Kassiopi," he replied.

Kassiopi!

Kassiopi where Jean and I had spent that idyllic fortnight before we split. Now why had Mario chosen Kassiopi I wondered. "It's quite a long way," I said.

"About one hour maybe," Spiro shrugged, "but I gotta get gas first."

"Who's idea was it to eat at Kassiopi?" I asked, "when there's all the restaurants we need right here in Corfu Town."

Spiro shrugged again, "Mario say Kassiopi," he said, "so . . . ," another shrug and a spreading of hands.

During that anniversary holiday Jean and I had found this delightful restaurant in Kassiopi. We ate there most nights and now here was Mario booking a table . . . . I thought, if all this is some kind of reconciliation scheme hatched up by the two of them . . . .

Spiro led the way out of the maze of streets that was the Old Town to the place where he had parked his battered old Fiat. I chose to sit in the back, partly for safety and partly because I was still tired from my flight and hoped to have a doze.

The flight from Birmingham had been in the early hours, a 'flight only' deal arranged by Mario. All the details had been in the large envelope I had to sign for on a chilly doorstep one morning together with a copy of a standing order which would credit my account with a generous monthly allowance, more than enough to cover all my domestic expenses.

There was also a handwritten note from Mario telling me that Spiro would be waiting at Corfu airport holding up a card with 'Mr Agnew' written on it. I was to introduce myself using my real name, all very cloak and dagger and I wondered why.

I had no sleep during the slow and bumpy journey north along the coast road. Spiro chainsmoked and I opened the window to dispel the fug, we spoke very little for the radio was turned up in order to be heard over the exhaust noise from the broken silencer. Once I tapped him on the shoulder, "what are those lights over there?" I asked pointing across the blackness of the sea.

"Albania," he said as he flicked a cigarette butt through the open window.

"They look very close."

"They are. So close I could spit there!" He laughed and reached for another cigarette as I sank back and tried to sleep.

We rolled into Kassiopi about nine and parked close by the harbour. "I have sleep now," Spiro announced tucking his head deep into the hood of his anorak and squirming down into his seat, his arms folded and, for once, not smoking.

"I think I'll stretch my legs for a bit," I said.

"Is OK. I be here all time," he mumbled.

I got out stiffly then reached inside the car for my fleece for there was a chilly wind blowing. The small, almost circular harbour was just as I remembered it, the boats tied up to the quay, bobbing and bumping together. The lights reflected in the dark waters and behind me the restaurants and tavernas, some already closed as it was nearing the end of the holiday season.

I had some time to kill so I walked round to the far side of the harbour and then back again past the sleeping Spiro to the other end. All the time I was thinking of Jean, the good times we had here during that holiday, and all the other good times before she met up with . . . . . Still, if it hadn't been the smooth talking bastard she was crewing for during those weekend sailing races, it would probably have been someone else.

I made my way to the restaurant Spiro had indicated. The restaurant Mario had specified, strangely the very same restaurant Jean and I had frequented so much that we had called it *our* restaurant. I was shown to the table Mario had reserved.

"Just soda water please," I replied to the waiter and sat awaiting my host. The table was set for four and I began speculating on the company. There had been three people on the boat, three that I saw anyway, there may have been more below. I wondered absently how many people it took to handle Mario's boat, it was a measure of my total ignorance of sailing that I assumed a larger crew to be aboard and I was to find out eventually just how few could do the job and just how quickly one can learn when one has to.

Yesterday after I had introduced myself to Spiro at the airport, he had driven me north to Sidari. That was another place Jean and I had visited during our holiday.

"You know Sidari?" I had asked Spiro.

"Sidari is my home village," he replied, "is now a bloody building site, you'll see." He had pulled up outside a two storey building near the centre and in spite of my protestations insisted on carrying my stuff up to a first floor apartment. He looked briefly around the place, nodded his approval and left saying he would pick me up the next day at 3pm, Mario's instructions he said.

I spent the rest of that first day lazing in the sun on the beach and most of the evening in the quietest taverna I could find taking a long time to drink three large scotch and sodas while skimming through the previous day's copy of The Telegraph. Eventually I went back to my accommodation and tried to sleep, the noise from the street and from a foul mouthed Liverpool couple in the apartment below gradually fading as sleep overtook me.

Next day I was up and about early, long before the late season holidaymakers showed themselves. I walked along the deserted beach past the sunbeds and beach umbrellas made ready for the sun worshippers to baste themselves. I found a restaurant serving full English breakfast and went inside and ordered. This was something Jean and I never did, if we went to Greece we ate Greek, if to Spain we ate Spanish, if to France? Well, there are limits. Anyway I was hungry, Spiro was not due to pick me up until 3pm so I had the entire morning to myself. I felt fresh and alive in spite of a relatively short sleep, it was a relief to be away from the air conditioned confines of that dreary London office with its petty bureaucracy and its power hungry minions, the only thing in its favour? The money.

The sun was not oppressively hot this late in the year, even so I stopped at a tourist shop and bought a cheap straw panama before strolling gently along the beach to Canal d'Amour and back to walk off my breakfast. I had decided beforehand to hire a bicycle so I made my way to a bike hire shop near the centre. To my surprise the proprietor was English and, in addition to repair kit and helmet, I was given a map with suggested routes marked upon it.

The map remained folded in my pocket as I pedalled out along the Peroulades road. I turned left after a while and left again until reaching the track that Jean and I had walked along that summer. Alternately riding and walking I made may way up through the olive groves passing the weirdly misshapen tree where I had taken her picture then along the undulating path where the old woman had been collecting olives, arriving eventually in Avliotes village. Once again I stood outside the small café where we had both grimaced over our Greek coffee.

Strange how this revisit was affecting me. Everywhere I looked reminded me of her, I could see her sitting there across from me, remember little things like when she dropped her keys and the waiter picked them up for her. It was all so long ago now and yet . . .

"Mr. Grayson?" I looked up from my reverie at the tall young man. He had a mop of black curly hair and a two day stubble of the designer variety. The black hair together with his deep set brown eyes and dark stubble made his weatherbeaten tan look paler than it was. I nodded and went to stand up but he waved me back to my chair, "you're waiting for Mario," he said blandly, "I'm afraid he's . . . . indisposed. You'll have to put up with me." He thrust out his hand, "I'm Neil. Neil Armitage, I help crew on Mario's boat."

We shook hands. So this was the nimble figure who had handled the sails at the bows and then dropped the anchor. I hoped that my face did not betray the disappointment I felt. I had been looking forward to meeting Mario all day, his disembodied voice on the phone or scrawled notes in the post had been my only contact since that reunion and now I was faced with a total stranger, a young man at that, whose dinner conversation would probably revolve around football or fast cars.

"Take a seat," I said, "indisposed you say?" I gave him a knowing look. Mario's exploits on the rugby field may not have been impressive but afterwards, after the loud and lewd songs in the baths as they washed off the mud and the blood and the sweat, back in the clubhouse, he and his mates could certainly drink some beer. Even at the reunion he must have drunk four or five pints to my one or two, so naturally I assumed his indisposition to be a hangover after celebrations to mark his safe and snazzy arrival yesterday. How wrong I was.

"I had to . . ." he paused, "he's not too well today. He asked me to apologise and keep you company and, well, fill you in on things but . . ."

"But?"

"Look Mr. Grayson, I understand you and Mario go back a long way, even so I don't feel I can tell you what his plans are. Anyway he hasn't told me all of it and even if he had I'd rather he told you himself."

"He invited me on a paid holiday," I said.

"Yes, well me too actually, but my function was rather obvious."

"And mine?"

"That's just it I don't know. You're no sailor he tells me."

"Far from it," I laughed and was on the point of telling him about Jean's passion for dinghy racing then I thought better of it. "No," I said, "the first I knew there was a boat involved was when his man Spiro picked me up this afternoon to watch your rather flashy arrival in Corfu harbour."

He smiled, his face creasing up, exposing white teeth their brightness accentuated by that black hair and stubble. "It was rather good," he said it without bravado, "we practiced it a lot."

"I guessed as much." I nodded to the other two place settings, "are more of the crew coming along tonight?" I asked.

"More?"

"I saw a woman on board and there are others I take it?"

"No," he smiled, "there are no others, just her Mario and me. I think she might have come along if Mario had been . . .OK but then again maybe not. She's gone shopping in Corfu Town," he added scornfully.

"Just like a woman," I said.

"As you say. Well, shall we order?" I had been so wrapped up in my memories of Jean that I had not even glanced at the menu and suddenly I realised how hungry I was having eaten nothing since that big breakfast. My eyes swept down the sections printed in English. I ordered saganaki to start, with Greek salad and lamb kleftiko to follow plus a jug of the local red wine.

"You said that your function was obvious," I said, "what did you mean?" He looked at me through a haze of smoke as he lit a cigarette and I had the distinct impression that he was thinking up an acceptable, if not entirely truthful, answer.

"Well boat crew of course," he replied, "I normally do the cooking on board. I speak Italian and a little Greek so I do the shopping and deal with the port authorities when necessary."

"You sound fairly indispensable."

"No one is that they say. Anyway Mario speaks Italian fluently but I expect you knew that."

"No I didn't actually," I said, "I know he could swear in Welsh and sing those foul rugger songs along with the rest of his Welsh mates. But that was when we were apprentices, a long time ago."

"But you knew he was Italian?"

"I knew he was of Italian extraction but I assumed it was generations back and he was just another Taffy with an Italian name."

The waiter brought the bread and I poured us some wine. I was keen to know the real reason behind Mario's invitation whilst enjoying a leisurely meal in familiar surroundings which harboured happy memories. "What are Mario's immediate plans, d'you know?" I asked.

"Tomorrow if he's . . . OK, I think he wants you to join ship at Corfu Town, then we'll sail round to Sidari and spend a few days there. He can tell you all about it then."

"Do you really not know what it's all about?" I asked.

"I know some of it," he admitted looking at me across the rim of his wine glass as if gauging the moment. "It goes back to World War 2 I believe. Something to do with a relative I think. And an icon."

4

A drop of wine fell from my open mouth onto the tablecloth. I knew almost nothing about icons, only that they were to do with religion and were usually worth a lot of money to those who collected them. "An icon?" I repeated.

"Yes, a very old one, from Italy he says. Stolen or liberated or looted, depending on your point of view, from a monastery."

"So has he got it with him? Is he trying to sell it or what?"

"He hasn't...look, I really think you'll have to ask him yourself. If he had been able to come tonight I'm sure he would have told you."

"Has he asked you not to tell me about all this? I mean, I know he's paying me to take this so called holiday but what with false names at the airport and now an icon possibly worth a fortune ...."

"I don't know that it is worth a fortune," Neil interrupted, "anyway, Mario's not at all concerned about its value. Monetary value that is." The waiter brought the saganaki, the smell wafting up and making my mouth water. It also brought back more memories of Jean and that far off summer.

"So what is he up to?" I asked, "this gets more mysterious by the minute."

"How well do you know him Mr. Grayson?"

"Jim please," I said. The young man was making me feel very old with his formality. "The thing is," I admitted, "I hardly know him at all really" and I told him about our chance meeting at the reunion four years back, our fleeting contacts during our apprenticeship and the way he had contacted me, presumably through Jean.

He looked thoughtful. "You see," he said, "I've not known him long but I do know him rather well. He's very theatrical, well you saw his arrival in Corfu harbour," I nodded. "I have heard some of his story and I know he is the one who would want to tell it to you. I don't know where or how but you must have made quite an impression on him all those years back. Unless you were the only one to recognise him at that reunion, who knows?"

I savoured another mouthful of saganaki washed down with more wine, Greek music came from somewhere triggering once again thoughts of Jean and the magic of the island. "Let me say this," he went on, "Mario is paying me also. I too have financial commitments and this cruise has already lasted two weeks, it could last another three, four even." I said nothing, savouring the wine, which was already having an effect due to my empty stomach. "I met him in Cardiff just over a year ago," he continued, "we got talking, he mentioned his boat and sailing generally and I crewed for him whenever I could." He looked wistful and there was a note of admiration in his voice as he added, "he's an exceptionally good sailor but then he has to be sailing in those waters."

"Which waters would they be?" I asked.

"The Bristol Channel," he replied, "and right up the Severn estuary, even to Gloucester. The tidal range is enormous, especially during spring tides and the currents . . ." he shook his head, "you have to be good to survive but then he's got the boat for it." He went on to describe the attributes of the Bristol Channel pilot cutter, most of it going way over my head. Mario's boat was based at Porthcawl, Neil told me, a small harbour on the South Wales coast. There was a family business connection there, a café or restaurant and Mario had an attic flat overlooking the sea.

The waiter brought the main course and I asked for another jug of wine, it was at just the right temperature with a mellow fruity smoothness typical of the reds of the region. I was feeling tired, it was the evening of the day after the flight, always the time when tiredness catches up and my lethargy was that much greater because of the wine.

Although intrigued by the secrets behind Mario's invitation I was becoming less anxious to know all about it as the serenity of the island soaked into me. This was how it had been with Jean, we had loved our stay here in spite of the rowdy tavernas which we usually avoided. The food the wine the twinkling lights across the harbour, it was all such a contrast to my frenetic London contract. I thought, thank god that's over for a while at least and not only was it all for free, I was getting paid as well.

"I've been thinking," I said at last, "Mario must be very well off to be able to afford to pay us both, plus Spiro, to help him do whatever it is he's doing."

"I think he's inherited money and property over the years," Neil explained, "anyway it hasn't cost as much as it would have to hire professionals."

"OK we're affordable but why? Why is he doing all this?"

"I'm sure he'll tell us when he's ready."

We continued our meal in silence. It seemed to me that whatever Mario was up to it was costing him plenty and there must be a payoff somewhere. Why else would he be paying out, especially for me, not even a sailor, cook or linguist and practically a stranger apart from a far off apprenticeship in an industry he had long ago forsaken.

"Is Spiro taking you back to Sidari?" Neil's voice broke into my thoughts.

"I expect so. He said he'd be waiting in the car, why?"

"Just wondered if you fancied a lift back on my motor bike."

"That's how you came here from Corfu Town?"

"Yes. It's a good one, 650 Honda. I hired it for a few days."

"My motor cycling days are long gone," I replied, "still, it's a nice night. OK, just don't go too fast."

After the meal I walked back down to the harbour to tell Spiro that Neil was giving me a lift back. "Is OK," he said bleary eyed, "I see you tomorrow." He passed me a plastic shopping bag containing the mobile phone charger and my binoculars before reaching for his flask of ouzo under the dashboard.

Once again I walked along the row of tethered boats, once again the thought of Jean and our distant relationship almost bringing a lump to my throat. I wondered what she was doing now, if her sailor boy lover was still part of her life. If I would ever see her again and if I did what my reaction would be.

I can't say that I enjoyed the ride back. The night was cold and the road tortuous. We stopped once and walked into an olive grove to relieve ourselves, there was no moon and the stars gave scant illumination to the gnarled trunks. The silence was overpowering, it was almost a relief to hear the distant sound of a motorcycle as some teenager returned home.

When Neil dropped me outside my apartment in Sidari I just thanked him and said goodnight. I turned in straight away and slept like a log.

5

I was awakened at 9am by a loud banging on the door. "Who's that?" I shouted.

"Is Spiro," he replied gruffly. I got up and let him in.

"I didn't expect you so soon," I said, "is anything wrong?"

"Is bloody Mario," he snapped, "he give me big bollocking."

"Why?"

"He say to me: 'where you fix up Jim with accommodation?' I say: 'my cousin has flat near cross roads. It got small cooker, nice bed and all that.' He say: 'I wanted him fix up in comfortable hotel, not some self-catering fleapit'. So I get angry. I say: 'My cousin got good apartments, clean apartments. Top holiday company lease from him, is not fleapit.'"

Mario was evidently feeling much better this morning I thought as I tried to suppress a smile at Spiro's discomfiture. "So what now?" I asked.

"You get packed," he replied, "I make arrangement for you. You pack up OK?"

I packed my case and hand luggage while Spiro paced up and down the small room smoking furiously. Finally he carried my stuff down to the street and I followed a few paces behind as he led the way to the big hotel. He had booked me into a second floor room at the rear of the building away from the noise of the street. It was small but I could see that it had recently been refurbished to a very high standard. As I was unpacking my things Spiro rang room service, he spoke very fast in Greek for several seconds before replacing the receiver, then he left with just a wave of his hand.

I wandered out onto my private balcony and sat down on a cane chair to admire the view. Below me the hotel pool was fringed with palm trees and surrounded by empty sunbeds. The small harbour with its motley collection of fishing boats was away to my right and the full sweep of the bay from Cape Drastis to the headland shimmered in the morning sun. The mountains of Albania, their tips already sprinkled with snow, loomed above the haze.

I still felt sleepy having been awakened by Spiro's frantic knocking and I must have dozed off because the next thing I remembered was the arrival of cereal with fruit juice and scrambled egg on toast. I ate it sitting at a small table on the balcony and washed the meal down with some excellent coffee which had obviously been freshly ground, I was beginning to appreciate Mario's generous hospitality. I spent the next hour or so unashamedly lazing.

About midday the mobile phone rang. I had completely forgotten about it and for a moment could not locate the bleeping, I eventually retrieved it from my fleece in the wardrobe and placed it to my ear. A familiar voice said "Hello? It's Mario. Where are you?"

"I'm sitting in this swank hotel admiring a wonderful view. All thanks to you I believe."

"That Spiro. What a wanker. Bloody Greek see, if he can keep things in the family he's happy. You comfy there?"

"It's luxurious Mario, what's the catch?"

"There's no catch boyo, just enjoy the holiday. Sorry about last night, I wasn't feeling too good see."

"When are we going to meet?" I asked.

"That's why I rang. Neil and I will be sailing around later today hopefully, I'll contact you soon. Get your mobile on charge for the next few hours OK?"

"OK." I rang off and plugged the instrument into the mains using the unit Spiro had left with me. Later I wandered down to the beach and hired a small outboard for a couple of hours, I headed out to sea then turned along the coast towards Cape Drastis. I got as far as the headland before a freshening wind kicked up a choppy sea and I turned back under the shadow of the towering cliffs and past the little coves and the bizarre rock formations.

This was something that Jean and I had wanted to do during our holiday but the boats had always been fully booked. Now, late in the season, there were only three of them in use, the others tethered in a string along the shoreline. I steered for the buoyed fairway between the shallows and cut the engine as the tee shirted blonde waded out to meet me. "Everything OK?" she asked in a Scandinavian accent.

"Fine." I stepped over the stern barefooted soaking my jeans to the knees then wandered along to the harbour carrying my shoes until I dried out.

There was no message from Mario that day. About 7pm Spiro rang me through the hotel switchboard and asked if I was OK. He was drinking with some friends down at the coffee shop near the centre but I declined his invitation to join them, I would have been like a fish out of water. At that time I had him down as a simple Corfiot peasant, another example of how first impressions can be misleading.

I enjoyed an excellent dinner in the hotel that evening sitting next to some English tourists who were returning home the following day. They were full of talk about their imminent return to the ratrace, about how marvellous their holiday had been but now it was back to real life. I felt a strange pang of homesickness listening to them, little knowing how long it would be before I would return. I drank rather too much brandy at the hotel bar and retired early.

The following morning was grey and misty. I went down for a late breakfast returning to my room some time after nine. I had forgotten to unplug the mobile from the charging unit so I did that and went out onto the balcony and sat facing the sea. Visibility was poor and the entire scene was one of dismal greyness, it was not cold but I still put on my fleece to keep out the damp. Gradually through the murk, which seemed to ebb and flow in intensity, I thought I saw a boat some way out from the harbour. I retrieved my binoculars.

As the small vessel came into focus I recognised it as a Mirror dinghy. It was being rowed quite expertly towards the harbour by Neil Armitage, Mario's boat was presumably anchored beyond the limit of visibility.

I watched as the boat rounded the harbour wall, it was hidden for a while by the gaggle of craft moored there before turning for the beach. As he neared the shore Neil gave one or two strong pulls on the oars forcing the dinghy well onto the sand and enabling him to step out over the prow without getting his feet wet. He started to walk towards the main street and I lost sight of him behind some buildings.

Some time later the room telephone rang and I picked it up to be told that a Mr. Armitage was in the lobby and could I come down. I packed some things in my hand luggage bag, locked the balcony door and went down.

"'Morning Jim. Sleep OK?" Neil looked fresh as a daisy, the dark stubble on his face no longer than it had been two days before. I wondered absently how he kept it like that.

"Fine thanks," I replied, "I take it you're going to row me out to meet Mario?"

"You saw me come in then. Yes, the cutter's about a mile offshore, the waters around here are very shallow. By the way I've had to do some shopping," he held up several carrier bags, "d'you mind?" I took the largest one, left my key at reception and we made for the harbour.

Neil held the dinghy steady as I clambered aboard and sat near the stern then he pushed off, stepped aboard and sat in the middle to take up the oars. "No outboard then?" I asked.

"No. Mario hates the internal combustion engine, so do I for that matter. Much better to exert oneself and it's quieter of course." He rowed us towards the harbour entrance past the string of moored yellow motor boats, one of which I had hired yesterday. The mist seemed to thicken as we rounded the end of the harbour wall and Neil paused in his rowing, looking down at a compass the size of a saucer mounted inside a polished mahogany box.

"They promised this fog," he said, "so I took a bearing on the harbour when we anchored last night. I'm just rowing out on the back bearing." Bearings and back bearings. That was a subject that came up later but there in the dinghy I just hoped he knew what he was doing and we could find Mario's boat.

Presently I glanced behind to find that the harbour had been swallowed up in the mist. We were afloat in a grey silent world then, only the splash of the oars and creaking rowlocks. Away to my right, in the direction of the unseen shore, came the occasional faint sound of a pneumatic drill and I remembered Spiro's comment about Sidari and building sites.

Suddenly, ahead and slightly to my left, the mist became darker and out of the greyness where the sea and the mist became one, the shape of the pilot cutter emerged. It was much bigger than I had imagined as it loomed above us. Neil came alongside grabbing the iron ladder which hung down from the bulwark. "Mario," he shouted, "we're back." There was no answer. He shot an anxious glance at me, "I thought he'd be up by now," he said quietly, "that sail up here yesterday was a bit much for him I think."

"Indisposed again I expect," I said smiling, "does he still put it away like he used to?"

"Put it away?"

"Beer," I said, "he and his rugger mates used to get through six or seven pints each after a match I believe."

Neil's face was serious as he sat holding onto the ladder, the sound of water dripping onto the deck above as the swirling mist condensed on the rigging. He said, "you *do* know what's wrong with him don't you?"

"Wrong with him?"

"I assumed you knew, that he must have told you."

"He hasn't said anything to me."

"I see."

"Well?"

We sat in silence for a few moments, the dinghy rocking gently, Neil glanced up at the empty deck then down at the compass sitting in its mahogany box. "You see," he said, "I am a qualified nurse. I work at a hospice in Cardiff and I met Mario while accompanying a patient for treatment at the same hospital he was at," he paused and looked me in the eyes. "Mario has lung cancer," he said softly, "it's terminal and it's at an advanced stage."

"Jesus Christ Almighty," I breathed.

6

Neil climbed aboard and I handed up the bags of groceries then, having tied the painter to the ladder, I followed. I felt numb. The revelation about Mario had hit me like a sledgehammer, now I understood the breathless voice on the telephone, the frequent coughing bouts while all the time his usual banter and good humour belied his condition.

I stood on the soaking deck waiting. Neil had gone below with the stores and was presumably attending to his charge. As I stood there the light seemed to intensify, I looked up at the masthead, at the courtesy flags hanging limply from the crosstrees. There was blue sky up there, the mist was low lying obviously and as I looked the sun broke through. It was as if an oven door had been thrown open, within minutes the mist was torn apart, it dispersed into isolated patches around the boat and even as I watched they evaporated under the heat of the sun. A voice behind me said, "ah, that's better," and I turned to see Neil emerge from below.

"How is he?" I asked.

"Still asleep. We'll leave him for now, can you give me a hand with the sun canopy?" So together we rigged the white canvass cover which gave shelter from the sun, now blazing down from a cloudless sky, then we erected a pair of deck chairs beneath it. "Fancy a swim?" Neil asked.

"Not for me," I replied, "I think I'd like a drink. Whisky preferably."

"I'm sorry to break it to you like that. I really thought you knew."

"There's no easy way to say that sort of thing. I'm just stunned."

"I'll get you that drink," he said and went below.

When he returned we sat under the canopy without saying anything for some time as I sipped at the drink. The deck was steaming as the sun dried everything out and I squinted against the glare as I admired the view over towards Roda. A breeze had sprung up fluttering the flags and ruffling the waters of the anchorage, I put my glass down on the small table Neil had set up between us.

"Fancy that swim now?" he asked but I shook my head. "Well I'm going in anyway," he said. He stood up and walked to the bow, stripped off all his clothes and dived in, naked as an egg.

A voice behind me said, "Fine body on him mind." I turned and there was Mario, holding onto the rigging for support. I stood up. "Sit down boyo, sit down," he said and he shuffled across and sank into Neil's deckchair. This was not the Mario I remembered. He was fatter and slower, he had a high colour and his grasp when we shook hands felt clammy.

"Can I get you anything?" I asked.

"A can of lager would go down a treat," he replied, "it's in the cool box down in the galley, you'll find it." I left him there watching Neil swimming around the boat, his crawl like his rowing, quite flawless. I envied him his youth and his athleticism. I found the cool box after a minute or so and returned with the lager, Mario opened the can and sat back, "well sunshine," he smiled, "we meet at last."

"Been a long time," I replied.

"Four years since that bloody reunion. Time flies as they say."

"You traced me through Jean yes?" I asked.

"Aye aye. Took some doing too, you move about a lot apparently."

"That's contracting."

"Sooner you than me boyo," he took a long pull at the lager and wiped his lips then he sat up. "Where's that silly bugger off to now?" I followed his gaze to see Neil some distance off, striking out across the bay. Mario pulled a small pair of binoculars from the pocket of his dressing gown and trained them on the swimmer. "Ah," he said, "he's making for that raft thing over there, that's where the tourists do their paragliding from during the season. He pointed and handed me the glasses. The platform was about half a mile away and I watched until Neil reached it, he hauled himself up onto it and lay there spreadeagled in the sun. I handed the binoculars back to Mario and he trained them on the raft, "posy sod," he snorted, "got no shame at all has he?"

"There's no one about though," I replied.

"He wouldn't care if there was," Mario took another swig from the lager can, "ah that's better, that cool box is worth the world." We sat looking across at each other. I don't know what Mario was thinking but I was remembering standing with a group of youngsters, Mario in the middle, receiving apprenticeship indentures from the local mayor. I have the photo still, somewhere amongst the stuff I brought to Coventry.

"Neil told me about . . ."

"About my complaint?"

"Yes."

"Ah well," he sighed, "nothing to be done about it see, so may as well carry on." He leaned back in the deckchair. "I reckon I picked this up when I was working at a foundry in the Midlands. They had this new fangled system, like a lost wax casting process but using something like polystyrene for the mould. Well, you can imagine the fumes that gave off!"

"You stayed on in the Midlands then?"

"For a while. I kept going back to Wales for family funerals, that's where the money came in, property and businesses disposed of and shared out, in the end I went back for good. Couldn't stand Midlanders anyway, work like buggery all week then it's car boot sales or bloody garden centres on Sunday. You're still there though, Coventry isn't it?"

"Yes."

"Where did you come from originally, I've forgotten."

"Kent."

"Ah yes, where they also had a mining industry once," he chuckled and then he began to cough. The bout went on for some time before he gasped, "do us a favour, bottom . . .bottom of the companionway . . . oxygen bottle . . .fetch it up by here for me." I was on my feet at once and fetched the bottle, I helped him with the mask before turning the thing onto the setting he had marked. He lay back for a while breathing the life giving gas as I watched him anxiously. Presently he removed the mask and turned off the cylinder, "you see," he said breathlessly, "there's something I've got to do."

"Is it something to do with this icon Neil told me about?" I asked. "I believe that's why I'm here isn't it? On this so-called holiday?"

"All in good time boyo," he said, "arrangements got to be made see and you've only just got here. Chill out, relax, switch off for five minutes, you're not in that bloody London office now." He drained the lager can noisily and put it down on the table. "See that island over there?" He pointed towards the northeast, "that's Erikousa, peaceful, quiet, none of this holiday resort stuff. The wind's got some strength in it now. As soon as Neil gets back we'll up anchor and away."

I looked across at the distant raft. There was no movement from Neil, he seemed to be as laid back as Mario, as unhurried as the island itself. I relaxed into the canvass of the deckchair.

A mobile phone warbled somewhere and Mario retrieved the instrument from his dressing gown pocket, he spoke into it. "Hello? Ah Spiro. Did you get fixed up?" He glanced at me smiling, "what sort? Bloody Toyota? I wanted a Range Rover," he paused listening intently and nodding from time to time. "Oh well that'll have to do. What about the other thing? Good. No that will be fine, see you."

He put the phone down on the table between us. The wind had pushed the boat around so that we were facing Mount Pantocrator, behind its towering bulk dark thunderheads were slowly building as the midday heat became even more oppressive. "Jim," Mario said suddenly, "what do you consider is the worst aspect of society? Hatred? Racial prejudice? What?"

"Hatred I suppose," I answered.

"No," he countered, "hatred you can fight, you can hate right back. Shall I tell you what I think?" I raised an eyebrow. "It's indifference," he asserted, "nobody gives a shit about anybody else unless they're very close, family or lovers or something. Everyone's too bloody busy to bother about anybody else, all paddling their own canoe to god knows where, when will people realise that they've only got each other, nothing else. That's what I like about that poser," he nodded towards the raft where Neil still lay stretched out in the sun. "He is the most compassionate person I've ever met. OK I know it's his job, as a hospice nurse I mean, but it goes further than that. He really cares, really *feels* for his patients and I don't mean just me, I've seen how he is with others."

"He always seems concerned about you," I said.

"He would be concerned about anyone, anyone at all if he thought they were in any sort of trouble, that's the kind of bloke he is," he paused, "mind you he *is* a queer."

"What? A homosexual?"

"Oh aye. Now that would have bothered me at one time, the thought of living cheek by jowl with a shirt lifter. Well, you remember how we all used to be about brown hatters?" I nodded. "I don't even think about it where he's concerned. I suppose we get more tolerant as we get older eh?"

Thunder rolled in the distance and I turned and watched as Neil stood up on the raft. He stretched and yawned before diving into the water and swimming swiftly, effortlessly towards us.

7

The anchor chain lay closely zig-zagged upon the deck as I stood near the bows waiting for Mario's signal. We were close to the shore of Erikousa Island in the lee of the low harbour wall running under foresail alone, Neil having struck the main about a quarter of a mile out.

Mario put the helm hard over and as we came up into the wind he waved and I kicked at the retaining pin. The anchor splashed into the clear blue water and the chain rattled out after it, the foresail came down smartly and suddenly everything was quiet, we were at anchor. The breeze which seemed to have such power when the sails were set was no more than a zephyr now. It had taken us most of the afternoon to sail across to the island. We had practiced various manoeuvres during the crossing, all for my benefit of course, and I had enjoyed every minute of it.

Between us Neil and I rigged the sun canopy once again and afterwards he said to me: "I'll get us some grub, you sit and have a chat with Mario, Greek salad with carbonara OK?" I nodded. I was extremely hungry, something to do with the fresh air and the exercise.

Mario and I sat upon the deckchairs beneath the canvass, two large glasses of gin and tonic with ice and lemon within easy reach. Corfu was invisible, enveloped by a menacing black cloud shot through from time to time by forked lightning.

"That's perfect," Mario said.

"Why?" I asked.

He winked mysteriously, "soften the ground a bit see, just as long as it don't go on for days. Mind you, I seen the forecast, it should be fine tomorrow or the day after. We'll see."

I sank back into the deckchair and sipped at the ice cold drink. I was thinking of the old days then, of an impecunious apprenticeship in a Midland town as foreign to me as it had been to Mario and all the others who had been drawn to the place because of its engineering reputation. I remembered a younger Mario, noisy and foolish as we all were then, carefree even, absorbing the skills of our trade almost without knowing it. And now. Now Mario, cheerful as ever, was sitting beside me. Dying.

My face must have betrayed my mood for Mario turned and punched me playfully on the arm. "Cheer up boyo," he said, "you've got a face like a German tourist. What's up?"

"Just thinking," I replied.

Neil appeared after a while and placed two large bowls between us. One contained Greek salad and the other the carbonara, the smell wafted up making my mouth water as he topped up our glasses before going forward to a deck locker.

"How did he conjour up that carbonara so quick?" I asked.

Mario spooned some onto a plate. "Microwave," he replied.

"All mod cons eh?"

"Only low power stuff. We've got limited battery capacity and no diesel generator, just solar panels and retractable wind generator to keep them topped up. That's why he's doing that." He nodded to where Neil was crouched amidships lighting a hurricane lamp. He tied it onto a rope then went to the base of the mainmast and hauled on a rope. The lamp rose up and hung swaying above the deck. "We've got an electric anchor light but out here that thing serves just as well and there's no drain on the batteries."

Neil fetched us a blanket each for it was getting chilly now that the sun had set and we all sat quietly eating, wrapped in our blankets and our own thoughts as the boat rocked gently in the gathering twilight.

"I expect you both want to know what this trip's all about eh?" Mario asked diffidently. We both looked at him without replying. "It makes me smile," he said quietly, "you see all the bloody tourists roasting themselves on the beaches, getting pissed in the tavernas, making fools of themselves in the discos. You see it all over the Med and yet how many of the sun, sand and sex brigade ever give a thought to . . . ." He shrugged and smiled, "still, we were all young once, young and foolish and probably totally thoughtless eh Jim?" He nudged me and grinned, his face capturing for a split second that youthful exuberance I remembered. "This trip," he said becoming serious, "it's all to do with my Uncle Benny. It's funny, he wasn't actually my uncle but I always called him that, anyway he died some time ago, keeled over in the billiard room of the Miners Welfare."

"What's that?" Neil asked.

"It's a sort of social club," Mario explained, "built by the miners for the miners back in the 1920's I believe, though what it does for their welfare I'm buggered if I know. All they did there was sit about smoking and drinking too much with the occasional game of pool or darts for exercise. That's all Uncle Benny did for years ever since the pit accident that put him on sticks, and his wife? Aunty Bronwen? She never ever complained, now there's true love for you."

"She still alive?" I asked.

"Oh aye. Aunty Bron's still alive and kicking. It was she who gave me Uncle Benny's diary and told me all the other things, the things he hadn't written down and told only to her. I was her favourite you see, she always found me some apple tart or rhubarb crumble when I went round to see them. So I promised her I'd come and do it."

"Do it?" I said.

"Do what Uncle Benny had always said he would do himself one day. Except he never would have. You know how people say things: one of these days I'll do this or go there, you know what I mean?" We both nodded. "He couldn't have done anything much after the accident in any case, and then he died. Anyway," he said softly, "I'll tell you all about it."

The night was closing in by then and the distant thunderstorm had gone. The breeze had subsided totally and all was still as we sat wrapped in our blankets in the glimmering dusk waiting for Mario to begin.

"Good old Uncle Benny," he sighed, "what a bloody character."

8

Guisseppe Benito Segadelli was the youngest child in his family. He had not been Christened Benito but took on that name himself in deference to Il Duce, Benito Mussolini, whom he idolised along with the dictator's Fascist ideals.

His elder sister's marriage was a sort of arranged affair. Not in the same way as a Hindu marriage perhaps, but similar. Their people were known to each other even though they lived quite far apart and it was not unexpected that she would marry someone from that family's region.

Benny remembered the ceremony well, that sort of occasion makes a lasting impression on a young child. He cried bitterly when his beloved sister went away to work at her in-law's cafe in the Welsh vallies. Some years later the war came.

When he was old enough Benny joined the Fascist Youth through whose auspices he learned to speak, read and write German. He learned so well that he was soon able to read Hitler's 'Mein Kampf' and he kept a copy by him, delving in from time to time to clarify a point or reinforce his faith. English he learned at school. His family were of mixed farming and fishing stock, they lived on the coast near Brindisi and Benny was equally at home dealing with crops and livestock or sailing his uncle's boat while they harvested the seas.

Benny's preoccupation with Fascism was more of a nuisance than anything else as far as his parents were concerned. They had little interest in politics but Benny's frequent trips to Rome with the Movement for this or that rally meant they were short handed sometimes. Still, they thought, he'll grow out of it. As for Benny, he could often be found in his tiny bedroom examining his membership documents (which he insisted on calling his 'papers') admiring the official stamps with the signatures scrawled across them, and the photograph, his photograph, below the symbol of the Roman axe and bundle of sticks, the fasces, from which the Movement took its name.

He was stunned when Mussolini was deposed in July 1943 and nursed a grudge against those who had engineered the coup. When the Allies invaded Sicily he was under no illusions that they would be pushed back into the sea but when that didn't happen, he resolved to take an active part in the defence of his homeland even if in a non-combatant capacity.

One day a military column stopped in the village and Benny walked up to a sergeant and snapped to attention.

"What d'you want young 'un?" the sergeant asked.

"I wish to join you, here are my papers," he handed over his Fascist Youth membership documents. "I can help the cause. In a non-combatant role of course."

The sergeant smiled. "Of course," he said and turned to an officer nearby. "This spring chicken wants to join our unit. In a non-combatant role if you please."

The officer turned to Benny. "Shouldn't you be at school or something?"

"I am too old for school, sir, and too young to join up." The second part at least was true.

"What about your parents, what have they got to say about this?"

"They have gone up north, sir. I stayed behind to help my uncle but now the harvest is over and I am free to leave." The lies rolled off his tongue.

The officer turned to his sergeant. "Well," he smiled, "we're going north too aren't we?"

"We're certainly not going south sir." They both laughed at some private joke which Benny did not understand but he did not know about the evacuation of Sicily at that time nor appreciate the significance of the rush north to defend Rome.

"Well sergeant, he'll be under your feet not mine, it's up to you."

"He can watch the pasta boil and be my runner," the sergeant said.

The officer glanced at his watch. "We leave in five minutes," he said.

Benny slipped back to his house to collect a few things, left a message with a neighbour to tell his parents of his action and was back sitting in the rear of the sergeant's truck as the signal was given to start up. The column rolled forward.

The sergeant was a brave man and did not deserve the fate that later befell him. He had seen action in Abyssinia and most recently in North Africa but his unit had been resting and training in a rear echelon until the fall of Sicily. He took Benny under his wing and some of the sergeant's resourcefulness, determination and forward planning must have rubbed off for Benny eventually rose to be pit overman until the roof fall that crippled him.

During the following days they acted as rearguard while other units overtook them and sometimes leapfrogged others who were watching their tails. Once they were strafed by Allied aircraft, two trucks were hit and rendered u/s and Benny attended his first funeral. It would not be his last.

Early in September they were ordered to set up a defensive position in undulating country, there were vineyards, some olive groves and rough grazing. To the right of the road the land rose fairly steeply but to the left less so, ahead the road snaked to a low summit. The officer set up a command post near the top with a field kitchen on the reverse slope, he delegated the deployment of the company to the sergeant then left to attend a regimental orders group some five kilometres to the north.

From what Benny could glean they were in a quiet sector of the front, at night, the flash and rumble of gunfire indicated where the main assault lay, nevertheless the sergeant was taking no chances. He split the trench mortar platoon into two sections, both were positioned behind some rocky outcrops hidden from the road and both had their weapons zeroed in on particular areas. The first was the road itself, near a bend about half a kilometre away slightly to the left. The other was a slight fold in the ground in open country between some vineyards to the left and boulder strewn rising ground to the right. Maybe it was just luck, but that was the way the attack eventually came.

It was late afternoon when they halted and by dusk all sections were dug in, the transport well dispersed and camouflaged, the 'phone lines laid and communications tested. Benny helped distribute the first hot meal for days, moving as unobtrusively as possible between slit trenches and ladling out the rations. He noted the disposition of the mortars, the machine guns and the riflemen, the entire shallow valley which was their sector was well covered.

The sergeant surveyed the scene through his field glasses. He stiffened instinctively as, in the failing light and at the limit of visibility, a vehicle appeared. It was driving slowly with dimmed headlamps towing a light artillery piece. It was at least four kilometres away, where the road emerged from an olive grove and it was alone.

Leaving a corporal in charge he led a detachment of five riflemen and a light machine gun section down to the road about two hundred metres on their left. With the machine gun set up and well hidden and the others under cover he walked down the road some distance, crouched behind some rocks and waited.

Gradually the sound of the approaching vehicle increased. It was in an intermediate gear and travelling at not more then fifteen kilometres an hour, as it passed him he could see why. One rear tyre was punctured, some attempt had been made to stuff it with straw and rags, the work of some enterprising front line fitter no doubt, but the rubber was splitting and the wheel rim was crunching on the road from time to time. At his signal a rifleman stood up on each side of the road, their weapons levelled.

"Shit!" The driver's exclamation was in Italian. Thank god, thought the sergeant. He stepped forward. "Where the hell have you come from? I thought it was only Yanks and Tommies now."

"We got cut off. We're trying to rejoin our unit."

"Got any ammo for that thing?" He nodded to the field gun.

"Not much sarge."

"How much?"

"Two boxes H.E. (high explosive) That's eight rounds. Box an' a half A.P. (armour piercing) Six rounds. That's the lot."

"Who's in command here?" The sergeant asked and a lance corporal slumped in the rear of the canvass topped vehicle roused up.

"Guess it's me sarge."

"OK. You're under my orders now," and he stood upon the running board and directed the driver off the road.

Although the field gun crew were dog tired, the sergeant made them work alongside his own detachment digging a gun pit, checking the field of fire, chocking up the rear of the gun to ensure adequate depression and camouflaging the position. All this by the light of a pale quarter moon in the chill of an autumn night. Benny kept up a supply of ersatz coffee and eventually saw the gun crew bedded down beside their charge having been fed and watered and excused all sentry duty.

In the cold light of a drizzly dawn the sergeant became instantly awake. Anxiously he peered out from under the tarpaulin and the camouflage netting. Yes, the sentry was still there keeping well below the skyline and stamping his feet to keep warm while standing in the shadow of a rock outcrop. All seemed quiet yet something had woken him.

Then he heard it and the hair on the back of his neck bristled. In the distance, brought faintly on the breeze, came the unmistakable squeaky rumble of tanks. At the same moment the field telephone rang, it was a sentry in one of the forward slit trenches, "sarge. I can hear tanks," he reported.

"Me too," the sergeant replied, "get everybody awake but stay hidden and no shooting until ordered."

"Right sarge."

Within seconds the entire company was ready, safety catches off, eyes peeled. The field gun was loaded with a precious round of A.P. the other five shells laid out ready. All this in complete silence apart from the muffled sounds of magazines being fitted, rifle bolts slid home and whispered orders. Nothing moved above ground, it had the makings of a perfect ambush.

Benny was asleep in the field kitchen dugout when the phone woke him. It was the sergeant. "Tell the cooks action is imminent. Get the medical stuff to hand. If there's any sign of Lieutenant Berni coming back, stop him in case he walks into this."

Benny was holding the instrument away from his ear so the others could hear. The corporal cook turned to him. "You'd better get down the road a way, ready to warn the lieutenant before he gets too close. Here." He thrust a bag containing some bread and cheese into Benny's hand for he well knew the effect of an empty stomach on a cold wet morning. "Off you go," he ordered.

Benny was only half awake as he made off down the slope. He headed for a small roadside shed used by the grape pickers and he sheltered there from the light drizzle, squatting in a corner eating his bread and cheese. He must have dozed for he was awakened by the sound of an approaching motorcycle. He shot out into the road.

"What the fuck . . .?" The dispatch rider swerved to a sliding halt and pushed his goggles up onto his helmet. "Who the hell are you?" he asked.

Benny gave a passable Nazi salute and produced his 'papers' he gestured to the ridge behind him. "There's action due in any minute up there. You mustn't go any further."

"Bollocks."

"It's true. I've been sent to warn Lieutenant Berni in case he stumbles into it." The man looked puzzled. He had just ridden from regimental HQ with sealed orders from Lieutenant Berni, yet here was this scruffy kid who had appeared from nowhere telling him what to do.

At that moment there came from the other side of the ridge a loud report followed immediately by a duller explosion. There followed a series of explosions which the dispatch rider knew to be mortars, then another loud report and explosion which sounded like 40 millimetre stuff.

He swung his machine around and tossed a sealed envelope to Benny. "Your orders," he shouted, "I'm off." And he tore off up the road, his rear wheel snaking on the wet surface. Benny tucked the packet inside his coat before making his way cautiously back to the field kitchen dugout.

9

After the sergeant had phoned the field kitchen he turned his attention to the coming action. As yet there was no enemy in sight, only the ominous sound of tanks coming from the south. He scanned the road through his field glasses and wondered what the hell was keeping Lieutenant Berni. One thing was for sure, this was his show now, he was the senior rank. He was in charge.

Then he saw them, emerging from the olive grove where he had first seen the field gun. Sherman tanks by the look of them, first one then a gap, perhaps one hundred metres, then another. There was another two hundred metres before a jeep appeared and well spaced behind it two troop carriers. Tommies probably, he thought.

Both tank commanders could be seen above the turret coamings, both with field glasses, both scanning the terrain. Seemingly at a signal the column stopped and the jeep raced forward to the lead tank. At first the sergeant thought they had been spotted but there followed a brief roadside conference. He guessed correctly that this was a probing exercise, a small if heavily armed reconnaissance unit forging ahead of the main force sniffing out any resistance.

He watched as the second tank struck off the road, ploughing across a vineyard before turning towards them when it reached the relatively clear swathe of broken country and heading straight down the muzzle of the field gun. It was followed by the jeep, which mounted a heavy machine gun, and one of the troop carriers.

The sergeant picked up the field telephone and spoke to the mortar section NCO. "When I give the order I want rapid fire on that fold in the ground. You all zeroed in?"

"Yes sarge."

"Very well." Next he spoke to the field gun commander: "I want that leading tank destroyed. You've got two shots at the most to do it. Don't shoot until the mortars open up, understood?"

"Got it sarge."

The sergeant waited until the troop carrier was hull down in the fold in the ground, by which time the Sherman was less than two hundred metres from the field gun and the crew were panicking. "I can't get it all in the bloody sight now," the gun layer was sweating and shaking, "come on mortars for Christ's sake."

The first tank meanwhile, followed by the second troop carrier was moving up the road keeping about half a kilometre behind its cohort.

"Open fire." The sergeant spoke quietly into the phone and as the first salvo of mortars went off the field gun commander shouted "fire!" The gun layer, whether startled or just edgy, missed the sitting duck before him. The round, instead of hitting the vulnerable area where the turret met the body of the tank, struck the left hand track. It disintegrated.

Meanwhile the mortars had straddled the troop carrier one scoring a direct hit. The vehicle exploded into an inferno of burning petrol and detonating ammunition, bodies and parts of bodies were flung in all directions. The tank, slewing on its good track, came to rest broadside on to the field gun which was already loaded with the second A.P. round.

This time the layer made no mistake. The round entered just below the turret leaving a small hole from which smoke emerged, there was no other indication of the internal carnage, the gun sagged down and the engine died. That was all.

It had all happened in just a few seconds but the jeep had already turned tail and was zig-zagging away. "Engage that other troop carrier down on the road," the sergeant bellowed down the phone to the gun crew. "Use H.E. this time."

It took the gun crew some time to re-align their weapon and the second tank had plunged off the road and was coming to the aid of its comrade by the time the first ranging shot exploded in front of the truck. It was close enough to persuade the occupants to abandon the vehicle and seek cover so that only the driver was injured when the next round blew away the rear axle and crippled it.

By that time the jeep had reached the road and a red very light went up from it. The tank immediately broke off the engagement and the remainder of the attacking force withdrew to the olive grove and out of sight.

Benny slithered into the dugout and handed the sealed envelope to the sergeant, he stuffed the packet inside his tunic and cranked the field telephone speaking to the corporal gun commander. "Wreck that gun of yours and prepare to move out," he ordered, then turning to Benny he said, "Get some dry rations distributed and tell the cooks we're moving." Then he led a small party down to the troop carrier. There were no survivors. The sight sickened him but he had seen it all before and this was war.

Benny helped with the rations and packing up the field kitchen while the gun crew did their bit. They rammed an empty shell case into the muzzle, loaded a round of H.E. tied a cord to the trigger mechanism then took cover in a slit trench and pulled the cord. The explosion sent the shell case flying and split the barrel like a pea pod then they removed the breech block and buried it in the latrine just to make sure.

In less than ten minutes they were strung out in a loose convoy on the road north, Benny sitting in the back of the open topped command car behind the sergeant and the driver. The rain had stopped but the cloud base had come down preventing the close support fighter bombers of the Allies from strafing them. They drove steadily for an hour through an empty landscape.

Eventually they entered a small village and what must have been a refuelling point. A small detachment of Werhmacht were loading jerry cans onto a half track. The sergeant halted the column and jumped down motioning Benny to follow him. "Thank god," he said, "we're getting short of gas. Can you spare us some?"

The corporal in charge eyed them suspiciously, shook his head and shrugged. The rest of his squad stood rooted, frozen in the act of loading or carrying the cans. Benny thought he detected a look of fear in their eyes. "Benny," the sergeant prodded him, "tell these dick heads we want some petrol."

There followed a brief conversation in German between Benny and the corporal during which it was agreed to let them have just two cans. The Germans were very short of petrol they said and Benny's lot would have to abandon one of their vehicles. While Benny was translating this for the sergeant the Germans clambered aboard the half track and made off, leaving the two cans at the roadside.

The sergeant supervised the disabling of the chosen vehicle after having its fuel siphoned out. Then they rested for twenty minutes while Benny distributed more dry rations and then the depleted convoy moved out.

They had travelled less than five kilometres when suddenly from behind a road side hut there emerged another German half track. The swivel mounted spandau and the soldier levelling it at them caused the Italian driver to skid to a halt throwing Benny onto the floor.

As he lay there he heard orders shouted in very poor Italian: "Don't move. Hands on your heads. Get down from your vehicles and line up." Slowly Benny stood up, then clambered onto the passenger seat and holding onto the top of the windscreen he shouted in German: "We are Italians. Italians not Yanks. Not Tommies. Italians."

A large sergeant with Afrika Korps flashes stepped forward and as he did so Benny could see they were surrounded by German combat troops. At the rear of the column another half track had pulled across the road. It too had a spandau pointing at them. The German sergeant said: "Who the hell are you? You German?"

Benny produced his 'papers'. "No sergeant, Italian. I am non-combatant but true Fascist." and he gave a passable salute to prove it. Just then an officer came up. He looked very young. Even to Benny he looked young. He wore the uniform of the SS. Immaculate. Polished. Terrifying.

He said: "Take this Eyetie sprog to the cook house and give him something to eat. He could be useful as an interpreter."

"Yessir," the sergeant replied and marched Benny off the road down into what had once been a vineyard. There were some mud walled barns in a clearing then the ground fell away towards a shallow valley. There was a well camouflaged mess tent between some rock outcrops and the sergeant led Benny inside. "Coffee and salami and some bread for my non-combatant Eyetie sprog," he shouted as they sat at a trestle table, then to Benny: "Now my young friend, where did you learn to speak the language of the Fatherland so well?"

Benny explained about the Fascist Youth and his admiration for Il Duce and his copy (now much dog-eared) of Mein Kampf. The ersatz coffee, salami and black bread came and he drank noisily from an enamel mug.

Suddenly there came from close by the sound of sub machine gun fire, just a short burst. It made Benny jump and the sergeant winced. There was something about the look on the German's face and then the shouts and curses in Italian from outside.

Benny leapt to his feet and ran from the tent, the German tried to grab him as he passed but failed. Outside he saw the Italian soldiers in a group under a tree. Some still had their hands on their heads as they sat, others were on their feet shaking their fists and cursing their captors all the time menaced by three Germans pointing their weapons at them. On the ground in front of a low barn lay the body of his sergeant and not six metres from him a German corporal, the schmiesser lowered, the barrel still. Smoking.

Benny took in the dreadful scene at a glance then flew at the SS officer. Benny barely came up to the man's waist as his small fists flailed at him. "You murderous German bastard," he screamed as the officer staggered back in shocked surprise, "you fucking Prussian swine. You Fascist Kraut pig." The officer regained his composure, punching Benny to the ground with his left hand as he drew his Luger from the shiny black leather holster with his right.

The Afrika Korps sergeant had been hot on Benny's heels, he dived forward and grabbed Benny by the scruff of the neck then, making sure he kept himself between the officer and Benny, he frog marched him back to the mess tent kicking him up the backside as he went. "You little Italian squirt," he bellowed, "how dare you attack an officer of the SS." Then over his shoulder, "sorry about that sir, he got away from me." Then to Benny: "You'll obey orders now. You're needed as an interpreter and don't you forget it," while under his breath he said, "you stupid sod. He was going to shoot you d'you know that?"

"I don't care," sobbed Benny. "The sergeant was my friend. He was a brave man."

They were inside the tent now and the sergeant thrust Benny down before his unfinished meal. He spoke more kindly, in a low voice. "Of course he was brave, he was a sergeant wasn't he? All sergeants are brave, otherwise they don't get to be sergeants."

Benny looked searchingly into the German's eyes. "Why did they shoot him?"

"Field Marshall Kesselring's orders"

"But we are allies," protested Benny.

"*Were* allies," the sergeant corrected him. "You're fancy new government made a deal with the enemy, a secret deal. Since the Salerno landings your lot are all, well, enemies of the Third Reich I suppose. So . . . ." he spread his hands and shrugged, "Kesselring has ordered all officers to be shot, other ranks to be sent back to Germany or wherever, to work for the good of the Fatherland."

"He was not an officer though."

"He was in charge. That's good enough for our SS friend." The sergeant stole a furtive glance over his shoulder as he said this. "Now finish your food and be quick. We're moving north soon." Benny ate in tearful silence as the sergeant lit a cigarette. "Lucky Strike," he said brandishing it, "got them off a dead Yank."

Benny had just finished eating when the officer put his head inside the tent. "Sergeant, get this Wop kid outside. He's got some interpreting to do." The sergeant crushed out his cigarette on the mud floor and motioned Benny to follow him. The officer told Benny what to say.

"My comrades," Benny began, addressing the Italian prisoners, "our new government has broken ranks with the Axis powers and has signed a separate armistice with the Allies. All Italian officers are to be shot and the rest of you will be transported north to work for the Germans. Distribute what food you have I don't know when you'll get another good meal."

Shouts of abuse came from the captives. The SS officer grabbed Benny by the shoulder shouting orders in his ear. Benny continued: "He wants four volunteers to bury our sergeant, the rest must get in those two lorries," he pointed across the clearing. "Good luck. Long live Italy." The officer cuffed him across the ear and Benny fell to the ground.

He picked himself up and helped with the burial He straightened the sergeant's legs and arms and closed his eyelids before removing his identity disc and going through his pockets the tears streaming down his face. Apart from a thin wallet containing a few lire and a photo of an elderly couple there was only the packet of sealed orders. Benny opened them and read the contents.

It was right what the Germans had said. The army was ordered to adopt a non-belligerent attitude to the Germans and surrender to the Allies if the opportunity arose. If only those orders had arrived sooner a whole lot of Tommies would still have been alive and so too would his sergeant.

"Get a move on with that grave." It was the SS officer. "I would leave traitors for the crows if I had my way. That's deep enough, get him in". He caught sight of Benny. "What's that you've got?"

"These were his orders, Lieutenant. He hadn't even opened them. He thought we were still on the same side. This morning he organised a brilliant ambush against the Allies he was brave and clever and . . . ." The officer snatched the papers from Benny and flung them into the grave on top of the sergeant.

"Fill it in," he ordered, "we're moving out."

The trucks with the Italian prisoners had been gone half an hour and Benny and his group were helping pack away the field kitchen equipment and the tables from inside the mess tent when there came the sound of a low flying aircraft followed by an explosion which shook the ground. The blast blew the tent flat and as they scrambled out Benny saw in the middle of the clearing a blazing half track.

The Afrika Korps sergeant emerged from a nearby dugout shouting orders. Somehow two jerry cans of petrol had been flung from the half track and lay on their side, intact but seeping fuel. "Grab those cans. Get them in a foxhole quick," he shouted. Two Germans sprinted across, grabbed a can each and dived back into the nearest slit trench.

The Typhoon fighter bomber which had made the attack did not return. It circled once then made off towards the south. Benny ran over to the German sergeant, "he's gone away I think," he said.

The sergeant squinted up at the sky, "for now anyway," the sergeant replied and he began running towards the burning half track. Benny followed.

The driver was just a smouldering shapeless mass indistinguishable from the machine he had been driving. A few metres away lay the SS officer. One leg seemed to have disappeared completely and half an arm. His scorched uniform, once so pristine, was smoking faintly. Incredibly he was still alive, his tongue moved in his blood filled mouth as he attempted to give orders to his sergeant, his eyes darting this way and that as if searching for the monster that had done this thing to him.

The sergeant bent forward taking the luger from the officer's leather holster. He cocked it and pointed. There was a sharp crack and the officer's head moved slightly. When Benny looked again there was a small round hole surrounded by a grey misty powder burn in the centre of the officer's forehead.

"You killed him," Benny gasped.

"He was already dead," the sergeant replied coldly, "you can see his injuries, I just finished it quicker." He unloaded the pistol, cocked it and squeezed the trigger, repeating the process a couple of times to ease the springs before slipping it and the ammo clip into separate pockets. "Come on," he said, "we've got to move out. We're going north to build the Gustav Line."

"What's that?" asked Benny.

"It's a line of defence for the Allies to break their teeth on. At least that's what Kesselring says. There's just one thing though, while they're breaking their teeth we could get some very bruised knuckles." He laughed but it was without humour. "Right young 'un, you travel with the cooks and take the burial party with you."

But there was no sign of the Italian prisoners. They had taken their chance during the confusion of the attack to vanish into the countryside. "No time to go searching now," the sergeant declared, "we've got to move, there's no telling how far behind we are."

The column crossed the Rapido river by the last remaining bridge only hours before the demolition charges were detonated and the sergeant reported to his regimental HQ.

Mario leaned over and placed his glass upon the table. "how much of that gin's left boyo?" he asked.

Neil reached down by his feet for the bottle and held it up to the soft glow of the anchor light. "Depending if you're optimistic or not," he replied, "it's either two thirds empty or one third full."

"Ah well," Mario smiled, "there's plenty more below if we run out"

"How old was your uncle when all this happened?" I asked. I was curious to know if such traumatic events at such an early age might have affected him in later life.

"Don't really know," Mario answered, "the age they put on his coffin was bullshit I reckon. He could have been anywhere between eleven and fifteen at the time" he paused, a faraway look in his eyes.

"What about this married sister of his?" Neil asked, "she'd have known wouldn't she?"

Mario reached for his glass and took a long sip at his gin and tonic, "I daresay she could have told us his real age," he agreed, "but . . . ."

Neil and I waited for him to continue. "But what?" I asked.

"Well I'm coming to that," Mario replied, his voice thick with emotion.

. . . .

The Afrika Korps sergeant kept the lad out of sight as best he could. Benny could pass for a German anywhere to hear him speak, it was his size that gave him away. Even the smallest combat fatigues swamped him so one of the cooks, a tailor's apprentice in civvy street, altered them to fit whilst giving plenty of room inside for bulky clothing to combat the coming winter.

One day as Benny was helping to fill sandbags for a roadside dugout three lorries came by. As the last one drew level the driver leaned out of his window and shouted across: "Hey sarge, I thought you'd still be brewing coffee for Irwin."

The sergeant straightened up from his task his face creasing into a smile as he recognised his old friend. "Hans, you old bastard," he shouted back, "now you know it was the other way around, Rommel used to brew mine. Anyway, I thought you were driving a crane in Hamburg docks."

"I was. Thought I'd be safer over here so I volunteered. Then what do they do? They put me in artillery and I'm driving truckloads of live ammo about. Typical."

"The bombing still bad back home?"

"Getting worse. Got some good news this morning though."

"What's that?"

"Been seconded to the Hermann Goering Division for special duties."

"That sounds bloody dangerous."

"That's what I thought until I found out what we were doing," he smiled, "we're off up there." He nodded towards the distant monastery, perched high upon its mountain top.

"To Monte Cassino?" the sergeant said, "what for?"

"To rescue precious artworks and religious artefacts from the wicked Allies. They're going to be stored in a safe place till the war's over."

"And how much of the stuff will find its way into Hermann's Bavarian chateau I wonder?" the sergeant snorted.

"My thoughts exactly," the driver replied.

The sergeant suddenly had an idea. Pretty soon now this area would become a battlefield, the Americans were already rumoured to be preparing for an assault across the Rapido River. Benny could not go south as a bona fide refugee nor could he go north. In fact he could not go anywhere. He was stuck in a war zone as an unofficial interpreter and could probably be shot as a spy by both sides.

The sergeant walked over to his old friend. "Look," he said, "do me a favour. There's this Eyetie kid, speaks German like a native, he's barely out of nappies. Could you take him up there? They'll take him in, he'll be among his own people. He'll be safe there. They won't attack the monastery."

The driver looked doubtful, "got any fags?" he asked. The sergeant passed him up his half empty pack of Lucky Strike, the driver took one and lit up. "Just open up the hood for me will you, if some bloody officer comes by I'll say the engine's overheating. Is this kid ready to go?"

"Can be in five minutes," the sergeant said as he struggled with the metal toggles and folded back the bonnet. The driver passed the cigarette packet back but the sergeant waved it aside. "Keep 'em," he said, "got a water bottle?" The driver handed it down and the sergeant unscrewed the cap before pouring a little onto the radiator. Steam began to rise. "That look convincing?" he asked.

The driver switched off the engine. "Doesn't fool me but it might fox an officer," he smiled. "OK, go and fetch this kid, I gotta get moving."

Benny listened to the sergeant's logical argument that he would be better out of the battle zone and up in the safety of the monastery, even so he was reluctant to leave the camaraderie of the front line unit for the unknown. His mind was made up by a ranging shot from an Allied twenty five pounder which whistled overhead and exploded about half a kilometre behind the line.

The sergeant gave him what little food they could spare, Benny packed it into the British Army respirator haversack he had been given. It was the same one that he would use years later to take his 'snap' on shift to the Welsh pit each day. "Now this," the sergeant said, "you never know when you might need it," and there in his hand was the SS officer's luger.

Under the sergeant's expert tuition Benny learned how to handle the weapon. He experienced the feel of the clip sliding home, the click of the safety catch, the strength of the cocking mechanism spring and how much pull was required to slide it back. Within a few short minutes Benny was loading and unloading, cocking and easing springs. He watched as the sergeant wrapped the pistol and the clip in separate pieces of oily rag and then in some remnants of British Army anti-gas cape so no water could get in.

"Keep these tucked away in an inside pocket somewhere," the sergeant said, "something to tell your grandchildren. How you got them off a dead German eh?" Benny didn't smile, he was thinking of his own sergeant, the one they had buried and a tear came to his eye. "Hey, come on," the sergeant punched his arm gently as if reading Benny's thoughts, "your sergeant wouldn't want you crying now would he?"

Benny shook his head and the sergeant fumbled in an inside pocket of his tunic. He was looking for something else, something extra to give this waif. Christmas would soon be here and he thought of his own family so far away. His fingers closed around the item he was searching for. It had been with him all through the North African campaign, the campaign which had started so well yet ended so disastrously. "Here," he said, "take this too. Just in case you get lost," and he handed over his beloved prismatic compass.

Hans was swearing as only Hamburg dockside crane drivers can by the time they got back to him. He had suffered a dressing down from an officer of the Hermann Goering Division for allowing his vehicle to overheat. It was a sign of deficient care and maintenance the officer had told him.

Hans was meticulous when it came to servicing the equipment under his charge be they crane or truck and he was very upset to be accused of slack maintenance. He was so upset that he almost lost his temper and told the man to piss off. Fortunately his military training prevailed so he snapped to attention, gave a smart Nazi salute and replied that he would catch up with the small convoy inside ten minutes. "Better get in the back," he said to Benny, "just until we get to the monastery. I'll tip you off when to get out. You'll just be another refugee then OK?" Benny nodded and with a leg up from the sergeant he scrambled into the rear of the truck where he hid himself among some empty ammo boxes and hessian. He heard the engine cover being slammed back into place and then the shouted farewells as the engine started and the truck lurched forward.

The journey was a slow and bumpy one. They passed through Cassino Town before commencing the long winding climb up to the mountaintop monastery. The temperature dropped appreciably as the altitude increased and Benny clutched his precious haversack and bundle of clothing hoping it would be enough to see him through the coming winter.

Eventually they drove through the monastery gates and he heard orders shouted and felt the vehicle reversing before finally stopping with a jolt. He peeped out of the rear canvass to find that they were backed up to a stone wall. The driver cut the engine.

"Name?" It was the voice of authority again, an officer probably.

"Weller, sir," Benny heard Hans reply.

"Got your ID?" A long pause.

"Here's your work ticket. You know what you'll be carrying?"

"No sir."

"Works of art. Pictures mainly, all nicely wrapped and labelled so drive carefully."

"I always do sir. Up to today I've been hauling live ammo." There was a hint of humour in the driver's tone but it was not returned.

"Remember this is the Hermann Goering Division you've been assigned to so keep on your toes." Benny heard the officer crunch away across the courtyard then the truck swayed and the door slammed as Hans got out.

"You awake young 'un?" Hans's hoarse whisper through the canvass tilt could be heard above the sound of him urinating against the rear wheel.

"Yes."

"I'm going to open the engine cover, check on the overheating. When you hear me close it, it'll be safe for you to nip out. Keep close to the wall behind the other trucks. Go left, that's towards the same side I'm standing, there's a bunch of scruffy looking Eyetie refugees, probably helpers or something. Latch onto them OK? Good luck."

And so for the next couple of weeks Benny helped load trucks with various works of art. Large pictures padded and wrapped in hessian, packing cases of various sizes containing religious artefacts all meticulously labelled and documented. Benny did not know it but the official Nazi propaganda film of the procedure, shown on newsreels around the world to illustrate the Third Reich's concern for the safety of those priceless treasures, included footage of himself!

Thanks to typical German efficiency it had taken only a couple of weeks or so to catalogue and pack the entire contents and now its transportation was a matter of urgency due to the Allied advance. Benny saw Hans once or twice more as he and his truck shuttled back and forth. They were taking the stuff to Rome, Hans confided, where it would be transferred to the Vatican for safe keeping. The German was convinced, however, that some of the smaller items would get 'lost' in transit and finish up on Goering's mantelpiece.

Eventually the loading was complete and Benny saw Hans for the last time, the big German shook his hand, "this is my last load kid, auf weidersehen."

"Ariverderchi," Benny replied.

"Huh? Oh yeah, I'd forgotten you were a bloody Wop you speak German so good. Anyway, look after yourself OK?" With that Hans climbed into the cab, started up and drove slowly away.

Benny had managed to attach himself to a group of elderly refugees who had persuaded the monks to let them shelter inside the monastery walls. Their numbers swelled as the weeks passed and the shelling came closer. They were safe as long as they stayed inside the monastery. No Allied shelling was directed at Monte Cassino and no German soldier was permitted inside, armed police at the main gate saw to that. Benny's main concern was keeping warm in the bitter winter weather.

Christmas came and went and the small graveyard beside the north wall sprouted more crosses as the older ones died of the cold and lack of food and the despair. Outside the walls the rumble of battle drew closer as the Allies broke their teeth against Kesselring's Gustav Line.

Benny remembered the slow and bumpy ride up to Monte Cassino, remembered peeping through the canvass tilt and seeing the in-depth defences, the Panzer tank turrets being concreted in at strategic locations, the engineers cutting deep caves into the rock faces from whence to harass the Allied advance. He imagined the desperate clash of wills as determined attackers met well dug in and equally determined defenders. At least he was safe here with all the other refugees, one day when the frantic tide of battle had rolled over them, they would emerge from their cellars and try to put this madness behind them.

During all this time he kept a diary. He wrote it in pencil, very small in Italian using a military notebook he had scrounged. Each day was dated each entry brief:

Buried two people today, an elderly couple, refugees from Cassino Town. The Brothers read over them. I made the cross for the grave.

A shell exploded near the eastern wall today. One of the monks was injured, I helped bandage his arm.

Found a safer place to sleep today. It is deeper down in an older part of the monastery. Some of the sick and older ones among the refugees will be brought down later. I help to feed and clean up after them.

New Year's Day 1944. Very cold at nights now. Food strictly rationed. I cry for my parents and pray for them every night. There is constant gunfire.

And so the entries continued through January, each day recording the hardship, the cold, the hunger and the despair experienced by the ever growing numbers of people seeking refuge within the ancient walls. Many had walked all the way from Cassino Town which nestled at the foot of the mountain and from which they had been evicted to enable the Germans to incorporate it into the Gustav Line.

The situation was desperate, but worse was to come.

11

The days dragged by, each one bringing the battle closer. The weather was atrocious, rain, sleet, snow and fog adding to the misery of the refugees. What it was like for the soldiers Benny could only guess. The monastery was taking more hits from Allied shelling and there were mutterings that these were not accidental.

Rumours spread of German artillery officers having been seen inside the building. Some said they had been carrying maps and binoculars. Certainly the armed police on the gates had been withdrawn but that was assumed to be for their own safety as the Allied shelling increased.

Benny would sit in his 'dugout' deep in the belly of the monastery and do his stocktaking. His possessions were few but every night he laid them out by the flickering light of the stump of altar candle he had commandeered. These few items were his entire world and the only things to link him with home were the tattered copy of Mein Kampf and his Fascist Youth membership documents, his 'papers', all of which he kept well out of sight of the other refugees.

He turned his sergeant's thin wallet over gently in his hands. A tear fell onto the scuffed and worn leather and he wiped it away quickly and dried his eyes. Once again he opened it and counted the few lire it contained and looked upon the old and kindly faces on the photograph. On impulse he slid the photo out and looked on the back of it. There was an address. A street name and number and the last line: Near Naples. He resolved that if he ever got away from this place he would try to visit them. Give them back the wallet and the money. Tell them of the brave sergeant. The sergeant who must have been their son.

He replaced the photo and packed the wallet together with all his other things back into the British Army respirator haversack. He eased the luger around from the small of his back onto his belly before blowing out the candle and curling up wrapped in his blanket upon a bed of straw.

Towards the end of January one of the Brothers took him aside. "Benny," he said quietly, "we have some wounded German soldiers. They were brought in last night. There are medical orderlies with them and they have brought food for us also. You speak their language better than most of us, can I ask you to be a go-between, sort of liaison officer?"

From cookhouse assistant to messenger boy to interpreter to fine art remover and finally now a liaison officer. Benny's career was certainly progressing he thought as he followed the monk down to a lower level to the place which had been converted into a makeshift sick bay.

There were beds lined up along both sides of the vaulted chamber. At the far end two orderlies were in the act of lifting a blanket covered body onto a stretcher. They carried it towards the entrance followed by a white coated man with silver hair who Benny took to be the Medical Officer. Benny and the monk stood aside to let them pass. The M.O. stopped. "Is this the boy?" he asked the monk in fluent Italian.

"Yes," the monk replied, "can I leave him with you? I take it we are burying this soldier with all the others?" The officer nodded. "I'll go with the burial party then," the monk said.

The officer turned to Benny speaking in German, "where did you learn to speak our language?" he asked.

"With the Fascist Youth sir."

"Ah yes, the Fascist Youth," the M.O. replied sarcastically, "like the Hitler Youth no doubt. Recruit them young enough and the Bohemian Corporal's got them for life." The officer snorted and turned away, Benny followed. "Down here," the officer said over his shoulder, "we deal only in medical matters. Politics we leave to others, got that?"

"Yessir."

"Had any medical training?"

"Just first aid sir."

"You can help corporal Schmidt here. Do as he says, watch what he does, ask questions when you must. Alright?"

"Yessir." And so Benny began his training as medical orderly. Training which, when practiced in the years ahead, would win him the trust and admiration of his fellow miners in the pit in the Welsh vallies. The pit which eventually crippled him.

On February 5th Benny's diary recorded: "Today many refugees from Cassino Town came to the monastery. The Brothers are frantic, there is nowhere for them to sleep. They bed down in any corner they can find. Some have brought food and blankets with them. The Germans are fortifying the town, commandeering houses, stealing food. It is a desperate situation."

Then came the morning of February 15th. The casualties had been coming in steadily over the past days and several of the able bodied refugees had joined Benny to help the hard pressed German medical staff. The M.O. could be found at all hours of the day and night red eyed and looking exhausted but doing the best he could with the injuries he had to deal with.

That morning, after disposing of the latrine buckets and the blood soiled dressings, Benny climbed to the lower courtyard for a breath of fresh air as usual. The day was bright and cold, a typical winter's morning. Benny breathed deep, savouring the cold clean mountain air as he made his way to one of the openings in the monastery walls where once a stained glass window had been before a stray shell destroyed it. He stood well back, a pace or two inside the massive wall where the tapering sides of the window opening narrowed to the splintered frame which still clung to the ancient stonework.

He felt tense and anxious. On such a serene morning as this there was no reason for such feelings. The sky was a clear blue without a cloud in sight, somewhere a bird sang. Then it dawned on him. The silence. The absolute silence. There had been other days when a lull in the fighting had brought relative quiet, but not like this. Small arms firing from somewhere would usually have shattered the stillness, or a distant rumble of artillery. Today there was nothing.

Then something caught his attention. Something in the clear sky to the south. He half closed his eyes to shut out the morning glare but could not quite make it out. There were specks in the sky, black specks as if a flock of birds hung there waiting to soar away or swoop to earth. They appeared to be stacked in groups. Groups of bird like specks, low in the morning sky, slowly, inexorably growing in size as they approached

In an instant Benny knew exactly what they were and in the same moment something inside warned him of their purpose and their mission.

He leapt down from the window and ran to the groups of refugees washing clothes in the shadow of the cloisters screaming his warning to them before dashing through the doorway into the garden outside the north wall where some others were digging potatoes. By then the quiet of the morning was overlaid with the ominous drone of the approaching bombers.

Buckets and bowls and overturned chairs lay where people had fled in panic as Benny re-entered the courtyard and ran for the stairs leading to his sanctuary. The air was vibrating with the deep thundrous roar of the aircraft as he reached the passageway and he was halfway down the second flight of steps when the first stick of bombs straddled the courtyard above.

The noise was like a nearby thunderclap and the ground shook beneath his feet as the second and then the third load of high explosive detonated above him. He stumbled and fell to the foot of the stairway as masonry showered down onto and around him. The normally dark passage to his left was lit from above where the roof had collapsed and the morning sunlight shafted down through the thick dust which was almost choking him. He crawled to the head of the next flight of steps covering his mouth as best he could with one of the field dressings which were now his stock in trade.

The bombing seemed incessant, the ground shaking and masonry falling. Dust was everywhere and he struggled to breathe through the cotton dressing. A near miss brought the wall to his right bursting inwards fracturing a water pipe and letting in light from somewhere above. He used the water to dampen the dressing before tying it around his mouth then, by the dim light filtering into the passageway, he saw the package which had been dislodged from the wall.

That first raid lasted about twenty minutes but to Benny it seemed much longer. It reduced the monastery to a ruin yet the outer walls still stood. But the planes came again later and yet again the next day and the next, shattering the labour of centuries to rubble and dust. However, Benny's hidey hole was intact as was the sick bay, safe and deep inside the mountain.

If conditions had been bad before they were now considerably worse. The bombing had killed a great many of the refugees from Cassino Town, their bodies lay buried in the rubble. Refugees and Wermacht shared what little safe space there was as the sick bay took in more casualties.

Above ground the Allied bombs had created the ideal environment for defence. Like in Stalingrad the ruins provided excellent cover for individual snipers or small groups to harass and delay the attackers, for if before there had been no German fighting troops allowed inside the monastery, now the place was crawling with them. Most were the elite Paratroopers charged with the final desperate defence of the mountain which commanded the approach to Rome. Now the only sounds were of small arms, grenades and mortars as the fighting became hand to hand.

Benny's 'dugout' was used now only as a storage cache where he kept all his things including the unopened package from the monastery wall. He slept in the sick bay whenever he had the chance.

On March 15th, just a month after the first devastating raid on the monastery, it was the turn of Cassino Town. Wave after wave of bombers droned overhead as they turned for base having dropped their terrible cargoes onto that wretched place. The sound of aircraft and explosions and the shaking ground seemed endless. Then, late in May, Benny wrote in his diary: "Tending German wounded today when Polish soldiers came into sick bay with bayonets fixed. One spoke good German. I pretended not to understand. Germans are now prisoners. Refugees told to prepare to be evacuated. Thank God."

Benny was with a group of refugees from Cassino Town. Together they had helped the medics tend the wounded, helped bury the dead, helped each other with the tasks involved in survival in this primitive hell below ground. Soon, they were told, there would be transport to take them down the mountain to what was left of their homes, but the days dragged on as the mopping up operations which followed the German withdrawal were completed.

Finally, some time in June, Benny collected his things from his 'dugout' and became just another refugee from the conflict. A conflict during which he had always believed that he would be on the winning side, a conflict against the wicked Allies in which the Axis powers would triumph, for he was still secretly a Fascist at heart although his views would eventually change. Now all he wanted to do was to get home.

But first there was the matter of his sergeant's wallet.

12

The lorry lurched to a standstill and the refugees clambered out. Benny emerged last, helping an elderly lady who had somehow become separated from the rest of her family.

She gasped and put her hand to her mouth at the sight that greeted her. The town was in ruins, no building had escaped the Allied onslought. Burned out military vehicles littered the place, bomb craters scarred the roads and groups of refugees together with German POW's were filling them in with rubble.

Holding tightly onto Benny's arm she led him to what was left of the home she had fled. Only half of the roof was still intact, all the windows had been blown out and the rear wall had collapsed. There they found the rest of her family and Benny left them foraging around in the ruins as he made his way to a group of American soldiers stood around a jeep drinking coffee.

"Hiya kid!" A tall swarthy man smiled down at him. He wore on his arm the distinctive three inverted stripes and below them the letter 'T' which Benny knew signified that he was a technical sergeant. "You want some candy kid?" the man asked. Benny shook his head. "Some crackers maybe?" He brandished a packet of biscuits. Benny shook his head again.

Another of the soldiers piped up: "Hey sarge ask him if he's got a big sister he wants to sell for a pack of Luckies." They all laughed except for the sergeant.

"You speak English kid?" the sergeant asked.

"Yes," said Benny, "I want a big tarpaulin, you got one?"

And so, with the help of a detachment of U.S. Army Engineers, Benny's new family got a temporary roof over their heads, *'courtesy of Uncle Sam'* as the sergeant said. The war had rolled over and past them, their town had been commandeered by the Werhmact and turned into a fortress and now, finally liberated by the Allies, it was in ruins.

Benny spent the following weeks helping to rebuild the house, he became expert at scrounging food and materials from the Americans and frequently acted as a go-between when some G.I. fancied a screw. Years later, in the all male confines of the Miners Welfare and after a few beers, he would tell of his days spent pimping for the Yanks. It was not a time for prudeness or the niceties of civilian society, there was a war going on, food and fuel were scarce except among the military and the sex starved soldiery were not slow to realise they were in a strong bargaining position.

Benny did alright out of the trade. He managed to amass a considerable quantity of American dollars whilst keeping his adopted family fed and watered at the same time. The money, in five and ten dollar bills, he carefully sewed into an undershirt which never left his back.

Soon Benny decided to move on. He announced his intention to visit the Italian sergeant's family near Naples and left on a southbound train from the bombed out station amid floods of tears from the old lady and her extended family.

When he arrived in Naples and emerged from the station concourse he was greeted by a bunch of ragamuffins trying to sell him a bicycle. They had two or three to sell, all undoubtedly stolen, and Benny spent a long time bargaining for their bottom price. Eventually he flourished a five dollar bill and they all stopped jabbering, mouths open and eyes wide. He stepped forward and took the best bike from the biggest lad, stuffed the note into the boy's shirt pocket and pedalled away.

He headed inland asking the way from time to time and towards dusk he entered a small town. Once again he opened the sergeant's wallet and checked the address and eventually he dismounted outside a house in a quiet suburb. He knocked hard on the heavy door and presently it was partially opened and he knew he was at the right house, the elderly lady was instantly recognisable from the photograph. "Yes my dear," she said, "can I help you?"

"I have some things belonging to your son," Benny replied, "can I come in?" The old lady stood back and swung the door open. The house was substantial. It spoke not of opulent wealth but rather of the solid middle class virtues of thrift and hard work, or so Benny thought at the time. The floors were of marble, the stair rail of wrought iron, the furniture old and polished from a previous generation. Pictures on the walls depicted Venetian scenes of antiquity.

"Something belonging to our son?" A man with the face of the other person on the photograph appeared.

"I have it here," Benny fumbled inside his army haversack and produced the wallet. The woman gasped as she recognised it. The man stepped forward and took it, he flipped it open and briefly examined the contents.

"How did you . . . .Where did you find it?" he asked.

"Could I have a drink of water please?" asked Benny.

The couple exchanged anxious glances and the woman said: "Yes, of course, you look exhausted." Benny turned to look outside at his bicycle leaning against the railings.

"That's alright," the man said, "I'll bring it around to the back," and he ushered Benny into an ante room before going out and closing the door behind him.

The old lady sat Benny down at a table that smelled of furniture polish and when her husband returned she said to him: "Would you run a bath for our visitor? I'm sure he would like one." She smiled kindly at Benny, "You'd like that wouldn't you?" Benny nodded. He could not remember the last time he had bathed and he had become so accustomed to the faint smell he exuded that he did not even notice it. The sergeant's parents had detected it immediately however. "Would you like some coffee?" the lady asked when her husband had gone.

"Yes please."

"I'll get you some," she said, "I won't be long."

Benny sat at the polished table, his British Army respirator haversack at his feet. It seemed that he had worn these clothes for years not months, they were as much a part of him as his very skin. Also he had not set foot in a real house since leaving home and never in one as grand as this. He wondered vaguely how to break the news of their son's death. It was no good beating about the bush he decided, he would have to come straight out with it.

Presently they returned and they all sat around the table with their coffee. The old lady spoke first: "Our son's dead isn't he?" she asked. Benny looked from one to the other in the bleak silence that followed before nodding his head. "We had word that he was missing," she said softly, "do you know how he . . . how he died?"

"The Germans shot him."

"I knew it!" The man's face contorted in anger as he smashed his fist into the palm of his hand. He placed the wallet on the table before him and emptied its few contents onto the shiny surface. "Were you there?" he asked.

"Yes," Benny replied, "he got his orders too late. The orders about the conspiracy with the Allies. He thought we were still part of the Axis but that cut no ice with the SS officer who gave the order to shoot him. He himself was killed soon afterwards," he added as if that made any difference.

"We should not have been part of the Axis Powers in the first place," the man snorted, "it was only that fool Mussolini got us involved. Now there could be civil war just like in Spain."

"Il Duce is a great man," Benny protested but even as he said it he could feel deep down that his Fascist sympathies were waning.

The man's face softened. He remembered he was talking to a child, a child who had probably been indoctrinated into Fascism from the day he could speak. "You go and have your bath," he smiled, "leave your clothes by the bathroom door. You look tired, you can stay the night, our son's room . . . ," his voice faltered, "our son's room is free."

Benny did as he was told and relaxed into the bath, its luxurious heat making him drowsy then, for the first time in many months, he enjoyed the comfort of a soft warm bed in a safe environment.

He slept.

. . . .

Benny awoke slowly unable to make out where he was. The room seemed huge and sunlight shafted in through the shutters. He stretched and yawned and rolled over. On a nearby chair he saw his clothes clean and neatly pressed and he realised that he was still wrapped in the towelling robe he had put on when emerging from the bath the previous night.

He lay for some minutes savouring the unfamiliar luxury until he became aware of the hard lump under his back. He retrieved the luger and clip of ammo still wrapped in their gas cape packaging and placed them well out of sight beneath the bedside cabinet. Presently there was a gentle tap on the bedroom door and the man's face peeped in. "You awake?" he asked.

"Yes."

"Come down and have some breakfast, your clothes are there," he pointed.

"Thanks," Benny replied and squirmed down into the bed as the door closed, unwilling to leave its soft warmth. Reluctantly he got up and dressed.

Suddenly he froze. His undershirt. The one with the money in. So impatient had he been to sample the warm inviting bath he had left it with all his other clothes outside the bathroom door. Neither that nor the haversack was to be seen. He took a long time to dress, carefully concealing the luger and its ammo under each armpit in the hand sewn shoulder holsters he had made from scraps of material during his months at Monte Cassino. The tapes criss-crossed his chest and circled his waist and he tied them neatly and securely at each hip. Presently he went downstairs.

Benny sat before the polished table and ate a light breakfast followed by some excellent coffee obtained through his hosts' contacts on the black market. The old lady fussed around the place tidying things, moving things and dusting things. There was no sign of her husband and all the time Benny knew they would want to know all the details of their son's death. Also there was the matter of his money and his haversack.

In later years Benny would relate to his wife Bronwen that, even at that early stage, he had a premonition of potential danger ahead. It was a sixth sense that had helped him avoid several pit accidents until his luck ran out with the roof fall that crippled him. He finished his meal in silence and soon the man returned and the woman cleared away the breakfast things then they both sat down facing him. "So," the man said, "what exactly happened?"

Benny told them his story from the time he joined the Italian army convoy moving north to the tearful departure from Cassino Town railway station but carefully omitting his lucrative pimping role. They both listened in silence except when he described the shooting, then the woman buried her head in her hands and sobbed. The man bowed his head and swore softly.

When Benny had finished they all sat quietly, no one spoke for a long time and Benny wondered when the subject of the money and his haversack would come up then, as if reading his thoughts, the man produced the notes and placed them in a neat pile upon the table. "My wife threw the shirt out," he explained and Benny just shrugged, it had served its purpose. "Now this," the man said and he placed the mysterious package from Monte Cassino Abbey on the table before them. "Do you know what's in it?" he asked. Benny shook his head. The package was wrapped in leather which was cracked along the edges where it had obviously been recently opened out, the thongs which had tied it he could see were freshly cut through. The man unfolded the outer cover to reveal a second layer of protection, some closely woven fabric this time and inside that, wrapped in silk, a flat rectangular object about the same size as his copy of Mein Kampf but much thinner.

"Do you know what this is?" the man asked folding back the silk covering. Benny stared at the object. On its surface there was a delicately painted and detailed representation of the Madonna and Child picked out in sombre shades of brown, deep ochre and black. It looked rather dull and somewhat depressing.

"It's beautiful," he lied.

"It's called an icon."

"Oh," said Benny.

"You say it was hidden in a wall in the Abbey?" Benny nodded. "My guess is that it was put there in about the 7th or 8th century to protect it from the iconoclasts."

"The iconoclasts?"

"They believed these icons to be the same as idols, that people worshipped them as such. So they destroyed them. Thou shalt not worship any graven image Remember?" Benny nodded trying to remember which commandment that was. "So if it is from that era it is very valuable. I have a few contacts in the art world, I could sell it for you. You could make quite a bit of money."

"I dunno," Benny said for he knew where it belonged. It belonged in Monte Cassino Abbey where he had happened upon it during the vicious Allied bombing which had reduced the place to rubble with him inside. "I've got enough money there," he said pointing to the little pile of notes on the table.

"What?" the man laughed, "two hundred and fifteen dollars? This thing could be worth . . ." he hesitated, it would not do to let this waif know the true value of his find, "well, much more than that."

Benny smiled inwardly. This man had obviously counted the money, his money, Benny hadn't had time to. Mentally he recalled the sweaty garment trying to visualise the number and the denomination of the bills he had so meticulously sewn into it over the weeks. He guessed the amount was about right.

The woman meanwhile had left the room. Out of the corner of his eye Benny had seen the man's slight nod and frown which had ordered her to leave. He was becoming increasingly uneasy about his sergeant's parents but then war often tests the integrity of even the most honest people. Things are done in wartime which later might appear shameful, a glance at the money on the table produced his own pang of conscience.

"Tell you what," the man said furtively, "think about it. You can stay here as long as you like. Where do you live?"

"Taranto," Benny lied. Fortunately he had kept his 'papers' well hidden along with the luger and its ammo ever since leaving the Abbey. He had heard how a great many people had turned against Fascism, if they had ever really embraced it in the first place, and he did not want his membership known. His proper address written upon that document was, therefore, a secret.

13

I heard it first. It was as if someone had dropped a pebble onto the canvass sun awning above my head. There was another and then another. Gradually their frequency increased as the heavy raindrops began to fall in earnest. "Come on Neil," Mario said, "do your stuff."

Neil shrugged off his blanket and went to front of the boat to where several white plastic bins, one inside the other, lay lashed to the gunwhale. He untied them before adjusting the ropes that held the sun awning so that the rainwater ran off in a steady stream at one end. He positioned a bin to collect this discharge.

"I don't pay for water at some fancy expensive marina when I can get it for nothing," Mario smiled, "and this stuff tastes better anyway."

"This Italian sergeant's father was a bit of a shyster then was he?" I asked.

"Mafia connections," replied Mario, "that's how they managed to get good coffee and plenty of grub during the war. Mind you, he wasn't as ruthless as some of the bastards. Uncle Benny was lucky to get out alive I reckon and that was thanks to the sergeant's mother."

Neil topped up our glasses in the glimmer of the swaying anchor light as the rain hammered on the canvass above our heads and poured in a steady stream into the bin while all around us the dark sea hissed with the sound of the deluge.

. . . .

Benny gazed out of the window. The walled rear garden was mostly in shade this early in the day but there was a garden seat and table at the far end beside an ornamental pond bathed in sunlight. The sergeant's mother re-entered the room carrying a coffee pot. "Why don't you go into the garden for a while," she said to him, "here, have another cup of coffee." She filled his cup and opened the French doors that led onto a small patio. Benny got up and went outside and made his way to the garden seat.

He sat before the garden table sipping his coffee. His bicycle was leaning against the high wall next to a heavy wooden door leading out to a back street, the door was bolted and secured with a large padlock. His mind was more troubled than it had been for weeks. When he was among the troops there had been the camaraderie born out of their common purpose. At the monastery there had been the close co-operation, the self sacrifice and the mutual compassion engendered through the proximity of and yet the isolation from the war being waged outside its walls. The war which finally burst in upon them so violently.

Here in this house he felt alone and vulnerable. Through the open doors he saw the man pick up the money and the icon and move across the room to a small bureau, he unlocked it and placed the objects inside before pocketing the key. The woman had followed him and they appeared to be arguing.

The sun rose higher and Benny became drowsy in the heat in spite of his overnight rest. He seemed to have managed with very little sleep for months but now, in the calm of this pleasant garden, he dozed. The shadow of the tall house moved across the garden, eventually shading him from the sun and he awoke with a start wondering, for a moment, just exactly where he was.

He got up and stretched. A hoe leaned against a small wooden shed near the padlocked door in the high wall. On impulse he walked across and picked it up and began hoeing the gravel paths and the soil around the shrubs where the weeds were sprouting. His thoughts strayed to his home and the crops they tended through the seasons and he longed to be back there. It seemed an age since he left and he was suddenly very homesick. He lost himself in the hoeing.

After about an hour he had cleared the garden of weeds, they lay in profusion all around, he walked to the shed and opened the door. Inside there was a wheelbarrow standing against the wall, some rope in neat coils and various garden tools hanging up on nails. He selected a rake and a narrow pronged fork and took them outside in the wheelbarrow. Twice he filled the wheelbarrow with weeds before depositing them on a compost heap behind the shed and then the sergeant's mother called him in for lunch.

The meal was a strained affair, the man spoke little and the woman fussed around too much. The atmosphere relaxed when they began to speak about their son. Benny had to re-tell his story about the ambush and the capture of the column and the unopened orders that could have saved both the Tommies and the sergeant. He helped with the washing up before asking if he could go upstairs for an afternoon nap. "Of course you can my dear," the woman said, "all those weeks in the fighting," she shook her head in wonder, "you must be exhausted. You go, I'll call you for dinner."

Benny closed the bedroom door behind him and sat upon the bed. He eased the pistol and ammo out of their makeshift underarm holsters and just held them, a feeling of reassurance gradually replacing his vague anxiety. He unwrapped the luger, cocking it and squeezing the trigger several times to get used to the feel of it again before placing it down on the bed beside him. He unfolded the piece of British Army gas anti-gas cape and the oil impregnated rag inside to reveal the clip of ammo. After some hesitation he slid the clip into the butt and set the safety catch before placing the pistol under his pillow and putting all the wrappings back under the bedside cabinet. He lay upon the bed for a long time unable to sleep.

Suddenly Benny heard a sound outside on the landing, he glanced at the door and saw the handle slowly turning. He quickly put his hand behind his head and under the pillow grasping the butt of the pistol while feigning sleep, his head on one side. Through partly closed eyes he could see, reflected in the mirror on the dressing table, the door inch open and the man's face peer in. "Benny," the man whispered, "are you awake?" Benny breathed slowly and noisily through his nose while secretly watching the door. The man withdrew, closing the door silently behind him and Benny relaxed his grip on the pistol.

He lay there for some time not knowing what to do. He almost wished that he had never come to find them to give them first hand news of their son's fate. They would have found out anyway in due course through official military channels but then it was the wallet he wanted to return, the wallet and the photo and the few lire, all that was left of their son's possessions. That was the point of his visit, to return those things to their rightful place.

He rose and tiptoed to the door, opening it as quietly as he could. From downstairs he could hear arguing and he crept to the top of the staircase so as to hear more clearly. "Promise me you will not call them," he heard the woman say, "at least not until tomorrow. The boy might change his mind."

"Don't you see," the man answered, "they are the ones with the contacts. They know best how it could be disposed of. I know of its rarity, I know roughly how much it could be worth but without their contacts it's no good. Even if he changes his mind we still need them."

"They are a bunch of criminals," she retorted.

"They are men of honour," he insisted.

"You know what they will do?" she asked, "as soon as they know this thing exists, as soon as they know it could be as valuable as you say?" She didn't wait for his reply. "They will take it from him, probably kill him to shut him up. After all who is he? A homeless refugee, a bicycle thief perhaps, a worthless urchin. Italy is full of them. He would not be missed. Would you want that on your conscience?"

"No of course not," he said quietly.

"And another thing," she went on, "how much would you get out of the transaction? A pittance no doubt. They always keep the lion's share."

"We've done well out of the black market. We never went hungry during the worst times did we? They did alright by us didn't they?"

"When you consider the people we helped to cheat and the risks we took we got little enough out of it," she replied, but I don't know the half of it. You always kept things from me."

"It is better that way. What you don't know can't hurt you."

"All I know is I've lost my son," she sobbed, "and all the good food, the expensive cigarettes and the Mafia handouts won't bring him back."

Benny withdrew quietly to his room and closed the door softly. He unloaded the luger and put it and the ammo clip back under the bedside cabinet wrapped in the coverings he had so carefully concealed them in over the weeks and months. His mind was in turmoil. The argument downstairs had not been resolved, the man could still contact his shady accomplices and Benny could, actually could, finish up in a river somewhere wearing a concrete overcoat.

He made his mind up. After surviving Monte Cassino he was not prepared to be sacrificed on the altar of avarice by Mafia thugs who called themselves men of honour. He moved to the bedroom window and surveyed his escape route.

There was his bicycle, a valuable commodity as street urchins across Italy were discovering. He pondered the best time to leave, if he rode during the dead of night any police patrol would be bound to investigate. By day he could bluff his way through by saying he was visiting an aunt or uncle in the next town but he would be visible to the Mafia men and their cronies who could easily be alerted to look out for him and probably had the vehicles, and the petrol, to patrol large areas.

But first he had to get his money and the icon out of that bureau then get himself and his bicycle out onto the street.

There was the rope in the shed he remembered. He could climb up the orange tree near the padlocked door, haul the bicycle up on the rope and lower it down the other side then slide down the rope and be away. Simple. He went and lay down upon the bed and was asleep within minutes.

It was dusk when he was awakened by tapping on the bedroom door and the sergeant's mother peeped in. "Would you like to come down for some dinner?" she asked.

"Thank you," Benny replied as he sat up collecting his thoughts, "I'll be down in a few minutes." She withdrew closing the door quietly behind her and Benny retrieved the pistol and ammo.

Presently he made his way downstairs and into the austere dining room. There were three places laid at the table, a steaming bowl of pasta placed centrally alongside a dish of tossed salad and a bowl of mixed fruit. The woman motioned Benny to his seat. "Did you sleep well?" she asked.

"Yes thank you," he replied, "it is a nice room, a comfortable bed. Your son . . . . ," he stopped himself from saying more. He was going to say that her son was lucky to have such a fine room in such a nice house. It was just making conversation but, in the circumstances, idiotic. "Your husband," he said, pretending to correct himself, "is he not eating?"

"He has gone around to some friends, a card game. It is usual on this day of the week," she replied. "Please help yourself, you must be hungry." Benny ladled some pasta onto his plate, it was mixed with diced meat, onions, peppers and mushrooms with a skin of crisp melted cheese on the top. He covered half his plate with that and the other half with salad, helping himself to some thickly sliced bread stacked upon a nearby plate. He certainly was hungry and tucked into the meal with gusto, the woman's plate looked empty by comparison and she seemed to peck half heartedly at her food. "Some wine?" she asked and without waiting for a reply she poured a generous measure into a glass before sliding it across the polished table to him.

Benny was no connoisseur, the wine they drank at home was rough and ready and of unreliable quality, this however was incredibly smooth, a deep red, almost warm to the tongue, mellow and fruity. In later years he often said he had never tasted better. It was, he correctly surmised, supplied courtesy of the Mafia.

The meal continued in silence until Benny finally pushed his plate aside and drained his glass. He declined the offer of a re-fill, he wanted to have his wits about him for his escape later. Through the open door he could see the bureau in the lounge and wondered how he could break it open quietly and whether to do it before or after getting his bicycle over the wall.

The woman too had finished although the amount of food she had consumed was miniscule. She pushed her plate away and sighed deeply. "Benny," she said, "what are you going to do with the icon?"

Benny glanced at her. She had a kind face, lined and wrinkled from the sun and her age. Sad eyes that looked to be always on the verge of tears, a thin neck almost scrawny. He did not know what to say. Until the previous day he had been unaware of the contents of the package he had retrieved during that first devastating air raid. It had just been something else to be in charge of along with the luger and the compass and the wallet. Vaguely in the back of his mind he had intended to return it to the monastery but when or how he had not considered. "It belongs to the Abbey," he muttered.

"My husband says it is very valuable," she replied.

"It still belongs to the Abbey," Benny insisted, "one day, when the war is over I could take it back there. They might be able to sell it to help rebuild."

The woman smiled. A lonely sort of smile as tears welled in her eyes. "And what if you lose it or someone steals it from you or you decide to sell it yourself?" Benny smiled inwardly. She and her husband and his thug friends were the very people intending to steal it from him if he could not be persuaded to relinquish it. How ironic was that?

It was his fervent wish that someday, somehow he would return the icon to its owners, the monks at Monte Cassino Abbey. He looked the woman in the eyes. "I won't lose it," he said defiantly, "I definitely won't sell it and if anyone tries to steal it from me I'll kill them!"

As soon as the words left his lips he was appalled at them. He had lived with violent death for months and yet the thought of killing anyone never crossed his mind. To say what he had and to mean it was a sobering and worrying development.

The woman never flinched. Her face even seemed to soften a little as she gazed at Benny. This slip of a kid who had endured so much, who had come all this way to return her only son's meagre possessions. She fumbled with the sleeve of her dress where it fitted around her wrist. "You are a brave boy," she said, "I was hoping you felt that way about the icon. Here, take this," and she handed him a small key, "in the lounge there's a bureau, open it with this. Inside you'll find the icon and your American dollars. Bring them to me."

Benny's mouth dropped open but he quickly did as he was asked and laid the items on the table before her. "Can you find your way back to Naples railway station?" she asked. Benny nodded. "Here is some money, there is enough to buy a ticket for Taranto and some more besides."

"But I have money," he said flourishing the dollars.

"Keep them out of sight for now. Give them to your parents perhaps. People will kill for American dollars. Take the lire, buy your ticket, third class of course."

"My bicycle," Benny groaned, "the garden door, the padlock . . ."

"I will unlock it for you but you must go soon. I will prepare some food for you to take, get all your things together. Be quick now."

14

It was dusk before Benny covered the twenty or so kilometres back to Naples. The city had suffered considerable bomb damage and Benny got lost once or twice when having to take diversions due to street closures caused by unsafe buildings. Eventually he arrived at the railway station to find the same bunch of urchins selling bicycles. Benny dismounted and walked up to the one he had dealt with previously. "You want this bicycle?" he asked.

"How much?" the boy asked, eyeing Benny shrewdly.

"You can have it for nothing."

The boy glanced at his friends in disbelief. "What's wrong with it?" he asked.

"There's nothing wrong with it. You sold it to me yesterday remember?" He thrust the machine into the boy's hands. "Here, check it over. I've got to find out what time the train leaves for Taranto." He brushed past them and hurried into the station.

So far so good he thought. If he had been followed by any of his hosts' Mafia friends the frequent diversions should have thrown them off the scent, if not, his encounter with the bicycle thieves would have been observed, they would be quizzed and paid to tell of Benny's planned destination.

He stood in the queue for the train tickets until his turn came. "Third class single to Brindisi please," he said and paid with the money the sergeant's mother had given him. The station was poorly lit and crowded with people, military police stood in pairs at various points and Allied service personnel seemed to outnumber civilians. Benny checked the departure boards noting the times and platform numbers. The Taranto express was due to leave in half an hour, there was no indication of a train for Brindisi. He sought out a railway official. "Brindisi," he said, "when is the next train?"

The man glanced up at the station clock. "Best to get the slow train to Foggia," he replied, "leaves in an hour. Then pick up the connection to Brindisi from there." Benny returned to scan the departure boards, noting the platform number for the Foggia train.

By that time the Taranto train was waiting and passengers were boarding, Benny walked along the platform right up to the locomotive. He stood watching the fireman shovelling coal into the firebox as they got up steam for the journey, the smell of hot oil and sulphur filling his nostrils. He was still concerned that he might have been followed so he decided on one final act to elude any possible pursuit.

He walked on past the locomotive to the end of the platform where there were no lights, in the semi darkness he peered out along the track, his eyes following the gentle curve of the glistening rails as they reflected the reds and greens of the signals. A couple of hundred metres out there was a linesman's hut shuttered and unlit. He turned back towards the crowded concourse and sauntered casually among the people until he was near the end of the train.

With only a few minutes to go before its scheduled departure he boarded the train and began to walk towards the front end. He managed to reach the front coach without being challenged just as the locomotive let out a long blast on the whistle and the train began to move.

The window was difficult to open but Benny finally managed it and wriggled through to hang by his fingertips with his toes on the running board as the train slowly gathered speed. He made out the dim shape of the linesman's hut as it slid past and then he jumped. It was extremely fortunate that he narrowly missed a signal gantry as he landed heavily beside a stack of railway sleepers. He lay still, his heart pounding, until the train's red tail light vanished into the night then he crawled back and crouched in the shadow of the hut. He checked himself over feeling the bruises and rubbing his shoulder where he had rolled onto his side and surmised correctly that he had suffered no broken bones.

His eyes were so accustomed to the darkness by then that the dimly lit station appeared glaringly bright. He picked out the platform from which the Foggia train would leave before retrieving the luger from his makeshift holster. He loaded it and set the safety catch before replacing it. If the Mafia were still on his tail he knew what he would do before he ever relinquished the icon.

The Foggia train was shunted into the station and Benny waited, trying to estimate the time before departure. Keeping in the shadows he crawled towards the train then, leaving it as late as he dared, he scuttled across the tracks up onto the platform and into a third class coach. He found an unlit compartment and settled down in the darkness his hand clasped around the butt of the pistol.

A whistle blew and the coach jolted forward then stopped, voices sounded outside and doors slammed but no one entered his dark sanctuary. Several minutes dragged by before the locomotive let out a short blast and the train began to move.

It seemed incredible that he was on his way home at last. A pang of excitement at the prospect made his stomach turn over. Homeward bound. The weeks and months away, with all the adversity and the danger he had endured, were of little concern to him now. Had he known what awaited him however he would have felt less euphoric. Presently he fell into a fitful sleep.

The journey to Foggia was painfully slow. They stopped at almost every station along the way and were sometimes sidetracked to let a faster train overtake them or to avoid bomb damaged track. Benny finished off the last of the food the sergeant's mother had prepared for him, washing it down with wine. He kept a little of the wine back for the last leg of the journey and the sun was well up as the train finally pulled into the station at Foggia.

It was midday before his connecting train arrived. Benny was dog tired by then and had to force himself to keep awake. The east coast express stopped only at Barletta and Bari before it steamed into Brindisi.

The taxi driver in the square outside the station concourse quoted a ridiculously high fare when Benny asked how much it would cost to take him home to his village. The war had certainly changed things and inflation was rife but his price was extortionate and Benny was in no mood to be overcharged. "That's too much," he retorted.

The man shrugged. "Please yourself," he said and flicked his cigarette butt past Benny's ear.

Just then another taxi pulled up, this driver had a friendlier face. Benny shouted across to him, asking him if he knew the village. "Sure I do kid," the man replied.

Benny pulled out a five dollar bill. "You take me there for this?" he asked.

"Jump in kid," the man beamed.

The first driver got out of his car. "Hey, the kid was my fare. You piss off."

Benny got in friendly face's taxi. "No," he shouted through the window, "you piss off. You were going to rip me off." Benny's taxi drove away and the shouts of abuse faded into the distance.

The taxi dropped him off at the end of the street, the street where the army column had halted and his adventure had begun. That all seemed to have happened in a previous life, a life where everything was black and white, where Il Duce was a national hero to be adored and worshipped. He watched the taxi as it diminished into the distance trailing a cloud of dust then he turned away and walked home.

The house was locked and shuttered when he got there. Around the back the chickens pecked and scratched in the run, the goat was tethered in its usual place, from beyond the screen of brush and scrub came the faint sound of the sea. He shrugged and wearily made his way to his uncle's place farther down the road.

He found his uncle and aunt hoeing in the back plot, they looked up as he approached. "Can I help you?" his uncle asked.

Benny looked from one to the other. "It's me," he grinned. The weeks of army rations had obviously agreed with him, he had grown up a lot in spite of the privations he had endured at Monte Cassino. "It's me," he repeated, "me, Benny."

His uncle squinted against the glare of the afternoon sun trying to reconcile this stocky youngster with the child he knew. Then recognition dawned. "Guiseppe, my little one," he shot an anxious glance at his wife who stood rooted to the spot wide eyed. "In the name of the Virgin Mary," he said crossing himself, "we thought you were dead. No word, no letter. Come and give your old uncle a hug."

All three clung to each other and Benny felt a surge of happiness to be home. It was to be short lived. He looked up at his aunt, at the tears streaming down her face, at his uncle's sad eyes. "Where are Mama and Papa?" he asked. "The house was all shut up but the animals were OK."

"We have been looking after the place," he replied, "come into the house, it is time for supper anyway." All three made their way into the dim coolness of the kitchen. "Sit down Guiseppe," his uncle said, "we'll have some wine." He reached a bottle down from the shelf and poured out three glasses as his wife brought out some salami and bread and cheese. They all sat down at the table, his aunt still tearful, her eyes downcast, her grubby soil stained hands folded in her lap.

"Guiseppe my boy," his uncle said gently, "I have something to tell you. It is bad I'm afraid." Benny looked from one to the other, a dreadful foreboding in the pit of his stomach. "Your Mama, your Papa. They . . . they are dead."

Benny said nothing for several long seconds. He looked from one to the other, his mouth open, shaking his head slightly, trying to take it in. "Dead?" he breathed.

"They were visiting friends in Brindisi," his uncle said, "there was an air raid. The house was hit. Everyone inside was killed, your parents, their friends, two children, the grandmother. It is the war," he added despairingly.

Benny buried his head in his hands and cried. He cried more bitterly than he had ever cried before. The war, the war, this bloody awful war. Death and destruction everywhere. He had lived through months of it and now to come home to this. In his despair he was inconsolable. That night and for many nights afterwards he cried himself to sleep.

Benny's aunt and uncle looked after him during the weeks that followed. He went to his own home every day and tended to the livestock but he lived at his uncle's place. Most afternoons after his chores, if there was nothing else to do he would wander over to the seashore and sit listening to the waves crying constantly while cursing god and Mussolini. There seemed to be a permanent lump in his throat but every evening he would put on a brave face as he sat with his aunt and uncle discussing the coming harvest or what they would take to market the following week. He never talked about the war or the Fascist movement of which he had once been an enthusiastic member. All that seemed so irrelevant now.

One evening his uncle said: "Have you ever seen anything of our tenants when you sit by the seashore?"

"Our tenants?"

"Over towards the north headland, you know that big patch of trees and scrub?" Benny nodded. "Well we've got someone living there. Haven't you noticed the smoke sometimes?" Benny shook his head. "Don't know who they are," his uncle added, "I've kept clear, could be army deserters. Anybody."

"How long have they been there?" Benny asked.

"I first noticed them way back last autumn."

"They've been there all that time? What have they been living on?"

"I don't know. I was tempted to take them some food, an occasional chicken or something but I never saw anyone, just the smoke. As I say they could have been army deserters, German special forces who knows? I stayed well away. They didn't bother me, I didn't bother them."

In the days that followed Benny made sure that his frequent visits to the seashore took him closer and closer to the area mentioned by his uncle. On one occasion he thought he could smell wood smoke but he saw no one, the copse of trees and scrub was too dense.

One afternoon a chilly easterly wind was blowing mist and rain inland, Benny was minded to give his excursion a miss but something told him to go in spite of the weather. The headland was a grey blur, the clump of trees shrouded in mist. The sea disappeared into the murk with no horizon to distinguish it from the leaden sky.

Benny stayed close to the sand dunes and low cliffs well back from the shoreline as he approached the trees, he crouched behind a clump of marram grass. This time there was no mistaking the acrid smell of wood smoke, he could actually see the grey blue wisps as they dispersed through the foliage. Suddenly a movement caught his eye and coming up from the water's edge was a boy of about his own age, in his arms a bundle of driftwood.

Benny froze and watched as the boy approached the trees, as soon as he disappeared into the bushes Benny was on his feet and sprinting in pursuit. He was only a couple of metres behind when the boy entered the tiny clearing.

The upturned boat was well camouflaged amongst the scrub and a crude hut had been constructed between two convenient trees, the roof a mixture of rough thatch and canvass sailcloth. A small fire burned before the hut and a man was grilling two fish speared on sticks. The boy placed the driftwood down beside the fire.

Benny pulled his pistol from under his coat and inched forward before stepping into the clearing. "Who are you?" he demanded. The pair almost jumped out of their skins and stood paralysed with their hands up, fear written all over their faces. The boy said something to the man who snapped a reply. Benny did not understand the language, he decided to try English. "Where you come from?" he asked.

The boy pointed towards the sea. "From Kerkyra. From Corfu." Just then an old lady emerged from the hut a blanket wrapped around her thin shoulders, she looked as terrified as they did. She said something to the man and they had a brief discussion in the same unintelligible tongue which Benny now realised was Greek. There was a further three way conversation as Benny looked on. Finally the boy, his eyes glued to the pointing luger, asked: "Are any Germans here?" Benny shook his head and the boy turned to the man and the old lady, "oxi," he said.

Benny slipped the safety catch on and put the pistol away noting the look of relief on the faces of the foreigners. "What are you doing here anyway?" he asked.

"Can my father do his cooking?"

Benny waved an arm, "yes, yes of course." The man resumed his task and the old lady sank down onto a makeshift brushwood bed just inside the hut. "We come here to escape from the Germans," the boy explained, "Italian soldiers they help us but when we land they go away, leave us. We hide here, make hut. You sure Germans gone?"

"Quite sure."

"My name is Yiorgo," the boy announced, "this my father and my grandmother."

"My name is Benny," he replied, "I live quite close. You are safe here, it is my uncle's land. I will bring him here to meet you tomorrow. You need not worry about the Germans, they are far to the north," he paused trying to think of the right thing to say. "My country has now been liberated by the Allies," he concluded.

The following day Benny brought his uncle to the hidden encampment, he also brought some bread and a couple of bottles of wine. It appeared that this small group had been living on fish caught at night and seagulls trapped during the day and they were all suffering from malnutrition. It was decided to move them into Benny's parents' place straight away.

They were overjoyed at their deliverance and showed their gratitude unstintingly. Yiorgo and his father worked tirelessly repairing gates and fences, hoeing, feeding livestock and a thousand and one things that needed to be done around the place. The old lady mended clothes, washed and scrubbed, cooked and cleaned and every Sunday they all went to mass.

One Sunday after the service, as they sat around the big table at his uncle's house, Yiorgo stood up nervously. "My father and grandmother want me talk for them," he said. "We have our boat," the boy continued, "we want go back to Kerkyra, to Corfu. But we are not good sailors. Can you help us?" Benny translated all this for his aunt and uncle.

"Do you know what condition their boat is in?" his uncle asked Benny. The boy shook his head. "I'd better have a look at it tomorrow then," he said, "if it's OK d'you think you could sail it over there for them?"

The prospect was an exciting one. "I reckon I could," Benny replied.

So the following day the men and the two boys inspected the boat. They pulled it out of the clearing and checked that it had all the sails and rigging necessary for sailing. Its long sojourn on dry land had caused the planking to shrink so that it resembled a sieve as far as water retention was concerned. They dragged it into the sea, sank it and weighted it down with rocks.

"What I'd like to know," Benny's uncle said to him quietly, "is why they came here in the first place."

"So why did they?" I asked as Neil topped up our glasses once again. A slight breeze had sprung up, warmer now that the rain had gone, swaying the anchor light and making the shadows dance about the deck. "Oh, that's a story in itself," Mario replied. "A juicy story too by all accounts, all about this little Greek kid's grandmother."

"Don't tell me," I said, "sex raises its head again I'll bet."

"You English are always so bloody cynical and unromantic," Mario chided, "it was love man. There is a difference."

Mario need not have told me that. Since Jean and I broke up I had lived the life of a reclusive bachelor. Apart from a brief liaison with someone at an office in Birmingham where I had been on a six month contract, I had been celibate. That particular girl was, I later discovered, on the rebound from a long standing relationship, I had been sympathetic, she had been receptive, I became genuinely fond of her and she was attractive, Her apparent vulnerability brought out my protective instinct. To be frank I fell for her but when her man came crawling back, she flew into his arms.

It took me several months to get over that. I was hurt and I missed her but, looking back, I'm not convinced it wasn't my ego that hurt rather than my heart. Anyway, from then on I steered well clear of apparently vulnerable females, on the rebound or not. That distant affair lay somewhere between love and sexual infatuation, with Jean it was love pure and simple. Even after all this time I still felt a deep inner sadness at her loss in spite of her betrayal. I sighed and took another sip at the gin, "so come on then," I grinned, "let's have all the sordid details."

"Well," Mario began, "on the face of it they were escaping from the Germans but they would not have been in any danger at all if it hadn't been for dear old grandma."

"How come?" Neil asked.

"Apparently she had unfinished emotional business as far as Italy was concerned," Mario replied, "this Greek kid Yiorgo had picked up all the details by listening in to grown ups talking over the years, kids are like that. It was one of those family secrets everyone knows about but nobody mentions. Yiorgo and Uncle Benny must have become real good mates because Benny got the whole story from him during the time they spent together. It involved Uncle Benny's childhood hero Mr. bloody Mussolini and his greedy territorial ambitions."

. . . .

By 1923 Yiorgo's grandmother had been ten years in a loveless marriage. Her husband was several years her senior and she had been promised to him from the age of five. Her wedding night had consisted of a painful loss of virginity followed by several more brutal and drunken penetrations all of which she bore with stoicism, believing it her duty. After the birth of her son, Yiorgo's father, her husband spent increasing amounts of his spare time at the local coffee shop playing cards or backgammon, usually losing money and always getting drunk, his sexual demands diminishing over the years.

That fateful summer she went to visit her sister in Corfu Town leaving her husband and his coarse peasant family for the rather more refined surroundings of her well to do sister and her professional husband. The break was most welcome, there she enjoyed a lifestyle of genteel sophistication totally outside her normal experience. Her sister had really done well for herself she thought but she felt no envy, no bitterness, just a simple gratitude that she was able to visit from time to time and escape the feudal drudgery of her husband's agricultural background.

That particular morning stood out in her memory. The explosions rattling the windows and shaking the buildings, the flashes from the distant warships followed by the scream and whine of the shells before the crumping detonations. The bombardment was directed at the Old Fort where the refugees were housed.

Her sister's husband had talked about the situation over dinner only the previous evening. How the government's misguided expedition against the Turks had been foolish in the extreme. How the Asia Minor disaster, as it became known, had cost many lives, had achieved no territorial gain and had landed Corfu with thousands of refugees, many housed in terrible conditions in the Old Fort now being mercilessly shelled by Mussolini's navy. The dictator had seized upon the chaos following the Greeks' abortive exercise to make his move.

Her sister's house was not the grandest but it was a cut above the rest. The upper windows commanded a view across the harbour and was convenient to the administrative centre of the town. It was therefore no surprise that, after the troops had marched in to claim the island for Italy, the house should be commandeered to billet junior officers of the occupying army.

To say it was love at first sight would be an overstatement but certainly the young Italian lieutenant and the former peasant girl experienced a strong mutual attraction. She stayed on at her sister's place for the entire month that Mussolini's troops occupied the island before pressure from the League of Nations forced an end to his grandiose dreams of expansion. The soldiers were forced to leave and the Corfu Incident, as it became known, passed into history.

Messages of concern from her husband's family in their mountain village were answered with reassurances of her perfect safety under the protection of her brother-in-law. There was no mention of the Italian lieutenant. That magic month spent in his company made a long lasting impression upon her. She ate out at up market restaurants and learned a little Italian, although they usually conversed in broken English. Not that there was much need for conversation. They made love by moonlight amongst the olive groves, on beaches, on grassy meadows even in her room when her sister and brother-in-law were out. The lieutenant was gentle and kind and considerate. All the things her husband was not. She broke her heart when the troops sailed away. Eight months later she gave birth to a baby girl. It was stillborn.

It was understandable then, that twenty years later, now a widow and again visiting her sister in Corfu Town, she was excited, pleased even that they were once again occupied by Italian troops, now part of the Fascist Axis powers. The sight of these young men in uniform stirred sad memories of the distant love affair with her Italian lieutenant and the dead child they had created together.

Her sister's house was once again commandeered by the military, once again it housed Italian officers. Her brother-in-law was furious and fumed in private at the Italianisation of the island. Many of his closest friends were schoolteachers, they were all sacked and replaced by Italians who taught the new Italian curriculum. Greek newspapers were banned and only one, printed in Italian, was published. He himself was lucky not to lose his job. As a local government official, however, he had to report, in Italian, to a superior appointed by the occupying power.

Since Italy's occupation of the island in 1941 Yiorgo's grandmother had visited her sister frequently, adding to her Italian vocabulary and harbouring a forlorn hope that her former lover might turn up again one day. That did not happen but she became friendly with the officers billeted at her sister's house. Where most of the household maintained a frigid politeness towards them, she conversed openly with their unwanted guests. It was from them they learned that Mussolini had been deposed and arrested on the orders of the Italian King. It was from them they heard of Italy's surrender after the Allied landings at Salerno.

That was when the nightmare began.

The Italian garrison on the island outnumbered the Germans but their orders were to remain passive towards their former allies. The Germans had other ideas, especially Field Marshall Kesselring.

When called upon by the Germans to surrender the Italians refused and what followed was the cause of the family's flight to Italy. The Italian garrison held out for weeks against mounting German strength. Finally, out of ammunition and by now outnumbered, they surrendered but not before much of Corfu Town had been reduced to rubble by Stuka dive bombers and artillery fire. One of the officers billeted at the house was an artilleryman whose battery was positioned on the coast. As soon as he heard rumours of Kesselring's murderous orders he and two gunners slipped away under cover of darkness. They swam for several miles before coming ashore and making their way cautiously to the house. It was still standing although every window was broken by blast. In the cellar they planned their escape.

"You know what Germans do?" Yiorgo asked Benny as they sat by the shore near the sunken boat. Benny shook his head but he knew the answer. "They shoot all officers and take other soldiers to be slave labour. Bastards." Yiorgo spat into the sand.

"So what happened then?" Benny asked.

"I working, collecting olives with my father near our village," Yiorgo continued, "and suddenly my grandma, she arrive with three Italians. One of them officer."

Against the advice of her sister and her husband, Yiorgo's grandmother had insisted on helping the trio escape. Driven by thoughts of her lost love she was determined to do everything in her power to repatriate these Italian soldiers in spite of their unwanted occupation of her homeland. Their uniforms were burned and all military identification destroyed or buried and clothes were grudgingly provided from the extensive wardrobes of her sister and brother-in-law. Then, with one of the gunners dressed as a woman and each carrying a bundle of belongings, they set off like refugees to walk to Yiorgo's grandmother's village.

No one took any notice of the two 'couples' as they trudged north. There were many others on the road in a similar state. Occasionally a military vehicle swept past in a cloud of dust and several open backed lorries containing Italian prisoners bound for internment or worse. Now in broad daylight close to town they were not conspicuous, later, during the hours of darkness and out in the country, it would be different.

"My grandma she know the old paths through the hills," Yiorgo explained, "even so it take two days and nights to get back. My father very angry. He say we all get shot if we caught."

Yiorgo's father was not just angry, he was terrified. He knew the penalty for helping the Italians would be a firing squad. He had heard about the Allies crossing the Messina strait having liberated Sicily, and knew that they were forging north towards Rome so, he reasoned, perhaps the best course of action would be for all of them to get over there as soon as possible. He tried in vain to convince his wife but she would have none of it. She fled in tears to her family in the next village imploring Yiorgo to go with her and swearing not to breathe a word about the planned escape or the Italian fugitives they were risking their necks for.

That night the six set out for the coast by the light of the moon. With Yiorgo's grandmother leading they kept off the roads, following the tracks through the olive groves which she had known since childhood. By dawn they were hidden in a thatched hut used as a shelter by the olive pickers on the hillside overlooking Roda. Yiorgo's father walked down to the village. He had a cousin who owned a boat.

It was mid afternoon by the time he returned. They had all slept for a while, taking turns to keep watch. His father had brought bread and cheese and wine and two roast chickens still warm from the oven. He explained by sign language helped by some Italian from Yiorgo's grandmother that this was all the food they had to last them until they reached Italy. The officer took charge and rationed it out.

It was agreed to try and set sail at dusk so, before sunset, Yiorgo, his father and grandmother together with the disguised officer set off for the village. Half an hour later the other two Italians, one still dressed as a woman, followed on to meet near the tiny harbour.

"I think my father say we all on run from the Germans," Yiorgo explained to Benny, "that why his cousin so helpful. He take away woman's clothes, dress all Italians like fishermen. Even grandma look like a man for no womans go fishing in Corfu. Then we get in three boats, all sail out together to look like normal fishing trip. We sail for Erikousa."

It was dark long before the little flotilla anchored off the north shore of the island. All the refugees transferred to one boat and the cousin tethered the other two together, hoisted the sail and set off back to Corfu. "You know," Yiorgo smiled, "is crazy. No one know how to sail. We have to learn as we go along."

"No one?" Benny asked.

Yiorgo shook his head. "Grandma, she have watch what my father's cousin do, so she take command. She take helm, tell Italian soldiers what to do," he smiled to himself, "is crazy," he repeated.

The wind was favourable and the night was clear. Steering by the stars they headed for Italy and by dawn they were out of sight of land. Towards noon the wind fell light and they ate some food and drank a little of the precious water they had brought with them. Around mid afternoon they sighted a sail to the south and an hour later the wind picked up. They resumed their course, which could only be estimated, and it soon became obvious that the other boat was on a convergent track. Soon they were within hailing distance. Yiorgo's father made signs for the Italians to remain silent as he stood up and shouted to the occupants in Greek. To his infinite relief they answered him in the same language and came up alongside.

"You know where they from?" Yiorgo asked. Benny shook his head. "They from Kephalonia. That down south from Kerkyra. They tell us what happen there."

The two boats lowered their sails and stayed alongside for a while, long enough for the strangers to relate the awful news from that island. As in Corfu the Italian garrison had surrendered to the Germans only this time, instead of transporting the prisoners, there was wholesale massacre of their former allies. These Greek fishermen had sailed through seas strewn with the bodies of Italian soldiers and, afraid for their own safety, had headed northwest away from the Greek islands. All this was relayed to the soldiers by Yiorgo's grandmother in faltering

Italian. Their grim faces showed that they understood. The two boats sailed on together until nightfall and as the first stars appeared it was obvious that their course was too far west. As the wind increased Yiorgo's grandmother altered course to the north before handing the tiller to one of the Italians and slumping exhausted in the bottom of the boat.

The wind continued to increase in strength and soon the stars were obscured by scudding low cloud. They let the sail out so that the boat heeled over less alarmingly and it was fortuitous that this action combined with the wind direction meant their course was leading them, more by luck than judgement, towards Italy.

At first light it could be seen that the boat was in a mess, all of them had been sick but at least no one had been lost. Of the other boat they had encountered there was no sign. By late afternoon they sighted land and before dusk they had beached the boat and dragged it up into a small copse of trees some way from the shoreline. They upturned the boat, fashioning an adjoining shelter from the mast and sails then they ate what little food was left, drank the last of the water and slept.

"When I wake up," Yiorgo said, "Italian soldiers gone. We not know if they captured by Germans. We stay hidden, catch fish at night. Then you come. Now we go home yes? Back to Kerkyra?"

"I told my uncle I would do it."

"Then it is a deal yes?"

"Yes." They shook hands on the seashore in the gathering dusk.

"If you wanted to hide something," Benny said, "Somewhere nobody would find it, where would you do it?"

"I know place like that," Yiorgo answered, "when you take us home I show you."

"Promise you won't tell anyone?"

Yiorgo crossed himself. "I promise on my mother's grave," he said solemnly.

16

Yiorgo's boat remained submerged for days. Each afternoon after they had completed the daily chores he and Benny would go to the shore just to see it there shimmering below the surface. They played together amongst the sand dunes and the scrub, attacking imaginary German machine gun nests, sabotaging imaginary fuel and ammo dumps, ambushing imaginary troop convoys and cutting the throats of imaginary SS officers.

As the day for their departure drew near Benny's uncle took him on one side. "Benny," he said, "have you thought about what you will do after you get these people home?" Benny had thought a lot about what he would do. Deep down he wanted to join his elder sister in the Welsh vallies but he had no idea how this might be achieved. There was a grieving sadness inside him that cried out to be comforted but no comfort could be found. When he was alone around the house he would talk aloud to his dead parents, reminding them of the days of his early childhood, telling them of his adventures and his plans to go and live with his big married sister.

One day, behind the dust covered clock that stood silent upon the mantelpiece, he found a faded picture postcard that she had sent home. The photograph showed the imposing waterfront buildings of the Bute Docks at Cardiff. He read aloud to the sepia portrait of his parents that stood beside the clock from the neatly written message they must have read themselves many times before, of the happiness she had found with her new husband. Of how they hoped to open a small café of their own with money borrowed from his family. Eventually he sank down at the table where, in earlier years, they had all sat and laughed and dined together and there he wept more bitter tears of grief until his throat ached and he could weep no more.

At last Yiorgo's boat was made ready. The planking had swelled through its long immersion so that when they had bailed it out and the sun had done its work, it was as dry as a cork inside.

"Have you got everything, Guiseppe my little one?" his aunt asked as they prepared to leave.

Benny shouldered his British army haversack, eased his home made shoulder holster into a more comfortable position and checked his inside pocket for the wad of dollar bills. "Yes aunty," he replied.

"You know you are welcome back at any time Benny," his uncle said.

"I know that uncle, I will write to you as soon as I can."

"Tell your sister we will look after the place as best we can. Good luck, God speed and a safe journey." With that Benny kissed and hugged them both and with tears in his eyes he climbed aboard. Yiorgo, his father and grandmother wept openly as they waved their farewells, their shouts of *epharisto* ringing in Benny's ears as the wind filled the sails and the boat heeled slightly, the wake bubbling out behind them as their speed increased. When next he looked back his aunt and uncle were just two tiny figures upon the beach though they were still waving.

The course Benny would be steering, using the German sergeant's prismatic compass, had been calculated from a tattered old school atlas belonging to his uncle. First they followed the coast until they came abreast of Otranto, that took them most of the day then as the dusk came on they turned away from the friendly shore lights and headed east south east into the darkness of the coming night.

They had no navigation lights, only a battered old electric torch but they were well provisioned with food and water plus several bottles of wine to celebrate their arrival. Benny could sense the family's excitement at the prospect of their return and in some odd way he shared it with them, his own homecoming having been such a tragic anti-climax.

The wind fell light as the night drew on and at one stage they were practically becalmed. No calculations had been built in to allow for leeway or sea currents and they could have drifted considerably during the hours of darkness nevertheless, at first light, as the breeze picked up, Benny resumed the course they had measured off that old atlas.

The sky remained cloudless and the sea calm, the breeze pushing them gently along. They spoke little, lost in their own thoughts as the sun climbed higher and the heat of the day built up. They took turns at the helm keeping the boat roughly on the heading which Benny hoped and prayed would bring them to their destination.

Dusk fell on the second day without sight of land or any other vessel. They had seen some smoke to the south in the late afternoon probably from some steamer just below the horizon, but that was all. The breeze remained fresh all that night and they were able to maintain a reasonable speed then, towards dawn, it fell away and their progress slowed. Benny insisted they keep to their course. He had no way of knowing what correction, if any, he should make to allow for drift or currents so, he reasoned, the course from the atlas was their best, their only, hope.

Around midday the breeze increased and their speed picked up again. Towards evening, away to the southeast, Yiorgo noticed a patch of cloud low on the horizon. To the east a continuous cloud bank looking like a mountain range stretched left and right as far as the eye could see. "You know what I think?" he asked Benny who was dozing at the tiller.

"What?"

"All that cloud bank, that is Albania. That little patch there," he pointed to the southeast, "that is Corfu." Benny glanced down at the prismatic compass. Yiorgo could be right. The direction was a good twenty degrees off course but the evidence of the cloud formations was a strong indicator in these settled weather conditions. They had been at sea plenty long enough to have covered the distance, even allowing for their slow progress. He pushed the tiller over and pointed the bows at the small patch of cloud. Slowly it grew in size as the daylight faded. Benny took a bearing on the cloud before the darkness swallowed it up and they kept on that heading as the breeze once again fell away during the night.

Before dawn Benny was roused by Yiorgo who was taking his turn at the helm. "Benny, Benny I see lights." He shouted.

"Where?" Benny stared blearily in the direction Yiorgo indicated and, sure enough, the distant twinkle of shore lights could just be discerned at the limit of visibility. They were plumb on the bow, in the direction Benny had set for their new course. "Keep aiming for them," he said and sank down to sleep once more.

At sunrise they were all wide awake. The island lay dead ahead, blue grey in the morning light, its hills mist covered, the highest point, Mount Pantocrator, shrouded in cloud. As they drew nearer a sandy beach could be seen stretching left and right for miles it seemed and behind it low lying marsh and scrub extended inland to the foothills of the high mountains. Yiorgo turned to his father, "Acharavi?"

"Nai," his father nodded and said something else to his son who turned to Benny.

"We almost at Roda," he said, "we steer to the right. There," he pointed, "around headland we see harbour." Benny adjusted the helm and sure enough as they rounded the point the tiny harbour slid into view.

The family reception at Roda was joyous in the extreme. Yiorgo's father's cousin had given up hope of ever seeing his boat again, to have his cousin back too was a definite bonus. After the drinking and the hugging and the kissing someone spirited a large car from somewhere, it was a taxi driven by a maniac Benny recalled later, who drove them all up into the hills to Yiorgo's village. Somehow news of their return had preceded them and Yiorgo's mother and all her family were there. The party went on for two days and would have gone on longer but for a chance remark by someone that the island was still ostensibly under German occupation.

The revelation brought Yiorgo, his father and grandmother down to earth with a severe jolt. If ever their role in helping the Italian soldiers escape became known they could still be executed. They were assured, however, that the troops occupying the island were Austrian and anti-Nazi and in any case the island was being administered by Corfiot officials with the invaders keeping a low profile. Then news came through in October that a Greek liberation force had landed at Messonghi beach, they marched into Corfu Town just as the Germans were leaving. Corfu was free again.

Ever since his arrival Benny had made a point of returning the favours that Yiorgo and his father and grandmother had done for his uncle and aunt. He helped milk the goats, collect the eggs and feed the turkeys, he repaired fences, hoed the crops, and helped with the olive harvest. He and Yiorgo slept in their own thatched hut, it was built of interwoven bamboo cane coated with dried mud, it had an earth floor and a small stove and was lit by a couple of oil lamps.

Every night before climbing into the old iron double bed they shared they would kneel on opposite sides and say their prayers, each in his own language. Benny would check his haversack with its precious contents and sleep would come quickly in the stillness of the mountain village.

One day Yiorgo said: "Benny, when you want to hide your treasure?" Benny looked his friend in the eyes, he knew he could trust him to keep the secret and he knew he must soon turn his mind to the problem of getting to England or rather to Wales and the *vallies* where his big sister and her husband lived. But what to do first? Arrange travel somehow? or hide his treasure ready for the day he would return and retrieve it and take it back to Monte Cassino Abbey? He decided that his first priority must be to hide it.

Yiorgo did not want his friend to leave but he listened patiently to Benny's reasons for wanting to get to England. He tried to imagine what life would be like if his own parents had been killed, it was only natural, he reasoned, for Benny to want to go and live with his married sister so he resolved to help his friend all he could. He knew his grandmother had a sister in Corfu Town and Corfu Town had a port. He had visited there a few times and seen the ships, if his friend wanted to get to England a visit to Corfu Town was essential. But first he had to help Benny to hide his treasure.

The following Saturday Benny was awakened before sunrise. Yiorgo stood framed in the doorway of the hut and behind him, munching on some hay, was his father's donkey. "I borrow her for the day," Yiorgo announced, "I got plenty water and hay, some food for us too. Come on, bring your treasure. We go and hide it someplace nobody find, okay?"

"How far is this place?" Benny asked.

"Long way. We back before dark though."

"I'll need a spade," Benny said, "to bury the treasure. That's what pirates do."

"Is okay, this thing do same," he flourished a British Army entrenching tool World War One vintage which had somehow found its way into his dead grandfather's tool shed. "You ready?"

"What about some breakfast?" Benny asked.

"I got some bread and some goat meat, we eat as we go along OK?"

"OK." They both got mounted on the donkey and, munching the food with one hand while holding on with the other, set off up the winding track through the olive groves. Yiorgo insisted on stopping every hour or so to rest the animal and let it drink from the canvass bucket they carried. At first there were streams or small waterfalls to fill up from, later as they climbed higher, they had to use water from the bottles and containers they had brought.

The day was hot, the sun blazing down from a cloudless sky but in the shelter of the olive groves it was not uncomfortable. By midday however they had left the olive groves behind and were climbing along dusty tracks bordered with stunted pine and bracken. The climb became steeper, the vegetation more sparse and all the time the road ahead clung to the valley wall as it wound upward. There was no shelter here from the unrelenting heat, no breeze disturbed the dry grass and the wild flowers that grew among the rocky outcrops dotting the hillside.

"Watch out!" Yiorgo reined the donkey to a halt as a metre long snake, his basking sleep disturbed, slithered off into the undergrowth.

"Can we rest for a minute?" Benny asked.

"OK. It's time she had another drink anyway," and they dismounted so that Yiorgo could administer the canvass bucket to their steed.

"How much further?" Benny asked as he mopped his brow and gazed up the valley to where the track hairpinned and climbed the other side.

"About another hour maybe," Yiorgo replied tilting the bucket so the animal could drain its contents. "This is worst bit, this and road up there," he pointed upwards to the track steeply climbing the opposite side of the narrow valley, "when we get up there maybe we get some breeze." They sat at the roadside for some minutes, wary of snakes, before continuing their journey.

They rounded the hairpin, leading the donkey now and trudged upward, tiredness causing their feet to drag sometimes on the stony surface. Benny glanced down the steep side of the valley, the road they had just negotiated was a dusty thread far below. They rounded another bend and the gradient decreased, wearily they remounted and soon they were passing through a shallow defile edged with stunted trees and boulders. At the top of the rise the road turned to the left, levelled out and then began to fall.

The donkey picked her way daintily down the gently curving track avoiding the biggest boulders and rough scree and Benny gasped at the sight that opened up before them. Yiorgo reined in the donkey. "You get down now," he said, "I go back to those trees we saw and wait for you in shade. Take this," and he handed Benny the old entrenching tool. "You got the treasure?"

"It's here," Benny patted the haversack.

"I wait for you back there. This good place to hide treasure, yes?"

"It's perfect Yiorgo, How did you know about it?"

"My grandmother she bring me here long time ago." He winked, "I think she come here sometimes with her Italian soldier," and with that Yiorgo wheeled the animal around and set off back the way they had come. Benny watched them climb the track and disappear around the bend, he knew he could trust his friend not to spy on his secret mission, then he turned and looked upon the incredible scene spread out before him. The entire area was overshadowed by Mount Pantocrator, he squinted up against the glare of the sky, at the squat shape of the monastery perched on the summit as he tried to decide upon a suitable hiding place, one that he could easily find again when he returned.

Almost two hours later Benny found Yiorgo asleep in the shade of a pine tree, the donkey nibbling at the coarse grasses nearby. He sank down beside his friend and closed his eyes. The job was done. The haversack was slung around his neck, the dollars safe in an inner pocket, the compass bearing burned into his memory. He dozed.

"Hey Benny, wake up!" it was Yiorgo shaking him, "it soon be sunset, we go now." They ate what little food was left and gave some water to their mount then set off along the track in the late afternoon.

The moon had risen, casting eery shadows through the olive trees, by the time they got back to the village and under the cold starlight of a late autumn evening Yiorgo lit the stove. They sat quietly before it lost in their own thoughts as they ate a light supper before going to bed.

17

A week after the expedition to bury Benny's treasure Yiorgo's grandmother announced her intention to visit her sister in Corfu Town. The family were all aware of Benny's desire to get to England and this visit was intended to help.

The ride into town was uncomfortable, sharing a bus with chickens and a goat did little for the well being of the other passengers. Benny's grandmother muttered complaints under her breath for the entire journey and, having disembarked at the terminus in the middle of Corfu Town, she spent ten minutes brushing herself and the boys down determined to be rid of the farmyard smells she insisted she could detect.

Her sister and her husband knew of Benny's help in bringing the three generations of the family safely back to the island and Benny was treated as an honoured guest. The husband, now retired, related the privations they had all endured since the Italian bombing of the town in 1940. How they had lived in the underground galleries of the Old and New Forts until the island surrendered to Mussolini's troops the following April. Benny listened intently to the old man's story as it was related piecemeal through Yiorgo. He in turn told of his subterranean experiences at Monte Cassino Abbey, of the bombing and of his role as medical orderly. He avoided telling them about the icon.

Corfu Town was still in ruins from the even more devastating bombardment exacted upon it prior to the Italian surrender to the Germans. Benny observed it at first hand, it reminded him of Cassino Town and, more recently, of Naples. He noted it all with shame and dismay while accompanying Yiorgo's great uncle down to the port. His feelings stemmed from the guilty feeling that he had somehow been a party to it by his support for the Fascist Axis.

The official in the port office scratched his head. Although unable to help in any official capacity, Yiorgo's great uncle knew that the man had been instrumental in securing unofficial safe passage for various refugees over the recent troubled times. The man was an old acquaintance and over the years they had both been guilty of bending rules in the execution of their various duties.

"Has he got money?" the official asked.

"How much does he need?" his old friend enquired.

The man shrugged. "Depends on the captain."

"Would a hundred dollars cover it?"

"American dollars?" the man asked wide eyed.

"Of course."

"This kid got that kind of money?"

"No. I have. Now how can we be sure he doesn't get dumped over the side as soon as the captain's got his money and they're out of sight of land?" Yiorgo's great uncle was taking no chances.

"What kind of people do you think I deal with?" the man asked in horror.

"Alright, I was only being careful. This war has brought all sorts of vermin out of the woodwork." The other man nodded but said nothing. "Anyway, at least I can trust you."

"Don't forget my fee," the man smiled, "twenty percent of the shipping price. And one more thing."

"What's that?"

"Your word that it remains a secret. If this gets out I get fired and lose my pension."

The two old friends shook hands. "When will there be suitable transport available?" Yiorgo's great uncle asked.

The official tapped his nose. "It might already be here," he whispered.

. . . .

The battered old collier had limped into Corfu harbour with engine trouble. It had been engaged on an Admiralty contract in the Mediterranean for the past four months and the captain and crew were getting homesick. Then, just as they were ordered to return to the UK for further duty in support of the Normandy campaign, the ancient vertical piston steam engine developed some serious faults.

Spare parts were a problem but a local marine engineering workshop on Corfu Town's waterfront came to the rescue and made replacement parts using existing undamaged bits as a pattern. It all took time however, the engine had to be stripped down and reassembly involved careful fitting to ensure acceptable running clearances of the moving parts. Benny was closely involved. Having been signed on as a fictitious fourth engineer he fetched and carried, held, pushed and pulled as instructed learning a great deal about steam engines and general engineering in the process.

Finally, having been ordered to return to Britain in ballast ready to take up their new role, the captain gave orders for some brief sea trials before granting Benny twenty four hours shore leave. Benny took the bus north to say goodbye to Yiorgo and his family promising to return one day when the war was over. For the last time they slept on the iron bed in the mud hut in the quiet of the mountain village and in the morning Benny shouldered his haversack and he and Yiorgo caught the bus back to Corfu Town.

They had a last meal together at Yiorgo's great aunt's house where Benny handed over one hundred and twenty of his precious dollars to the great uncle who was responsible for dealing with the port official then they all walked down to the harbour where the ship had already got steam up for the long leg to Gibraltar. Benny stood at the rail waving to his friend and his elderly relatives until the bulk of the Old Fort hid them from view.

The chief engineer nursed his engines along, never going beyond three quarters ahead and fussing about them all the time, getting Benny to watch this or oil that or listen for little noises or feel here and there for vibrations. At one point the captain and the chief had a fierce argument about whether to put into Valetta in Malta to investigate overheating in a drive shaft bearing. In the end the captain agreed to heave to and allow the offending bearing to be stripped down. The cause was found to be a restricted oilway. When it was cleared and the ship got under way again, the temperature remained normal.

They stayed at Gibraltar for several days under orders from the Naval authorities. Rumours that they were to be diverted to the Pacific theatre of operations almost caused a mutiny but eventually they resumed their homeward voyage. Benny learned that they were actually bound for Wales itself to pick up a cargo of coal destined for a secret location for bunkering Royal Navy ships.

The Bay of Biscay lived up to its stormy reputation and Benny did succumb to sea sickness for a day but after that he was not affected in spite of the mountainous seas. He would stand clutching the rail staring in awestruck disbelief as a wave the size of a large house would rear up alongside them, towering like some menacing monster that threatened to swamp them. Then suddenly they would be lifted up onto the crest looking down into a deep watery valley and all the time the engines throbbed away, turning the screw that was pushing him towards his big sister in this mysterious place he knew only as the *vallies* in the distant country called Wales.

Benny spent most of his time in the engine room, even when off watch he preferred to be there watching the gauges, making tea for the duty watch and keeping warm. Now that they had left the kinder climate of the Mediterranean, being up on deck was like standing in a draughty refrigerator. He had brought with him all the warm clothes he had and they were barely adequate. One day in an unused locker in the crew room he found a discarded donkey jacket. It was dirty and paint spattered but it was also warmly lined, had several inside pockets and nearly fitted him. He commandeered it.

As they neared the Western Approaches he could be found, clad in this new acquisition, standing in a sheltered spot below the bridge scanning the horizon for a glimpse of this land he knew of only through his sister, the land where the *vallies* were, where people sang hymns and dug coal out of the ground and bought ice cream, cigarettes and cups of coffee from his sister and her husband in their little café.

He was standing thus at dusk one day when the island of Lundy in the Bristol Channel came into sight. As the daylight faded he watched the lighthouse flashing its warning and he sensed that they were nearing their destination. He went below and climbed into his bunk and soon he was asleep.

Benny awoke to the sound of the anchor chain running out, it was barely light and he could feel the chill of the day even down in his cabin, he got up and dressed then went up on deck. There was a cold wind blowing from seaward and the sky was overcast. They were anchored in a deep bay, to his right a sandy beach backed by sand dunes stretched into the distance, behind the dunes a wide coastal plain ended abruptly in steep sided hills, some bare some tree clad. Farther down the coast where the dunes faded from sight there were the faint outlines of dockside cranes. Directly in front of him there appeared to be a river mouth with leading lights and training walls each side and inland, the smoking chimneys and factory buildings of industry while faintly, between two rounded hills, a distant oil refinery glistened grey in the dull morning air. To his left the unmistakeable clutter of a huge dock complex with cranes and oil storage facilities and further to his left, way round almost behind them, a headland with an island lighthouse.

Benny groped in an inside pocket of his donkey jacket and pulled out the picture postcard his sister had sent back to Italy. He switched his gaze from the picture to the scene before him as he read again the picture's inscription. Wherever he was this was definitely not Bute Docks, Cardiff. He went below again and sat upon his bunk puzzled and slightly disappointed.

As a special treat the captain allowed Benny to have breakfast with the officers. They were awaiting the pilot boat which would deliver the man who would guide them into harbour. The tide would not be right for another hour so they all relaxed over coffee when they had eaten.

"Where are we exactly sir?" Benny asked the captain. "This isn't Cardiff is it?"

The captain, a stocky Welshman, wiped some coffee from his beard with the back of his hand. "Cardiff boyo? No indeed." He reached across the table helping himself to a cigarette from the mate's packet. The steward came in just then and topped up their cups and Benny's question went unanswered. He sat deep in thought not listening to the conversation around the table which dwelt mainly on their homecoming and how much leave they had accumulated.

He had his sister's address on a letter she had sent him soon after her marriage, it was possible, likely even, that she would have moved to the new café they were considering buying. Still, the old address was his only starting point. He unfolded the old letter trying to decypher the unfamiliar wording of a language he did not understand. The one word that always took his eye when scanning the address seemed to leap off the page again now – *Duffryn* – such a strange arrangement of vowels and consonants he thought.

Just then he felt the slight impact as the pilot boat bumped alongside and heard the shouted greetings as the man climbed the rope ladder to the deck. He asked the chief engineer if he could stay topside as they were conned up river. "I'll do better than that young 'un," the man said, "I'll see if the old man will let you operate the telegraph."

And so it was that Benny stood upon the bridge of a battered old coal ship as it was guided up the Neath River in South Wales by the river pilot. The captain stood at the back of the bridge, the ship was under the total control of the pilot now. It was he who ordered changes in direction to the helmsman, it was he who ordered changes in speed to Benny who rang them through to the engine room. Slowly they inched upstream in the slack water of a high tide to slide through the open dock gates into the floating harbour that was Briton Ferry Docks. They berthed alongside a timber jetty beneath the towering steelwork of a coal chute and Benny rang down 'finished with engines' on the telegraph. The captain ordered the steward to serve rum all round.

After the pilot had disembarked, the captain sent for Benny in his cabin. "Well boyo," he beamed, "here we are in good old Welsh Wales so I've done my bit. Where do you go from here?" Benny showed him his sister's address but it meant nothing to the captain whose home was in Newport in the county of Monmouthshire, in fact none of the crew was local. "I wish I could help you boyo, you've been a damn good fourth engineer, only thing is we don't carry one. Still, the people at the Labour Exchange won't know that, so here, take this." The captain handed Benny his Merchant Navy papers. "They're forged of course," the man said, "but they should be enough to get you a National Insurance number. Once you've got that you'll be one of us like. You got any lire?"

"Some."

"Good. An Italian without lire would seem odd. Now your granddad, or whoever he was in Corfu, asked me to give you this, you can't get far without money." He produced three English pound notes, old and well used. He glanced sideways at the boy, "I reckon you might have some dollars tucked away too, eh boyo? Well, take my advice, put them in the bank along with the lire the first chance you get."

"Thank you sir," Benny took the notes.

"We load coal this afternoon then we're off with the first tide tomorrow. You can stay aboard tonight but you'd better be away early in the morning OK?"

"OK." They shook hands and Benny went below to get his things together.

18

With the captain's permission Benny watched the coal loading operation from the comfort of the bridge. It was warm there and he was shut away from the clouds of coal dust that accompanied the process.

He followed the progress of the loaded coal wagons as they approached the hoist, watched as the clamps went on before the wagon was hoisted bodily to the top of the structure to be tipped upside down, its contents emptying into the chute and cascading in clouds of black dust into the hold. As each compartment filled, the ship was moved along the wharf by the steam winches until she lay almost to her plimsoll line in the black scum covered waters of the dock. The operation took all the rest of the day and continued under shrouded floodlights until the hatches were replaced and the dockside shift ended.

Benny watched for over an hour. The empty wagons were returned to the inclined track to roll down under gravity before being coupled into a train for return to the pit. Suddenly Benny reached for the binoculars hanging from a wheel spoke. He trained them onto the line of wagons and adjusted the focus. There it was, painted in bold characters on the side of some of the wagons: Powell Duffryn. That unreadable word again *Duffryn*, it was part of his sister's address, he retrieved the letter once again from the inside pocket of his donkey jacket just to make sure. Now he knew what he was going to do.

Towards dusk he collected his evening meal upon a tray and took it to his tiny cabin to eat it alone. He was more than a little apprehensive. Here on board ship he was safe, he got fed three times a day and did a job he enjoyed among people he had grown to like. Tomorrow was a step into the unknown. He was a foreigner from a country which, until only recently, had been at war with the one he was about to set foot upon, he had no map, no idea how to get to the *vallies* this mysterious place that his sister had travelled to after her marriage, all he had was the letter she had sent containing an address he could not read.

A lump came to his throat as he remembered the old days before the war, before his big sister went away, when they would all sit around the table after church and talk about the week just gone or the week to come and the arrangements for market day or when the weather was right for fishing. All the ordinary day to day things that life consisted of then.

His mind drifted back over the months since his fateful and impulsive decision to join the military convoy. Tears welled in his eyes as he remembered the brave sergeant whom the Germans had shot and the German sergeant who had been so kind to him, he thought of all the things he had seen and done, all the people he had met, the places he had been. Now he was here, in the country they called Wales, the country where his big sister had gone to live. It all seemed unreal, unbelievable. He took his tray back to the galley.

"Hey, you gonna leave tomorra?" The Chinese cook asked.

"Yes."

"Look I got stuff for you. Some fruit, Tinna bully beef, tinna milk, some bread, some cheese. All in bag. Cap say OK," he handed Benny a large brown paper carrier bag. "Hope you find your sister OK, good luck."

"Thanks Chiang," they shook hands and then Benny made his way back to his cabin to re-pack his haversack ready for the journey.

He lay upon his bunk for a long time unable to sleep, the ship lying unnaturally still in the darkened harbour. Through the riveted steel plates of the hull the noise of industry still penetrated, the quickly accelerating clanging of buffers as rail trucks were shunted, the metallic rumbling of a nearby rolling mill, the roar of a blast furnace, the screaming whistle of a locomotive hauling an express bound for London followed by the rhythmic clatter of the wheels over the rail joints. During a brief lull in this cacophony came the sound of a town clock striking midnight. Benny got up, donned his donkey jacket and shouldered his haversack. He took a last look around the cabin before picking up one of the blankets from his bunk. It was time to go.

Benny stole down the gangplank and paused under the shadow of the giant coal loading hoist. He surveyed the mass of sidings before crossing the perimeter path and ducking under the nearest line of coal wagons searching for the empty ones, the ones he had seen earlier, the ones displaying the logo Powell Duffryn. He climbed stealthily into the first one he found then, wrapped in his blanket, he lay down upon the coal dust and, using his haversack as a pillow, wrapped himself in his blanket and waited.

After what seemed an age there was a vicious jolt as the locomotive snatched the wagon into motion, it was followed by another less violent one as the coupling to the following wagon took the strain and slowly, noisily the train gathered speed. Benny had no idea of the time but that did not matter, he was on his way. The final leg of his long journey had begun. He pulled himself up to peer over the side of the wagon. He was about half way between the engine and the guard's van, part of a long train of empty coal trucks. The smoke from the locomotive turned crimson as the firebox was opened to shovel more coal on and way up ahead a signal glowed green in the darkness. They were approaching a brightly lit signal box but before dropping down out of sight he looked back to see the now distant coal hoist outlined against a sky shot through with an orange glow as a blast furnace was tapped. They clattered on and soon left the industrial areas behind, he lay gazing up at the stars which twinkled with stark brilliance in a freezing black sky as the train wound its way along wooded vallies gradually climbing into the hinterland. He slept.

When Benny awoke, dawn was breaking. He was stiff with cold even wrapped in his thick blanket which was dusted with snow. He struggled to stand up clutching the blanket about his shoulders and stamping his feet. With movements clumsy from cold and fatigue he somehow managed to climb out of the wagon and take stock of his surroundings. The train was parked on a siding, one of many adjoining a colliery the pithead gear of which loomed out of the morning mist some distance away. As he watched, the winding gear started to turn and he stood fascinated as the wheels began to rotate, slowly at first, then faster and faster, the spokes accelerating to a spinning blur atop the steel framework.

The mine was located in a shallow valley, to his left he could hear a babbling stream rushing between banks lined with dead bracken and the sides of the valley rose gradually on either side clad in pine and birch and stunted oak before giving way to the barren mountain tops.

At the rear of the train Benny noticed smoke coming from the chimney of the guard's van, he made his way there limping slightly with stiffness and cold. With difficulty he managed to climb up to the covered platform at the back of the vehicle and knocked on the door leading to the enclosed section. There was no reply so he tried the door, to his surprise and joy it swung open and he was met by a wall of warm air, he quickly went inside and closed the door.

There was a bunk and a small table and chair and in the middle of the floor an iron stove giving off a welcome glow of heat. Benny sat down and stretched his feet towards the stove, he sat thus for a full ten minutes until the chill of the night had left him. He assumed correctly that the guard had gone home, his night shift completed, and he had left the stove, well banked up with coal, for his relief. Benny knew that the man could turn up at any moment but he decided to take the risk and eat some of the food that Chiang had given him in comparative comfort.

Even a cold breakfast of corned beef and cheese with bread and butter put new life into him. He re-packed the remainder of the food in his haversack, rolled the blanket up tightly and slung it around his shoulder like a bandolier then, reluctantly, he left the warmth and comfort of the guard's van and made his way across the rail tracks to the road leading up the valley.

The turning pithead wheels had signified a shift change but by the time he emerged from the guard's van the old shift had gone home and the new one was already underground, consequently he saw no one along the road as he walked to the village which was about a half a mile further up the valley.

He passed the first terraced cottages and soon came to an imposing Methodist chapel opposite a public house. The sign hanging above the pub door proclaimed it to be The Brynhyfryd Arms. He glanced up, perplexed at the incomprehensible combination of letters. As he passed, the front door opened and a young girl emerged, she was carrying a wicker basket covered with a cloth, their eyes met for an instant and she smiled at him. Benny felt his colour rising as he smiled back at her before striding on looking right and left for the street name written on his sister's letter.

It was still early morning and the village was quiet. The girl's footsteps sounded inordinately loud behind him on the flagstoned pavement and they seemed to be coming closer. Benny stopped and pretended to read the name on a street sign hoping the girl would pass by. But she didn't. "Can I help you?" she asked.

Benny looked at her. A combination of black hair and blue eyes was something new to him as was the knitted tea cosy-like headwear. "I er I try to find my sister's place," he stammered.

"Where do she live then?"

"I have address," he showed her the letter.

"Oh," she smiled, "I live in the next village down the valley from there. Why are you over by here then?"

Benny took the letter back. "See?" he pointed to the word he had seen on the coal wagons, the one he recognised but could not say, *Duffryn*. "I see name on coal trucks for this village, so I come here."

The girl looked puzzled for a moment then the realisation of what Benny meant dawned upon her. She shook her head smiling kindly, "You'll see Powell Duffryn on coal trucks all over the place boy, they own pits everywhere. No, you're in the wrong valley altogether. Come on we got to catch a train, it's only ten minutes through the tunnel under the mountain see. You got any money?" Benny nodded. "What's your name then?"

"Benny."

"Mine's Bronwen. You're foreign aren't you?"

"I am Italian."

"Let's see that letter again." Benny passed it across. "Oh I know that place now. Soon as you said you was Italian I remembered that address. It's that Italian café, that's on Hill Street see. That's your sister's place is it? Well I never," and so she prattled on as they walked to the small valley station. Bronwen bought the tickets with Benny's money and they boarded the push and pull train, talking and laughing together like children, which they were, and acting for all the world as though they had known each other for years. The engine let out a shrill whistle and they began to move, in no time at all they were swallowed up in the darkness of the tunnel but Benny hardly noticed, then they were in the open again, in bright sunshine in the next valley. So lost were they in each other's company that Benny missed his stop, got off at Bronwen's village and had to walk three miles back to Duffryn.

He found Hill Street and realised it was aptly named. The houses and shops clung to the mountainside on his right while on his left a terraced footpath paralleled them, the steep drop down to the railway on one side was protected by a cast iron post and rail fence with tall gas lamp posts every hundred yards or so.

Benny found the little café. He stood before it, leaning against the railings on the opposite side of the road. He had come so far, looked forward to this day for so long, he stood savouring the moment, trying to imagine what his sister would say when her little brother breezed in from out of the blue.

The shop front looked extremely imposing to him, two large plate glass windows with lace curtains halfway up discreetly screened the tables inside, across each window in gold and black script the curved signwriting proclaimed the establishment to be Cavalli's Café. Benny walked across the road.

He lifted the latch on the brass door handle and pushed but the door was firmly bolted, there was a bellpush which he pressed but could not hear any sound from within. He waited a few moments and was about to press it again when he heard a window slide open and a voice from above shouted: "We're not open yet. Two o'clock it is. OK?"

The strange combination of English spoken in a mixture of Italian and Welsh accents confused Benny for a moment then he stepped out onto the road and looked up to the open window and the man leaning out. "It's me, Guiseppe," he shouted in Italian, "your little brother-in-law. Where's my sister? I've come a long way. I've come to the *vallies*."

The man at the window frowned. The ragamuffin in the street below, with the rolled up blanket tied like a bandolier across his chest looked more like a Jarrow marcher. He blinked in the sunlight and rubbed his eyes leaning forward to take a better look, his face creased into a smile, "Guiseppe? Is it really you?"

"Yes Giovanni it is really me. Now are you going to let me into your swanky café?

The man's face clouded, his smile fading. "Guiseppe my little one. Wait a moment I'm coming down."

The café door opened and Benny stepped through. His brother-in-law hugged him tightly for what seemed a long time. The room smelled of disinfectant and stale tobacco smoke, Benny noted the tables set out neatly around the room each with four cane backed chairs, each with a neat table cloth. He knew there was something wrong, his sixth sense once again coming into play. "Where is Gina?" he asked.

His brother-in-law held him at arms length looking searchingly into his face, his eyes brimming with tears. "Guiseppe. Guiseppe my little one. How can I tell you?"

Benny looked into his brother-in-law's eyes, they looked empty. Desolate. Lost "Giovanni," he said softly, "she is dead isn't she?"

His brother-in-law sank down at the nearest table his head in his hands. "I miss her," he breathed, "Oh God how I miss her. And all because of this crazy war and that bastard Mussolini."

Benny felt a momentary pang of anger to hear his former hero spoken of in such terms. It subsided quickly, his blind juvenile infatuation with Fascism seemed now to belong to an earlier existence. "What happened?" he asked.

Giovanni sat listlessly staring at the floor. "Things were great," he began, "father had a good business, we were going to expand then," he paused, shaking his head, "then Italy declares war. Business gets bad, people throw stones, paint slogans, spit in the street. That's OK, we can cope with that. Then the police come, they intern papa and mama, they say they going to deport Gina and me."

"Deport you? Where to?"

"To Canada I think. Anyway we don't get there, the bloody ship, The Andorra Star, she gets torpedoed. I survive and Gina," his voice dropped to a whisper, "Gina, she get drowned, and you know the worst thing?" Benny shook his head. "Gina, she is with child, our bambino."

Benny stood in shocked silence clutching his brother-in-law's shoulder, feeling the slight movement of subdued and furtive sobbing. He felt totally empty and alone. During all his long journey to the place he knew only as the *vallies* he had felt excitement at the prospect of seeing his elder sister again whilst harbouring a secret dread at having to tell her about their parents. Now both the excitement and the dread were irrelevant. He was alone in the world apart from his uncle and aunt back in Italy. The whole point of his journey was invalid. Without his sister the future seemed bleak indeed. "What happened to your mama and papa?" he asked.

"They get released," Giovanni replied, "yeah they release them when they tell the authorities about my brother. When they tell them how he was at Dunkirk with the British Expeditionary Force, when they tell them how he got decorated for bravery." He banged his fist down hard upon the table, "when they tell them that he's not a fucking Fascist and neither are they!"

"Where are they now?" Benny asked gently.

"They're visiting my uncle down in Aber."

Benny stood irresolute, a cold emptiness seemed to engulf him. Another strange foreign place name adding to his sense of isolation. After a few moments he asked quietly: "Can I stay with you for a while?"

His brother-in-law looked up, an expression of shocked surprise on his tear stained face. "Stay? Of course. Guiseppe my little one why do you ask? You are our family now. We all live above this café like before. We have a room in the attic, it was all done out ready for . . . ," his voice trailed away then he sighed and shrugged, "it is yours my little one for as long as you want it," and the warmth of his hug gave Benny a surge of reassurance about the future. He looked out through the net curtains, down the valley to the distant steam and smoke of the pit where Bronwen's village nestled, in this place he had travelled so far to come to, this place they called the *vallies*.

"And the rest is history," Mario smiled. "Uncle Benny worked at the café until Bronwen's people got him a job in the pit. They walked out together until they were old enough to marry and they lived in this little end of terrace miners' cottage for as long as I can remember."

"Did they have any children?" I asked.

"No. That's why I was her favourite. We were not really related but she and her family treated me like the son they never had. I can still taste her apple crumble." He drained his glass and placed it upon the table. "So now you know why we're here."

"We do?" Neil asked.

"Well yes. To complete Uncle Benny's unfinished business of course. Find this bloody icon and get it back to the monks at Monte Cassino Abbey. I promised my Aunty Bron remember?"

Neil and I exchanged glances. So this was the reason for our Mediterranean cruise. I admired the tenacity of purpose which Mario had sustained to bring us to this point. It had become an obsession with him which was understandable in view of his condition. I wondered absently what I might become obsessed with if I were given six months to live. The answer in my case was easy, see Jean again. Just once.

"The gin's all gone by the way," Neil said, holding the empty bottle up to the glow of the anchor light.

"It's time to turn in anyway," Mario said, "here give us a hand to get below." So Neil and I helped him to his bunk before clearing the deck. The rain had stopped and the stars shone down with a fierce brilliance. We emptied the plastic bins into the fresh water tanks and stowed the sun canopy ready for the morning.

19

We got up late, weighed anchor about midday and slid gently away from Erikousa Island. There was only a light northeasterly breeze and Mario had Neil and me jumping about pulling on ropes and hauling up sails until we had every available piece of canvass helping us along. "It's times like this," Mario said as he stood at the helm, "I wish we had an iron topsail." I paused in the act of coiling down the mainsail halyard.

"An iron what?"

"A bloody engine", he explained, "mind you it wouldn't be right. It'd be like having a Model T Ford with power steering and ABS." He smiled to himself and adjusted the tiller causing the boat to heel a little even in the light wind. "Neil," he shouted, "fancy going below and fixing us some brunch? Just a sandwich to chew while we're creeping along like this." Neil waved an acknowledgement as he finished flaking down the chain ready for the next time we dropped anchor.

The previous night's storm had moved away and there was an unaccustomed chill in the breeze. The heavy rain had cleansed the atmosphere so that the Albanian mountains stood out clear and bright on our port side and Corfu looked deceptively close. From time to time Mario checked his mobile phone for a signal, swearing loudly each time there wasn't one before slipping the instrument back into the pocket of his fleece. Presently Neil appeared with two thick cut ham and tomato sandwiches on an enamel plate and we stood silently chewing as we made our slow passage.

After a while Mario said: "Here Jim, take the helm. I'm going below. Call of nature." It was the very first time I had held the tiller. During the previous day's practice I had acted as crew, pulling on various ropes as instructed and finally dropping anchor at a signal from Mario. This was different and I was somewhat alarmed.

"What do I do?" I asked. "How do I keep the thing on course and what is the course anyway?" I pointed to the compass in its mahogany box sitting on the deck near Mario's feet.

"Listen boyo, it's a piece of piss. Don't look so bloody panic stricken. We're on a broad starboard reach right?" I nodded uncomprehending. "That means the wind's coming from the right hand side slightly to our rear. See the pennant up there?" I followed his pointing finger to the masthead where a mall triangular flag streamed out. "That's not the actual wind direction," he explained, "it's the resultant of the wind combined with the movement of the boat through the water, it should fly roughly parallel with the boom, that's sailing according to Mario bloody Franzoni anyway," he said grinning. "Just grab hold of the tiller a minute. Don't worry about the compass course just keep the bows pointing at Mount Pantocrator. See it? It's the big peak with the radio masts on. Hold the tiller now."

He relinquished his grasp and I felt for the first time the inexplicable thrill of contact with the sea through the rudder blade running deep in the gently forming wake and up through the long curved wooden tiller to my hand.

"Now move it away from you a bit," he ordered, "now towards you." I did as he said and watched as the mountain top moved backward and forward across the bows. "That's it," he beamed, "keep doing that. First one way then the other, you'll soon get the feel of it. Just keep us going more or less in that direction. I won't be long," and with that he went below and I was alone on deck, Neil having gone to wash up and prepare some food for later.

The breeze had strengthened now that we were away from the shelter of the island and the boat was heeling a little more. I continued to move the tiller as Mario had said, noting the effect and beginning to relax and enjoy the sense of controlling this wooden monster with a touch of rudder first this way and then the other watching as Corfu gradually grew in size and keeping the mountain roughly on the bow.

Mario returned before long, steadied himself against the windward bulwark and checked his mobile. "At bloody last," he said as he was now apparently within range and tapped in a number. "Spiro? Where are you? Right. We're headed for Roda. Drive over there and park near the harbour if you can. OK?" He listened for a moment or so. "That's great. We'll anchor off and I'll send Neil in with the dinghy. You should be able to get that thing in OK it folds up doesn't it? Yeah. And the other thing? Good, see you in about an hour." He put the phone away.

I said: "In an hour? We'll be there before that won't we? That's Roda over there isn't it?" I pointed towards the cluster of houses and apartments nestled around the small harbour, vehicles could be clearly seen moving along the coast road, it certainly did look close. I remembered visiting the place on one occasion with Jean, the narrow street with the tavernas the tourist shops and the restaurants. It all seemed so long ago now.

"Yes that's Roda," Mario replied, "and it's further than it looks. That rain's made everything look a lot closer. We should be there in less time than that though. I'm just giving Spiro some leeway. You tired?"

"A bit. That was quite a story."

"Let's hope it's got a satisfactory ending," he said grimly and the fact that he used the word satisfactory and not happy was not lost on me.

Mario showed me how to turn into the wind when we were about half a mile offshore and as the sails began to flap Neil let go the anchor and between us we got all the canvass down and stowed. I gave him a hand to launch the Mirror dinghy and presently he set off for the harbour where we could see Spiro standing, holding the stuff Mario had asked for.

While Neil rowed towards the harbour Mario and I arranged a table and chairs on the deck. I picked up the compass, closed the lid and stowed it under the cross bench before bringing my binoculars from my bunk. The visibility was too good to waste and I turned towards the island and adjusted the focus.

The slopes of Mount Pantocratora were rock strewn and totally treeless, its foothills sparsely covered with grass and stunted trees. I spent a considerable time scanning the area but could make out no road or track above the treeline which petered out gradually from olive grove to pine to scrub. By then Neil and Spiro were close alongside and I put the glasses down, tied the dinghy's painter to a cleat and helped to get them and their mysterious cargo aboard.

Neil clambered up first clutching something like a golf club bag. He disappeared below with it as Spiro handed me up a folded wheelchair which Mario regarded with some distaste. Spiro clambered aboard, his stocky bulk tilting the boat slightly, before unfolding the wheelchair.

"Well?" he said looking across at Mario.

"Well what?"

"Look," he said, "you ask for it, I get it, now we try it. Yes?"

"Yeah, I bloody suppose so." Mario walked over and sat heavily and with obvious reluctance into the wheelchair. "Well come on then", he chided, "do your stuff." Spiro sniffed and began wheeling his charge around the deck. "Not too close to the edge you sod", Mario shouted, "you'll have me in the bloody drink."

"Don' give me idea", joked Spiro. "You gonna try by your own?"

"How many times have I got to tell you," Mario scolded, "it's *by yourself* or *on your own*. Got it?"

"Whatever. Now I let go," and Spiro gave a gentle push. The wheelchair rolled along the deck and Mario grabbed the wheel pushers, managing to come to rest just inches before his head would have struck the tiller. We watched as he practiced up and down the deck, starting, stopping, turning and all the time Spiro was watching like a hawk ready to jump to Mario's aid should he get into trouble.

Mario had practiced for some time, putting a great deal of effort into trying to master the technique as could be seen by the beads of perspiration standing up on his forehead. Eventually he stopped, panting heavily, before the inevitable coughing bout. We managed to get him down the companionway and onto his bunk where Neil could administer the oxygen. Then Spiro and I went up on deck and sat at the table.

Spiro lit a cigarette and muttered something unintelligible in Greek under his breath, out of the corner of my eye I saw him surreptitiously cross himself. It was obvious to me then that he knew of Mario's condition and I didn't want to get onto that subject so to break the uneasy silence I said something about tourism being a good thing, particularly the new concept of ecological tourism. That set him off.

He gave a derisory snort and glared across at me his face wreathed in cigarette smoke. "What you call it?" He demanded, "Ecological Tourism? No such thing. Just tourism." I had obviously touched a raw nerve. "You know the three rules of tourism?" he asked. I raised a quizzical eyebrow and shook my head. "Rule one?" he said stabbing the table with his finger. "Find some place in the world which is totally unspoilt. Rule two? Spoil it, totally. Rule three? Move on to the next place." He fell silent and took a final vicious drag on his cigarette before flicking it over the side where it hit the water with a brief hiss. He picked up my binoculars and trained them towards the west, his elbows resting on the table for support. Presently he put them down and sighed deeply. "You know," he said, "every time I looks at my village, my eyes they become tearfuls."

"At Sidari?" I said. "Why?"

"Why?" he repeated. "Look through these, you'll see why." He thrust the binoculars into my hands and I trained them on the distant shoreline. "See that?" he said softly, "that coast is unique for Corfu, for Greece I think, even for Europe, maybe whole world. Who knows?"

I thought of my boat trip the other day, the fascinating sea hewn sculptures of the coastal cliffs, the cavernous sea filled tunnel of Canal d'Amour. Maybe he was right.

"In UK that would be designate what you say? Heritage Coast? Protected, untouched. Only slow erosion of sea to disturb it. Here? Here we put out sunbeds, use bulldozers to cut terraces to accommodate even more sunbeds and let the tourists trample around everywhere." I glanced across at his embittered face. "Then what about hinterland?" he went on, "behind the coast was acres of swampland, floodplain, habitat. What they do? they fill with hardcore and build hotels, tavernas, car parks. Then they wonder why place get flooded."

"But surely," I countered, "tourism brings in money for the local economy?"

"For what?" he snapped back.

"Well, for roads, drainage, general infrastructure"

"Infrastructure! That is another what you call? Buzz word?" He fished a pack of cigarettes out of his anorak and lit up. "Listen. There was nothing wrong with infrastructure before bloody tourism. Roads was OK, drains was OK, then suddenly we need all that. I tell you what tourism brings shall I? Greed!"

This subject was obviously his hobby horse. Mario had said he was an environmentalist and I had laughed because he was also Greek and whoever heard of a Greek environmentalist? Now my chance remark to break a strained silence had unleashed this tirade. I shifted uneasily in my chair. He would just have to get it off his chest and I would just have to listen.

"This how it work," he went on. "Parents say to grandparents- *hey we got land, we could build accommodation, get some of this tourism action.* Grandparents say - *OK you go ahead but leave us alone to live in hovel we always lived in. Place you was brought up. We got satellite TV, fridge, washing machine. We got all we need, you go ahead.* So the parents go ahead, they make money, buy new car, spoil kids, buy them motor bike. Turn them into," he paused, searching for the right word. "Turn them into . . feckless bastards. They don' have to work, they just hand around being . . . feckless."

"Well," I began, "it's the same in England, fecklessness is the new religion. I remember once . . . ." But Spiro cut in again.

"Jus' look at this place," he sighed, "along road sides, in ditches, everywhere there is enough plastic bottles to reach to moon and back ten thousand times. You must have seen on your bike ride other day."

"I was too busy watching out for maniac drivers to notice," I countered.

"Hah, maniac drivers. I know we have those. You know what I think? Today's maniac drivers is yesterday's spoilt feckless bastards."

"Anyway we have a litter problem in England too," I said, "and we have anti-litter laws. What a joke that is. When Jean and I came here first we were disgusted with the plastic bottles and all the other stuff littering the roadsides. You know what? It's even worse in England now, anti litter law or not."

Spiro wasn't listening to me. "I have good idea sometime," he said, "there is machine I think. It is full of balls you know it?"

"Full of balls?"

"Sorry. I not engineer. It break things up ver' small." I looked across at him as he struggled to remember the name of the contraption he had in mind, struggling also with an unfamiliar language. "It like long metal tube, it spin round slowly, balls inside roll about, break up anything inside yes?"

"Oh you mean a ball mill."

"Nai, ball mill. Well, I got idea. Collect all plastic bottles, give them mighty dose of ultra violet to make them brittle, put them in ball mill to crush them up small then use all the bits as filler stuff for concrete, it save on destroying mountain for gravel and sand an' make concrete glisten too maybe, yes?"

"Maybe." I considered his idea. It was obviously impractical, economically unviable and probably would not work anyway. I said nothing more.

Presently he went on: "You ever wondered what happen to mountains of rubbish created every year by tourists?" I had, but kept my mouth shut. "They should burn it," he asserted. "It would reduce volume of stuff by over ninety five percent."

"I know that, Spiro, but you try and open a waste incinerator anywhere in the UK the environmentalists would have a fit. It might be the same here."

"Why they have fit?" he exclaimed spreading his hands. "They burn peoples' bodies don't they? Why not peoples' rubbish?"

Just then, thankfully, Neil came up on deck. "Mario's asleep," he announced. "I've fed him a small plate of stew, he wasn't very hungry. He should sleep all night now."

"What about our expedition?" I asked.

"He suggested we should do it tomorrow," Neil replied, "start early he said, there's a good weather forecast apparently."

"I got Toyota gassed up," Spiro said.

"How long will it take to get to this place?" I asked.

Spiro pursed his lips before flicking his cigarette end over the side. "Less than an hour," he said. "Jus' one thing. He can't handle that chair. I gotta wheel him. OK?" He looked searchingly at us both in turn, his swarthy face, black hair and piercing dark eyes demanding rather than asking. Neil and I nodded our agreement. It was obvious that Spiro was extremely fond of Mario and felt very protective towards him. I wondered absently how far back their friendship went and how they had met.

As the evening light began to fade Neil produced a bottle of Metaxa 3 star and some soda water and we sat around the table talking quietly and drinking. From below came the mouthwatering smell of a vegetable stew Neil had prepared that morning and I suddenly realised how hungry I was.

"Shall I fix the anchor light?" I asked. Neil nodded and I fetched the hurricane lamp from the deck locker, tied it to the rope as I had seen him do the previous night, lit it using Spiro's cigarette lighter and hauled it up above the deck. Then we sat and enjoyed the stew with thick slices of fresh bread that Neil himself had baked and by the time we went to our bunks, having bedded Spiro down on the deck with a blanket and mattress, the brandy bottle was empty.

20

I awoke early the next morning to hear Spiro clumping about the deck above my head followed by the unmistakeable sound of him urinating over the side. I lay savouring the cosiness of my bunk and the gentle movement of the boat as it lay quietly at anchor and wondering what the day had in store for us.

It would be Mario's day. He more than any of us had invested money and effort and of course time, his most precious and scarce resource, in preparing for it. He more than any of us would be affected by its outcome. To find the icon and return it to its historical home had been the pipe dream of his uncle, a dream Mario had promised to make reality for his widow. For my part, I had become infected by the romance of the whole affair. It was as if we were about to cross a time bridge and unlock a piece of history. I yawned and got up.

Neil did us proud with a full English breakfast served on deck as the morning sun warmed us. The sky was flecked with cloud and a gentle breeze slatted the halyards against the mast. We all mucked in with the washing up, except Spiro who slouched near the stern smoking and chatting in Greek on his mobile.

I packed an old fashioned basketwork hamper with bread, cheese, tinned meat, fresh fruit and tomatoes, some bottled water plus a couple of bottles of wine while Neil tended to his patient in his small cabin, assessing his fitness for the day ahead. As I was about to close the hamper he came out and surreptitiously slipped in a bottle of champagne and four carefully wrapped glasses. He at any rate was optimistic about the outcome of our mission. Finally we all clambered down the iron ladder into the dinghy taking with us all the things Spiro had brought aboard the previous evening, we cast off and Neil rowed us ashore.

"You sure you know the way?" Mario asked Spiro when we got to the Toyota.

"Sure I know way. I tell you plenty times."

"OK, OK. I'll sit up front with you, Neil and Jim in the back, that alright with you?" We both nodded and loaded the wheelchair and the hamper and the 'golf club bag' behind the rear seats. There were also a spade a garden fork and a Corfu hoe, items that Spiro had presumably loaded up the day before. I clambered in beside Neil and fastened my safety belt. The vehicle was extremely comfortable and high off the road affording good all round visibility. Spiro started up and the powerful engine purred away under the hood as we moved off, threading our way through the village before edging out onto the road to Acharavi.

The road wound along the coastline with the mountain bulk always on our right and after some miles we turned off and began to climb. Before long we entered a village and Mario said: "Stop here Spiro I need a leak." Spiro pulled over onto a piece of waste ground alongside a taverna and leaned out of the window to chat to some locals who were seated on the veranda. Mario got out and walked over to the veranda steps, he turned and shouted to Spiro: "Ask these guys if it's okay for me to use their bog will you?"

"I already tell them. You go ahead." Mario waved and I watched as Mario climbed the steps so pitifully slowly. Neil and I exchanged glances, our eyes saying much more than any words. "Poor bastard," breathed Spiro before murmuring some unintelligible Greek. Once again he crossed himself hoping that we did not notice.

Soon we were on our way again, driving through shady olive groves, past the occasional small village or farmstead or olive picker's mud hut, the road twisting and turning, slowly gaining height as it zig- zagged upward. My ears popped from time to time as the altitude increased and soon we left the olive groves behind and found ourselves climbing through scrubland or following the sides of treeless vallies which became narrower and steeper the higher we got. I looked back and the sea was a distant silver haze almost indistinguishable from the sky it reflected.

"How much bloody further, Spiro?" Asked Mario.

"No' much," he replied, "ten, fifteen minutes we be there." And it suddenly dawned on me that Spiro had not smoked since our journey began, I was on the point of mentioning it then I realised why. Beside me sat Neil, at his feet a holdall inside which I could see a small oxygen bottle and mask. Spiro obviously knew better than to smoke in the same vehicle as Mario.

By then we were climbing a narrow road along a valley the sides of which were strewn with rocky outcrops, small bushes, heather and coarse grasses. I glanced up to my right and saw where the road continued, slanting ever upward. Then we rounded the sharp hairpin at the head of the valley and soon I was looking down upon the road we had just negotiated. At the next bend the gradient decreased and we were passing through a shallow defile edged with stunted trees and boulders. At the top of the rise the road turned to the left, levelled out and then began to fall.

Spiro braked carefully and we crept down the gently curving track as gradually the whole of the huge bowl shaped settlement opened up before us. No one spoke, we were all struck dumb by the sheer scale and incongruity of the scene spread out before us in the bright sunlight of that autumn afternoon.

Mario gasped: "Bloody hell Spiro is this it?"

"Nai, this is Ano Perithea.

"Who the hell built this place all the way up here?"

"It is Venetian town. Or was. They must have been fed up with coastal pirate raids and came up here to be safe."

"Just like on Majorca," I said, "the ports are on the coast and the towns are several miles inland. Less vulnerable to surprise attack from pirates."

"Yeah but up here?" Said Mario, "How did they feed themselves? A place this size for god's sake, just kitchen gardens? Where's the water all the way up here?"

"Look up there," Spiro answered, "That Mount Pantocrator, town is in this hollow, we get plenty rain now and again so they could collect it, store it, maybe wells too, I don' know. Venetians they clever bastards."

We all fell silent. The scene was surreal. A whole small town, or rather the ruins of one, was nestled in this hollow high in the hills. Looking all around, all that could be seen was mountainside. Mount Pantocrator with its radio masts and the square block of the monastery towered above everything but surrounding the place on all sides were smaller hills, all bare of vegetation, some bearing the signs of terracing but the whole place hidden from the coast. Nowhere from the remains of the ancient town was the sea visible and therefore, obviously, the town was completely invisible to marauding pirates. Also by the time any raiding party could reach such a place they would be exhausted, be disadvantaged by fighting uphill and the defenders would be warned well in advance and have their defence strategy thoroughly rehearsed.

Eventually Spiro broke the silence: "I want smoke and piss," he announced. He switched off the engine and got out to perform the actions he described in reverse order. Neil and I got out too and stood in awe gazing around at the scene of silent decaying buildings, ruined churches, crumbling archways leading to abandoned houses and over all the absolute silence. He turned to me, "bloody spooky place this," he said quietly, "it's okay now but imagine being here alone at midnight, no moon, mist everywhere. Gives me the creeps even in broad daylight."

Mario meanwhile was studying some sort of map. He had spread it across the dashboard and was scratching his head over it. It was about A3 size. Eventually he called Spiro over. "What d'you make of this?" he asked. "I know Uncle Benny drew it from memory so it can't be too reliable but look, it shows Pantocratora, it's got this road or track coming in. What are these crosses? Churches or something? And these archway looking sketches? And which way's north for chrissake?"

Neil turned to me, "this gets more like Treasure Island all the time," he breathed, "did you know about the map?"

I shook my head and shrugged, "this is all new to me," I said.

Mario beckoned us over: "Hey you two, stop bloody whispering and come and see if you can suss this map." Mario struggled out of the vehicle and laid the map on the bonnet where we could all see it. It was the sort of map a child might draw, the features indicated by a mixture of symbols and small drawings. Towards the bottom of the sheet a larger and more elaborate sketch of an archway had a line drawn from the centre of the arch to the right hand corner of a square block which was shown at the top of Mount Pantocratora, obviously representing the monastery. A number was printed along that line with the letters deg after it.

"What I don't get," said Neil, "is these other smaller drawings of archways. That one's got 1. printed under it, the next one 2. and the big one with the line coming from it's got 3. under it. What's that all about?"

Spiro lit another cigarette. "Look is simple," he said. "That block on top of Pantocratora, that is monastery okay? Then the third arch in from edge of town is where he hide stuff. From there the right hand wall of monastery on Pantocratora should have that bearing. Look, I have compass. We check." He took a prismatic compass from his anorak pocket and looked again at the map. "Come on," he said, "I drive."

We all clambered back into the vehicle and Spiro drove at walking pace down the track into the sparse ruins of the town. We passed the first archway which had been the entrance to a large church. The building was roofless but the bell tower still stood although there were no bells. The second archway stood on its own, it was quite small and behind it there was a raised flat floor like area as if a building had once been there but no walls survived. The third archway was a solid and imposing entrance to a large mansion of a place, the roof was a threadbare tracery of sun bleached timbers the windows simply rectangular openings devoid of frames or shutters. Spiro stopped and we all got out.

"Shit!" It was Mario.

"What's up?" Neil asked.

"The monastery," Mario said, "where is it? You can't even see the bloody mountain from this archway."

He was right. The building blocked out the view to Mount Pantocratora completely. Spiro stood holding his compass, a bemused look on his face. I left them and wandered back along the track taking in the silent and empty desolation of the place. I agreed with Neil, the place was spooky right enough. Ghostly shells of buildings, staring window openings, crumbling boundary walls of weed filled gardens. I passed the second archway, paused and walked back. It was not an imposing structure, rather squat with a large stone plinth before it. It looked solid, immoveable, permanent and it was in full view of Pantocratora and the mountain top monastery.

I continued my stroll back along our route towards the first arched entrance to the ruined church. Off to my left, on the other side of the track and half hidden among briars and ferns, two stone stumps protruded. I walked across. A bright green lizard shot away from under my feet as I trod gingerly through the undergrowth wary of snakes. There flat among the vegetation, as if it had been pushed over by some giant hand, lay a perfect masonry arch. I shouted and waved for the others to join me.

It took some time for Mario to be convinced that number two arch was really number three. The fact that Uncle Benny had drawn the fallen second arch on the same side of the track as numbers one and two was the stumbling block. "Look," I said, "he probably did a quick sketch in this diary of his then did the map later, maybe years later and he made a mistake, forgot the actual layout or even didn't think it mattered. Or maybe the track went the other side then. Anyway let's just check this compass bearing. That should prove it one way or the other."

That set off another argument. There was a prolonged discussion about the bearing written on the map. Eventually Neil did some figuring with a pencil and suggested that Uncle Benny, possibly in an attempt to confuse illicit treasure hunters, had written down the back bearing. That is the compass bearing of the archway from the monastery and not the other way around. This explanation relied on Neil's assumption that Uncle Benny's figure six was actually a zero.

Spiro's patience finally ran out. "For fuck's sake," he implored, "we got metal detector don' we. Let's jus' do a search!"

Spiro strode back to the Toyota discarding his current cigarette before turning the vehicle round and heading back. He stopped by the disputed archway and got out, lowered the tailgate and grabbed the 'golf club bag' from which he withdrew a metal detector. He fitted headphones and switched the thing on, testing it by placing a pocket knife on the ground and passing the probe backwards and forward over it. Finally he nodded. "Is OK," he announced.

He got a reading almost at once. A spot just in front of the stone plinth and in line with the centre of the archway produced a strong reaction. Neil and I fetched the tools from the back of the vehicle and Neil started to dig. The ground was very stony and he exchanged the spade for the garden fork which soon struck metal about a foot down.

"Be careful," Mario shouted, "we don't want to damage anything." Neil put the fork aside and scraped the stony soil out using his bare hands.

"What the hell is this?" He exclaimed and we all peered into the hole. He had carefully uncovered the detached head of a British army entrenching tool. His fingers closed around the 'pick' end of it and he pulled it out.

We all stared down at this rusty relic before exchanging puzzled glances tinged with disappointment. "Uncle Benny you bastard," breathed Mario. He turned to us, "you know what the crafty sod's done? He's laid a false trail. Spiro, check all around this bloody archway just in case." Spiro replaced the headphones, picked up the detector and began a systematic sweep around the stone plinth and Mario said: "Let's have something to eat," the disappointment in his voice almost tangible.

The sun was well over its zenith by then but the heat was still oppressive, the settlement cupped in this high mountain hollow was a natural sun trap. Mario sat on the running board while Neil used some of our precious water to clean his hands which left me to unpack the food hamper. By the time I had done that, Spiro had drawn a blank and we all sat in the vehicle with the aircon full on eating our lunch.

Spiro finished first, he got out and stood disconsolately gazing up at Mount Pantocrator. I watched him place a cigarette between his lips then pause in the act of lighting it. Suddenly he threw the unlit cigarette aside, picked up the detector and crammed the headphones on before walking over to the hole Neil had dug. He passed the instrument over the hole and immediately shouted out. It sounded like *Eureka*, which was to be expected I suppose.

The rectangular biscuit tin was about six inches farther down. It had been wrapped in a piece of British army anti-gas cape, tied with rope which disintegrated as we withdrew it from the ground. We looked on as Mario eased the lid off.

The fact that the lid was not rusted on was due to a thick greasy deposit around the rim which Spiro identified as a mixture of feta cheese and olive oil. Inside the tin another package enclosed in gas cape material yielded the leather wrapped icon which was carefully repacked and placed in the shade. Last to emerge were two separate packages, one obviously containing the pistol, the other the ammo clip. Each package was wrapped in grease proof paper, inside which a covering of some kind of cotton fabric impregnated with olive oil had kept the items totally free from rust.

"Good old Uncle Benny," breathed Mario his eyes brimming and behind me I heard the pop as Neil opened the champagne.

After filling in the hole and replacing the turf we stayed on for an hour or so exploring the place, Mario seated reluctantly in the wheelchair and grumbling about the bumpy road surface as Spiro pushed him about. Incredibly there was a taverna tucked away among the ruins and some of the houses were occupied or being renovated. "Probably soon be a McDonalds an' a helipad for tourists," grunted Spiro.

Eventually we walked back to the Toyota and finished off the food and the other bottle of wine and the heat had gone out of the day by the time we began our return journey. Mario was asleep before we had travelled a couple of kilometres.

We left him asleep in the vehicle when we parked by Roda harbour while we transferred the recovered items back to the boat. Neil paid Spiro for the wheelchair, an item which he said would probably be necessary before too long. Everything else, the tools, the metal detector and the unused water we left for Spiro. "What you do now?" Spiro asked as we returned to shore.

Neil paused, resting on the oars for a moment. "Mario's knackered. It's been a long day. I think we'll sail around to Agios Stefanos tomorrow before heading for Brindisi. His job's not finished yet," he nodded toward the shore and the sleeping Mario. "I am afraid when it is done he might switch off and . . well, just fade out."

"How long he got?" asked Spiro.

Neil shook his head. "They gave him six months. That was eight months back so, who knows?"

"He make it back to Wales?" Spiro asked. But Neil merely shrugged and bent once again to the oars.

We had to wake Mario when we got back to the Toyota and help him into the dinghy. Then it was a difficult job getting him up the ladder onto the cutter. The effort brought on another coughing bout so Spiro and I got Mario below while Neil sorted out the oxygen and other medication.

By that time it was getting towards sunset, the town itself was already in shade and the boat's shadow stretched across the waters of the bay. We came up on deck and Spiro leaned against the tiller while I sat on the cabin rooflight. "How long have you known him?" I asked.

"Mario? Not long, about five years. He come to Corfu for holiday. We meet in taverna, we get pissed, we talk. We talk a lot. He good bloke. I go to England one time, sorry Wales. I stay with him. Some place he call the *vallies*. Everyone friendly, everyone get pissed a lot. Then he take me to this place Porthcawl. He take me out in this boat. He good sailor, he good bloke."

We fell silent. The sound of the water lapping against the hull was the only sound, the coughing from below having ceased some minutes before. The evening closed in and I said goodnight.

21

The following morning, much to my surprise, Mario was up and about early. Spiro had left the night before to return the Toyota to the car hire company in Corfu Town and I pictured him driving back to Sidari in his battered old Fiat smoking as usual and listening to the car radio.

We all had a light breakfast and Mario pored over the charts for some time before we got under way. The day was warm and sunny with a favourable wind so under Mario's command we set sail and headed out to sea towing the dinghy astern. We anchored off Agios Stefanos before midday and Mario and Neil went below while I lazed unashamedly on deck, soaking up the sun.

Jean and I had visited Agios Stefanos during our holiday on the island and as I looked across at the small harbour and the village crowding down to the beach my thoughts again turned to her.

"Jim!" It was Neil, his head appearing above the coaming, "can you come down. We've got some planning to do." Reluctantly I roused up from my sunlit reverie and clambered down the companionway. Neil and Mario sat at the chart table each with a can of lager within reach. "Grab a can and sit down," Neil said.

"This is the situation," Mario began, "I've e-mailed the Monastery with the good news about the icon and . . ."

"I didn't know you could e-mail a monastery," I said.

"Well, what I mean is I've been in touch with my contact in Cassino Town. The Town Hall people there were most helpful, all done by email of course. Anyway they put me onto this chap who's got connections with the Abbot and ever since I decided to go for this he's been my go-between. I've asked him to arrange for someone to meet us at Brindisi so we can return this artefact. Once that's done we can all bugger off home."

"The thing is," Neil added, "it could take some time for an answer, then we've got to arrange a time and date, then we've got to get there. You've still got your things at the hotel in Sidari haven't you?" I nodded. "Well, I'll row you ashore and Spiro'll drive you there and back. He's taken my motorbike back and paid all the bills we've incurred since we got here so we'll be free to leave."

The thought of sitting in Spiro's smoke filled Fiat again did not fill me with joy but I was in their hands. "How long will it take to get to Brindisi?" I asked.

"Huh, how long is a piece of string? Depends on the weather," Mario said. "And the bloody crew," he added pointedly glancing at me.

"Jim's pretty competent now," Neil said defensively. But Mario said nothing, just took another swig from his can as I sat savouring the cool beer and wondering what the voyage would be like. All my sailing practice had been in relatively sheltered waters. I knew Brindisi only from the air. On my flight out we had already begun our descent to Corfu by the time we passed over that Italian town. By sea it was a different matter. We would be out of sight of land for several hours I surmised, in open sea without an engine and with a disabled and dying skipper.

Mario's mobile bleeped and he pulled it out of his dressing gown pocket. "Hello Spiro you old bugger," he smiled, "where are you? Right. Well get over to Agios Stefanos to pick Jim up OK? He's got to get his stuff from the hotel. When? OK we'll have some lunch now in that case, give me another bell when your nearly here. Epharisto!"

"What happens after Brindisi?" I asked.

"We set sail," Mario said, pausing for dramatic effect and sweeping an arm across the chart in a triumphant gesture, "for Porthcawl!"

Neil and I exchanged glances. "How long will that take?" I asked.

"Depends," Mario replied. "My best guess is three to four weeks."

"As long as that? How long did it take you to get out here then?"

"Ah well that was different, I hired a yacht delivery firm to sail the boat to Gib then we flew out and joined ship there."

"With the woman?"

"No. She was one of the delivery firm's crew, when the others returned to the UK she stayed on to help us sail to Corfu. She has relatives here."

"I remember Neil telling me. So how come the firm could spare her?" I asked.

"These delivery outfits don't have employees. People just get on their books and if a job comes up they get a phone call, if they're available they do the job. She was paid by the firm for the leg to Gib and I paid her for the rest. You could put in for a job like that now Jim, you're practically 'competent crew'. Better than that bloody design office."

I smiled. That bloody design office seemed to belong to another world. "You want a hand with preparing lunch?" I asked.

Neil shook his head. "You get back up on deck. Make the most of the sun. I'll rustle up something." I gave Mario a hand to get up on deck and we both sat finishing off the lager. The day had become overcast but there was a warm breeze.

After a while Mario said: "I won't be happy until this thing is finally handed over, then I'll feel I can face Aunty Bronwen."

"Did she ask you to come out and do this?"

"No. She just told me the story, showed me the diary, and fed me apple tart and rhubarb crumble every time I visited."

"So you said you'd do it."

"That's right but I only said it to please her, I don't think I would have ever really done it if it wasn't for . . . ." his voice trailed away.

"Your complaint?"

He glanced across at me and nodded slowly, a wistful expression on his face. "It tends to focus your mind onto the limited time available to realise your ambitions. I've said a lot of things, made promises I didn't keep. Haven't you?"

"Too many I'm afraid."

"Well this was the one I had to keep."

We lapsed into silence for a time, finally I asked: "Why did you involve me Mario?" I looked him straight in the eye and thought I detected a flicker of a smile.

"We go back a long way," he said. "Remember that reunion? Did you ever go to another one?"

I shook my head. "I'm not sure if there ever was another one."

"There probably wasn't," he sighed, "all those years, all those blokes. All that industrial skill down the bloody pan. We had a good time that night, re-living the past. Met some blokes I hadn't seen for ages." He shrugged, "I dunno why I asked you Jim, maybe it was because your ex missus and me had such a good chat about sailing."

"I'm glad you did anyway, it's been quite an experience."

"It's not over yet boyo, not by a long chalk. There's no bloody yacht delivery firm on the way back, no fear. This time it's us all the way if you're up for it."

"I'm getting paid aren't I?" I smiled, "and as you said, it's better than that bloody design office."

Neil came up from below, a bowl of Greek salad in one hand and a large plate of something called a meat meze in the other. Tucked inside his shirt was a bottle of red wine. That lunch that day, sitting on deck fanned by the warm breeze coming from the shore still sticks in my mind. For one thing Mario was in good form, full of the devilment I remembered from the old days. Then there was the food. Neil's Greek salad was delicious, the meze of cold meats mouth watering, the wine smooth and full bodied. We lingered over it for almost two hours until Spiro rang to say the was leaving Sidari. The journey to Agios Stefanos would take him less than thirty minutes he said so, reluctantly, I drained my glass and pulled the dinghy alongside.

As Neil was rowing me ashore I asked him why Mario always anchored offshore when there were harbours available. "I used to think he was too tight to pay the berthing fees," he replied, "but I think it's got something to do with the fact that he's got no engine. It's usually more sheltered in harbour, so he might have trouble getting out in light winds. Also he might have trouble getting into such constricted areas, could damage other boats for instance. Much simpler to anchor off, provided the weather's OK of course."

Spiro drove me back to the hotel and I packed my bags and checked out then he paid the bill in cash and pocketed the receipt. "You want drink before you go back to boat?" he asked.

My first reaction was to decline but that would have been anti-social. Spiro had been a key player in this venture. He had met me at the airport, fixed up my accommodation, escorted me up to the New Fort and around Corfu Town, been my chauffeur and my guide. Spiro had arranged the hire of the Toyota and driven us all up to Ano Perithea. He had organised the wheelchair, paid the bills and been a general dogsbody for the entire operation. I would have to buy him a drink.

We left my cases at reception and crossed the street to a local bar. Before I had a chance to object he ordered a large Metaxa and soda for me and the inevitable ouzo and lemonade for himself. "I wanted to buy these," I complained.

"Barman on'y spik Greek," he replied, "you spik Greek?" I shook my head. "OK. So shut the fuck up. Yammas." He raised his glass.

"Yammas." I responded and sipped at the brandy. Then we went and sat at a nearby table. "When did you find out about Mario's condition?" I asked him.

"He e-mail me few months back. Give me all gen as he call it. He want my help to do this thing. I say OK, we know each other long time now. I wish I could do more but," he gave his usual shrug as he lit his usual cigarette, "once you all leave here I not see him again I don' think." He stared into his glass of ouzo, a thin smile on his lips, his eyes glistening.

"What will you do after we've gone?" I asked. "We seem to have kept you pretty busy what with one thing and another."

"I help with olive harvest I expect. I do part time lecture in Corfu Town, I teach some English. Not very good."

"Mario tells me you have a degree in Environmental Studies."

"Yeah. Everybody laugh when they find out. Greek environmentalists are, what Mario say? Like rocking horse shit?" He looked puzzled. "What that mean?" he asked.

"It means they're quite rare," I replied and Spiro nodded comprehendingly.

"How long you know Mario?" He asked.

"We were apprentices together. Long time ago. A long time."

"You going to sail all way back to England with them two?"

"I assume that was one of the reasons I was asked to come."

"They good sailors but, . . .Mario, he not well, he getting worse. You better be plenty tough to help them through." I nodded, smiling, little knowing how prophetic Spiro's words were. "Jus' one thing," he added.

"What?"

"Once you get icon delivered let me know somehow. Write or phone or maybe email my cousin. He got scuba diving business near Nissaki, I give you his email address." He scribbled it on the back of an envelope and handed it to me. "Why I ask you is this, I think I know this Yiorgo that Mario's uncle Benny knew."

"Mario told you all about him then?"

"Sure. He tell me when I visit him in Wales. I meet Benny's widow too, Bronwen she called. That mean white breast in Welsh, you know that?" I shook my head. "Anyway, I know this Yiorgo's village, he must be very old now, may even be dead. If not he be glad to hear about this treasure he helped Benny to hide way back then, so will his family." I nodded, thinking about that older generation of people now almost forgotten who had endured the war and all its personal tragedies. Of the beautiful islands under a cruel occupation, of an ancient city mercilessly blitzed, of a medieval abbey wantonly bombed to rubble.

Then I saw Spiro visibly wince, obviously at the same thing that had roused me from my melancholy reverie, for the coloured spotlights had begun to flash and the three scantily dressed English girls near the bar had begun to sing quite badly from the words on the screen. The karaoke had begun.

We had another drink which I managed to pay for and the sun was low over the olive clad hills behind the town before we left. We picked up my luggage from the hotel, crossed the street to the car park and got into Spiro's old Fiat.

The drive to Agios Stefanos was noisy but smoke free as Spiro did not light up, much to my surprise and relief. We drew up by the harbour and phoned Mario. Neil came on the line and then he appeared on deck and waved to us. We watched as he clambered into the dinghy and rowed steadily towards us. By the time we got back to the cutter the lights were coming on in the houses and tavernas. "Mario's got a reply from Cassino Town," he announced as we drew alongside, "we sail for Brindisi tomorrow."

The rest of the evening was spent in unashamed drinking with some eating thrown in from time to time. Neil did us proud with food as usual, with sandwiches, cold chicken, ham rolls and the inevitable Greek salad, we sat on deck beneath the swaying anchor light as the moon rose over the Albanian mountains. Mario turned in after midnight and soon afterwards Neil rowed Spiro ashore so he could drive back to Sidari. I was thankful that I was not his passenger this time as I surveyed the empty bottles littering the deck.

22

The next morning Mario called me into his cabin. It was extremely small, taking up only half the width of the cutter. His bunk lay fore and aft near the centre of the boat, his computer, fax machine, radio equipment and GPS display were ranged on a shelf along the starboard side. There was a large metal cabinet from floor to ceiling with the word medical stencilled on the door and next to that a portable toilet in an alcove with the curtain drawn back.

"You've been to Corfu before haven't you boyo?" he said, "so you'll know the score regarding bog paper."

"Don't put it down the loo you mean?"

"Right. Apparently when we Brits ruled the roost around here we installed a sewage system which was rather less than adequate. All down to the bore of the pipes being a bit small." I knew about this of course and it had never posed a problem. I was well used to making a small neat parcel of soiled tissue paper and placing it in the bin provided. "Now then," he continued, "the same applies on board this boat. No bog paper down the loo. The last thing we want when bein' tossed about on the 'oggin is having to unclog a blocked up crapper."

"I understand."

"That's my bog, there in the alcove. That works on the bucket and chuck it principle. Neil sees to that god bless 'im. If he can't cope for any reason how do you feel about doin' the job?"

I suppose he had to ask the question. Three men in a boat one of whom was going to become increasingly immobile posed problems of mutual survival, the thought of becoming a medical orderly was not too daunting if that was all it entailed. The real fear was if Neil, for whatever reason, was unable to administer Mario's medication. Then I would be worried. "I'm not squeamish," I replied, "I expect you'd do the same for me."

"No I bloody wouldn't," he retorted with a grin.

Neil stuck his head in that point. "Time for your medication, Mario."

"I'll wash up the breakfast things," I said and withdrew to the galley.

I had coffee on deck later while Mario slept. His rest periods were becoming more frequent, presumably due to his medication or maybe just to his condition. I sat pondering on the voyage ahead while Neil swam naked around the boat. I had once again declined his invitation to join in. Earlier Spiro had been pressed into service for the very last time. Neil had insisted that we re-provision before leaving the island and Spiro was at that moment in Corfu Town loading up his Fiat at the supermarket. Neil was, among many other things, the quartermaster and he had read out a long list to Spiro on Mario's mobile. The weather was overcast, the wind light so it looked as if we would not be sailing today in any case.

I was getting restless. The cutter's deck was large but I soon tired of pacing up and down. When Neil finished his swim and clambered out I asked him if he would row me ashore so I could have a wander around. "You can do that," he replied. "There's the oars in those brackets on the bulwark. I'll pull the dinghy alongside." And so my first clumsy attempt at rowing got me, eventually, into the harbour at Agios Stefanos.

I found the café that Jean and I had visited during our holiday and sat for almost an hour over a cup of coffee served Greek style, that is accompanied by a glass of water. I tried to ignore the slight lump in my throat that the memory of her provoked and surreptitiously wiped away the beginnings of a tear in my right eye.

Our separation had not been acrimonious in spite of everything. I had been angry beyond words at her betrayal and we both knew our relationship had to end but when the solicitor handed us our cheques I still remember the look on her face. I saw it in my mind's eye again now, sitting there in that little café. Was it a look of remorse? Of apology? Or just a sad reflection of what might have been if she had not succumbed to that man's undoubted charms? I smiled to myself. Who was I kidding? Succumbed to his charms indeed! She was probably as up for it as he was.

Eventually I got up and strolled around the village for a while until the sound of Spiro's Fiat drew me back to the harbour. We loaded the provisions into the dinghy and, luckily, Spiro took up the oars thus sparing me the embarrassment of demonstrating my inept sculling. We drew alongside the cutter.

"Ahoy Mario," Spiro shouted, "we're back with enough food to feed a fuckin' army."

Mario appeared at the rail, bleary eyed but smiling. "Spiro you old bastard. What would we do without you?" Between us we unloaded the dinghy, forming a chain with Neil at the far end stowing everything in its place below.

I helped Neil with preparing the evening meal down in the cramped galley. Up on deck Mario sat with a glass of wine while Spiro, keeping well downwind of him, chainsmoked as usual. We could hear them talking quietly together, probably for the last time, I thought sadly.

Spiro declined our offer to stay for the meal and Mario and I stood watching in the gathering dusk as Neil rowed him ashore. A final wave before he climbed into his Fiat was the last we saw of him. I was not to know it then but I would meet him just once more, unfortunately in much more sombre circumstances.

Mario went below as soon as his tail lights disappeared and I helped Neil hoist the Mirror out of the water and stow it in its inverted position over the cabin rooflight. Neil and I ate in silence in the cramped saloon that evening while Mario ate alone in his cabin.

We set sail at first light next day. As soon as we were clear of the island the wind increased and Mario estimated we were making at least six knots. Our course was approximately northwest and we soon hit a considerable swell. We breakfasted on fruit juice and toast followed by coffee and as soon as I had eaten I took the helm from Mario.

I suppose the first signs of abdominal discomfort occurred within two hours of sailing and as Neil was handing up mugs of tea through the hatch I knew that I was close to retching. Seasickness is a particularly nasty experience. The French call it mal de mer but in any language it is a desperately unpleasant sensation. Mario could see it coming and grabbed the tiller as I dived for the rail and deposited my breakfast over the side. Neil got me to drink some milk and eat a few biscuits. Within five minutes that too was feeding the fishes.

I spent the next four hours below on my bunk alternately eating dry bread and drinking anything that Neil put in front of me and then retching it all back into a bucket. I felt like death and must have looked it. The remainder of the day passed in similar fashion. I was of no use as crew and as night closed in I fell into an exhausted sleep.

I awoke next morning feeling hungry. In my hand I clutched the remains of a dry crust I had tried to eat the night before. I ate it immediately sitting on the edge of my bunk. Neil lay opposite me asleep in his bunk so I assumed Mario was at the helm. I had a raging thirst and made my way unsteadily to the galley where we kept the filtered rainwater. I steadied myself against the sink and took a draught of the cold liquid, not too much in case the sudden chill should give me stomach cramps. The boat was rolling incessantly but I did not feel sick. I made my way to the foot of the companionway and began to climb but the hatch was closed. I slid it back enough to get my head out and surveyed the deck. It was deserted.

My first panic stricken thought was that Mario had been swept overboard as we slept and I stumbled back down the steps and along the passageway to rouse Neil. As I passed Mario's cabin a loud snore emanated from within, I snatched the door open and there was Mario, fast asleep on his bunk, mouth wide open. My footsteps must have roused Neil who poked his head out of our cabin. "Who's sailing the bloody boat?" I asked. "There's nobody on deck."

"The tiller still lashed?"

"Lashed?"

Neil stood holding the door frame, he seemed to be feeling the boat's movement. "It's OK," he said, "we're still hove to. Is it light yet?"

"Just about."

"How do you feel?"

"Not too bad actually. Bloody hungry."

"Just have some cereal and a glass of milk. It doesn't do to overload your stomach."

"I wasn't much use yesterday. I never felt so terrible."

"You're over it now, hopefully. Once your brain gets accustomed to the movement your body adjusts. Trust me."

"What's this about the tiller?" I asked.

"We're hove to. That means the sails and the rudder act against each other so we don't go anywhere much. We'll be drifting downwind at about 2 knots."

"Nobody on watch though. What if we hit something, or something hits us?"

"Nothing to hit out here, we're miles from any land. Then Mario's got this gismo that can detect another ship's radar beam. It registers the direction it's coming from and if that bearing remains fairly constant it means something's bearing down on us and sounds an alarm."

"That's bloody clever."

"I told you, this may be an old boat but it's crammed with micro-electronics. Look, you grab some breakfast and I'll get us back on course, you relieve me in half an hour."

I ate a large bowl of cereal followed by a thick slice of bread spread with some honey I found in the galley. The boat's movement gave me no trouble, all traces of nausea seemed to have vanished. I felt wide awake and fit for anything. Presently I struggled into a waterproof and went on deck.

"Good breakfast?" Neil asked. He was sat on the bench we had secured athwart the boat for Mario, the tiller tucked under his armpit.

"Lovely."

"Not feeling sick?"

"Not a bit."

"Want to take the helm?"

"Yeah. What's the course?"

"Don't bother about a course. We were pushed quite a way downwind last night, I want to get as close to the wind as possible now, that will point us almost due north."

"I thought our course was northwest."

"It was, before we hove to. We must have drifted quite a way south. Here, take the tiller. Now push it away from you a bit. See the front of the foresail start to flutter?" I nodded. "That's called luffing, you're getting too close to the wind, steer off a bit, that's it. See the fluttering's stopped. So don't worry about a course, just steer as close as you can to the wind so that there's no luffing."

With that he left me at the helm. Once I turned into the wind too much and the boat almost stopped, I over corrected and it heeled over alarmingly. Eventually I managed to get it about right and I spent the next hour or so adjusting the tiller so that the boat was within a few degrees of luffing. That seemed to produce the highest speed.

Eventually Neil relieved me, sitting on the cross bench with a mug of tea in one hand and the tiller in the other. "Mario wants to see you," he said, "he wants to give you a lesson in navigation."

I went below to where Mario sat in the main saloon, before him on the table a chart was spread out. There was a notepad covered with scribbled calculations and a thick book entitled The Mediterranean Pilot. "That's where I reckon we were when we hove to last night," he said pointing to a pencil cross on the chart. "And that's where we were when we got under way again this morning. Now I reckon we're here."

He pointed to a series of crosses with a time and date marked against each together with the initials EP1, EP2 and EP3. "Those are our estimated positions," he explained.

"How did you figure that out?" I asked.

"A process called dead reckoning," he replied, "taking into account estimated or measured speed, prevailing currents, wind speed and direction and a bit of intuitive guesswork."

"Amazing. And how accurate is it?"

"Ah now then boyo. You want to see a bit of magic?" He grinned that boyish grin of his. "Follow me." He led me into his cabin and sat before the shelf containing his electronic equipment twiddling knobs and pressing buttons. Lights flashed and a digital display glowed green before some paper began to feed out of a small printer near his keyboard. Mario tore it off and peered at it, grunted something then brushed past me and made his way back to the saloon. I followed.

He transferred the longitude and latitude from the print out onto the chart then sat back. "There," he said with satisfaction, "that's where we are now." He had pencilled in a cross within a small circle with the words actual posn. alongside it together with the time. "We're only about ten miles out. Not bad considering it's the first time we've used the GPS since we set out. I can calculate a course to Brindisi now and email them our e.t.a. That's estimated time of arrival to you bloody landlubbers."

The rest of the day we took turns at the helm. Neil and I did two hour stints to Mario's one. Food consisted of soup in a mug with thick slices of bread and butter every four hours interspersed with tea or coffee served in the same mugs. That night the wind fell light and we were not making much headway, about three knots by Mario's estimate. He switched on the 'electronic speedo' as he called it and the readout glowed, varying between two and three knots. "I've a good mind to heave to again," Mario remarked, "but maybe we'd be better to keep going. We'll keep the same watchkeeping as before, maybe the wind'll pick up again." And so we sailed on gently through the night. The wind, such as it was, had veered a little so we had to steer by the compass instead of the luffing sail. Neil had rigged up a small light and the course, according to the antique graduations on the face of the compass, was North Northwest. I don't know about the others but during my stint at the helm our course varied considerably either side of that.

Towards dawn Mario came on deck to relieve me. He stood holding the rigging, sniffing the air like a fox. "D'you see that?" He exclaimed. I followed his pointing finger. "That's the loom of a lighthouse." The distant horizon showed as a dark line as a momentary glow, almost imperceptible it was so faint, appeared and disappeared rhythmically. Mario started to count out loud, measuring the time lapses between the looms. "You OK on the helm for a bit longer?" he asked.

"Yeah, I'm OK."

"I'm going to have a look at the chart, see what light that is," and he went below. I concentrated on keeping the boat on course, occasionally stealing a glance in the direction of the light. As the minutes ticked by it seemed to increase in intensity or maybe that was just my imagination.

Presently Mario returned with a hand bearing compass, and took a bearing on the light before disappearing below once again.

Slowly, imperceptibly, the blackness of the night became dark grey and soon I could define the foresail and the bowsprit, then the intervening deck and the bulk of the upturned Mirror dinghy lashed down over the cabin rooflight. After a while Mario came back. "I'll take her now," he said and sat down on the crossbench. "Got to alter course a bit. I got that lighthouse sorted, we got to steer west nor'west." He took the tiller and I watched as the compass needle swung and the boat came onto its new heading. "Better wake Neil up to get some breakfast on the go. I'll be OK here for an hour or so."

I went below and clamped the kettle onto the stove and brewed up some tea taking a mug through to Neil. "Mario says to wake you to make breakfast but I could do that if you like." I said.

"No, you're alright. I've had a sleep, you're just off watch. I'll do my usual dawn concoction. You take a mug of tea up to Mario."

"Dawn concoction?" I said, raising an eyebrow.

"It's called cheesy-hammy-eggy," he replied. "You'll like it." By the time I got back on deck it was full light. The sky was overcast, the sea grey and uninviting. Mario sat hunched over the tiller, the collar of his bulky waterproof turned up, his head encased in a grotesque bobble hat. I handed him his tea. He gestured towards the west. On the distant horizon a pinpoint of light flashed in a constantly repeated sequence, I guessed it was the lighthouse whose loom we had seen earlier. "The wind's getting up a bit," he said, "with a bit of luck we'll be in Brindisi by nightfall."

23

Neil's cheesy-hammy-eggy was delicious. He cooked it in a deep wok-like pan beating the eggs together with the chopped up cheese and ham and liberally laced with pepper and salt and, of all things, rum. "The day the Navy scrapped its rum ration," Mario remarked, "Nelson must have turned in his grave." The meal certainly was a morale booster after a long night and as the sun began to break through the overcast I surveyed the distant land with a degree of excitement.

Neil took the helm as Mario went below to his satellite phone and fax to make the final arrangements for handing over the icon to its rightful owners. I sat on the other end of the crossbench, the sun warm on my back as the boat rode the swell. All my seasickness had gone and the motion seemed so natural I hardly noticed it. "How is Mario?" I asked. "He seems to have perked up a bit since we set off."

"He's buoyed up by the thought of completing his task of course," Neil replied, "but I've increased his dose of steroids too. That could account for it."

"Isn't that dangerous?" I asked. And the look I got in return told me how stupid a question that was. To try and cover up I asked: "What are the chances of him getting back to the UK?"

Neil thought for a moment. "About fifty fifty," he said.

"What happens if . . . ." my voice trailed off.

"Go on."

"Well, what happens if he . . . if he dies while we're at sea?"

"It would depend where we were. We've discussed it of course. He dearly wants to get home but if he doesn't make it he wants a burial at sea."

My mind conjured up a scene out of The Cruel Sea, a heaving deck, hatless sailors and a Naval Chaplain saying the words. The prayer book would close and the Captain give an almost imperceptible nod to the burly seamen at each side of the board, they would lift and the board would tilt and the canvass bags with their lifeless weighted contents would slide out from under the flag and splash into the cold grey water. I shuddered. "Let's hope he makes it back," I said.

Towards nightfall we anchored south of Brindisi. Mario had arranged for us to be towed into the up-market end of the local yacht marina the following day about noon. "We could have sailed in," he grumbled, "but

I expect because we've got no engine they're afraid we'd bump their precious bloody yachts."

Neil produced an appetising stew for our evening meal, which we all ate together on deck then he did all the washing up by himself and turned in. Mario and I, wrapped in blankets, sat on deckchairs as the rising moon cast our shadows across the dark water.

"I had a girl once," Mario said softly, "whenever there's a moon I think of her." He topped up his wine glass before handing the bottle to me. "You ever been to Wales?" I shook my head. "Ah Wales," he breathed, "the drizzly rain, the lights reflected on the pavements, the crowded pubs, the singing. The pithead gear turning, the slag heaps towering. But walk a few hundred yards up the mountain and it's a different world. Stunted oaks and tall ferns, craggy outcrops and gorse, sparkling streams and marshy hollows. That's where we used to go Ruth and me."

I glanced across at him and his eyes were fixed upon the dark shore, his mind a thousand miles away. "My first girl she was. Her friends used to tease her because she fancied me. Me, short fat Mario Franzoni of the Eye-talian café in Aber. 'Ruth do fancy you Mario,' her friends would shout out to me after school. 'When you goin' to ask her for a date then?' So one day I did and she blushed and said yes."

We had forgotten the anchor light. I wanted to get up and fetch it from the locker and light it and then hoist it up on its rope but I was afraid it would interrupt Mario's reverie. He continued, quietly re-living the memories of his youth: "We used to walk out together. We never talked much, it seemed to be enough just to be together. We'd walk up through the woods out onto the mountainside and sit on a drystone wall somewhere looking down on the valley listening to the coal trains shunting, watching the steam rising. We were both part of it see, part of the place and the people yet we were remote from it, way up there in the cool clean air above the squalid industry we both depended on."

"Her father a miner?"

"Oh aye, and her grandfather. Later on her brothers too, same pit as uncle Benny. We'd sit there until dark, until moonrise. Then we'd walk back down and I'd see her home, well, to the end of back row anyway."

"Back row?"

"There were two rows of houses where she lived see, front row and back row. She lived in back row. Three kisses then, the last one being the longest then 'nosta cariad' till the next time."

"Did you ever . . . ?"

"No. Nothing like that. Christ we were only school kids."

"School kids are at it like rabbits these days Mario."

"So they say."

"I'd better rig the riding light," I said and as I hauled it up to sway above the deck I asked: "What happened to her?"

"To us you mean. We both grew up, she met someone else. She got married. We used to see each other now and again, just passing in the street you know? I often wonder if she remembers those walks up the mountain, if they meant as much to her as they did to me."

We fell silent. I often wondered the same thing about Jean and me. If some of the things we did and the places we went to were as significant to her as they had been to me. I had never thought to ask her and now it was too late.

When we had finished the wine I helped Mario to his bunk then sat out on deck for a while longer thinking about Jean. Funny what Mario had said. It was the same for Jean and me, we had no need to talk, to make conversation. There was a comfortable togetherness in our relationship that transcended mere words. Such a pity it had to end the way it did.

Next morning we all had a light breakfast after which Neil and I got the towline prepared. Mario was on tenterhooks, he sat on the crossbench dishing out orders or advice or criticism until Neil swore at him and told him to shut up or go below and let us alone to get on with it. About eleven thirty the towing launch drew alongside.

The skipper of the launch seemed to have different ideas from Mario about how to tackle the tow and they argued at considerable length in Italian before we set off with Mario at the helm. It was quite a way to the yacht marina and when we finally tied up to a floating pontoon it was after one o'clock.

The sun was oppressively hot and there was no sign of a welcoming party. The towing launch, its job done, sheered away, the skipper giving a peremptory wave as if glad to be free of us. Mario said: "Can you two get that sun canopy rigged again? I'm bloody roasting."

"D'you want the deckchairs?" I asked.

"Yeah, and get a can each out of the cool box." When we had done that we all sat under the canopy, sweating and drinking lager. There was still no sign of anyone from the monastery. "Bloody siesta time I expect," grumbled Mario. Midway through the afternoon a white minibus pulled up at the marina office. Four figures emerged, the first in a grey lightweight suit, the others in long black habits. "About bloody time too," breathed Mario. That was the signal to make myself scarce.

This was Mario's day. With Neil standing by to look after him he could do this thing for his uncle Benny, I would just be in the way so I collected the empties and tidied the deck before going below.

I lay upon my bunk dozing, vaguely aware of the slight movement of the boat as the welcoming party came aboard. I must have slept then for I was awakened by raised voices on deck. Mario's was the loudest, then someone else in a conciliatory tone then Mario again more irate this time. It was all in Italian except for Neil apparently trying to calm Mario down. The argument, if it was an argument, ended in the inevitable coughing bout with Mario being helped below by Neil and having oxygen administered. I lay there for a while wondering what to do and eventually Neil came in and sat upon his bunk. "What was all that about?" I asked.

"Much ado about nothing really," Neil replied. "They brought some Vatican expert along to validate the artefact and Mario took umbrage."

"I should have thought that procedure was normal," I said, "any charlatan could turn up with a fake. Remember the Hitler diaries?"

"Exactly. The thing is they wanted to take it away, that's what annoyed him."

"How else could they verify the bloody thing then?"

"Well, that's what finally calmed him down. They've got some fancy carbon dating kit in the minibus, plus this king pin expert so they could have it sorted in less than an hour. Anyway, in view of Mario's condition I persuaded them to leave it until tomorrow." So it was that we had to endure another twenty four hours sweating it out in Brindisi. By that time Mario had recovered. He had been on the phone to his contact in Cassino Town who had confirmed the authenticity of the icon and arranged the ceremonial handover for midday. This time I decided to stay on deck.

The whole thing was fairly low key although there was an Italian TV News unit there to film it. Mario was in his wheelchair and Neil pushed him along the deck to where the Abbot and his entourage graciously received the icon. It was photographed by Vatican staff and a short speech followed. Finally the Abbot gave a blessing, laying his hands upon Mario's head before making the sign of the cross.

We watched as the dignitaries made their way along the pontoons back to the minibus. Quite a crowd had gathered curious to know what was going on and Mario glanced up at the wind indicator at the masthead. "Let's get the hell out of here," he said. "Neil, hoist the foresail. Jim, cast off forrard. Let's show this lot we can do without a bloody towboat." He wheeled himself aft and struggled out of the wheelchair onto the crossbench. "Hold the foresail aback," he shouted to Neil and as I cast off, the sail filled and the cutter swung out from the pontoon. "Let go!" He commanded and Neil let the sheet run through his hands. The sail spilled wind and the cutter swung round more slowly. "Let go aft." This to me and I cast off the rope that secured us to the pontoon.

Mario put the helm over and Neil hardened up on the sheet and then we were sailing as sweet as you like down the fairway between the moored yachts under foresail alone. "Jim," Mario shouted, "get the main up. Quickly now, let's show 'em a clean pair of heels." And he threw his head back and laughed, bringing on a coughing bout which fortunately lasted only a minute or so, then we were out of the marina, heading south along the coast butting into the swell.

Mario was in his element, I could see that. He was singing one of his foul rugger songs, something about Jerusalem and a certain harlot from that city. Between verses he took a swig at a gin bottle eventually hurling it, empty of course, over the side before breaking into the chorus from The Sloop John B. The sun shone and the wind carried us along at around six or eight knots.

The wheelchair had fetched up against the starboard bulwark, I collected it, folded it up and stowed it below. Neil was in the galley making sandwiches and filling vacuum flasks with weak tea. "How is Mario Lanza up there?" Neil asked, "he's in good voice I hear."

"He's in excellent form," I replied, "who gave him the gin bottle?"

"He's got his own supply stashed away. He's on a high right now. He's completed his self imposed task. By tonight he'll be totally knackered. You watch."

Neil was right. Long before nightfall Mario was exhausted and I took the helm while Neil took him below and got him settled down and it was dusk before Neil came back on deck. Soon we were abreast of Otranto and we turned south. "After we round Capo San Maria di Leuca our course will be southwest," he announced, "Mario says we can lash the tiller then and let her sail herself." He placed the mahogany boxed compass upon the deck. "We'll be crossing the Gulf of Taranto," he said. "It should take us all night and most of tomorrow." I said nothing, I just hoped, as I had several times during this voyage, that he knew what he was doing. As I remembered it from my school atlas the Gulf of Taranto was a deep bay. If we steered too far west we would simply hit the toe of Italy wasting precious time. Too far south and we would not see land before we sighted North Africa.

"You get your head down for a couple of hours," Neil said, "I'll stay on deck and keep watch." I went below and lay upon my bunk but I could not settle. After an hour or so I looked in on Mario, he was sound asleep so I went to the galley and made some coffee for myself and Neil and took it up on deck. The night had closed in and we were sailing easily. Neil sat with his back against the windward bulwark shielded by the spray dodger, I passed him his coffee and sat beside him. "Can't sleep?" he asked.

"No. I don't know why, I'm tired enough."

"Sometimes gets you like that, a long sea passage I mean." I looked back and the loom of a lighthouse showed on the horizon. Apart from fleeting glimpses of the stars that was the only light we saw all night.

24

Neil and I took turns keeping watch through the long hours of darkness. Towards dawn he woke me from a deep sleep with a strong cup of tea laced with rum. We both sat on our bunks while the cutter plunged through the waves yawing slightly, as the lashed tiller kept us to our approximate course. "Give us a shout if you see any land," Neil said, "I'm turning in for a while," he rolled onto his bunk and before I reached the cabin door he was snoring like a pig.

I was well wrapped up against the chill dawn wind, even so it took half the cup of rum tea before I stopped shivering. I sat on the windward side as Neil had done, sheltered by the canvass spray dodger my harness clipped to the rail wire. There was nothing to see except the heaving grey wave crests approaching in endless repetition for us to soar up and then slide down the other side. They seemed enormous to me then but that was before Biscay. I think if I had known about that I would have jumped ship at Gib and gladly walked home.

The wind held steady in strength and direction so that the tiller arrangement could be left alone, allowing us to maintain our course. The hours dragged by, my mind numbed by the constant switchback movement of the boat and the awesome sight of the waves' remorseless advance. Occasionally I dozed, brought back to consciousness by a rogue wave or flying spray. Once I dropped the empty mug and only just prevented it from going overboard.

I began to wonder how long this apparently endless purgatory could be endured. Neil had said we would not sight land for at least twelve hours and that was assuming our course had not veered so far south so that we could miss Sicily altogether. I had a vision of a doomed ship sailing into eternity on an endless sea manned by corpses shrivelled and mummified by the sun and the wind. I shuddered, hoping and praying that Mario's GPS was functioning correctly.

The day passed slowly. I was relieved first by Neil and then Mario. When off watch I fell into a dreamless sleep on my bunk and each awakening brought me to semi-consciousness and a feeling of weary unreality. I lost all track of time, the sun broke through the overcast now and again and it was low over the western horizon when we finally sighted land.

We found a sheltered anchorage south of Crotone on the toe of Italy, hoisted the anchor light and turned in. I slept for a solid twelve hours and awoke to the sounds and the smell of breakfast being cooked. Mario was up on deck sunning himself for the day was fine and clear. I joined him. "Sleep alright boyo"? he asked. He was slouched in a deckchair near the tiller using the cross bench as a table for his cup of tea.

"Like a log."

"We'll have to keep these long sails to a minimum," he said, "lack of sleep can be a killer. Trouble is, the nights are closing in, we've got less and less daylight this late in the year. I'll have to plan coastal hops in daylight as much as possible. Ah breakfast."

Neil appeared at the hatch a plate in each hand. I took them from him and handed one to Mario and we sat in the sun tucking in to cheesy-hammy-eggy once again.

It took us four days to reach Reggio di Calabria. The winds were generally favourable and we sailed from dawn until dusk always with the Italian coast visible on the starboard side. Mario had marked an anchorage for each night on the charts and we usually managed to drop anchor in his chosen spot before darkness closed in. We had arranged the watches so that the last one before anchoring would be either Mario or me, leaving Neil to prepare the evening meal. Somehow he managed to create something different each day and the meal was always accompanied by a bottle of wine and followed by a game of cards or backgammon before retiring.

The night before we reached Reggio Mario had gone to his cabin and I sat with Neil in the small saloon. Neil was smoking, something he rarely did below deck, the smoke curling up through the skylight as the boat moved restlessly at her anchor. "He's doing very well," he said presently, "that larger dose of steroid seems to have given him extra strength."

"What are his chances now do you think?" I asked.

"Of making it home? Still fifty fifty. You see the tumour's still growing. It's pressing on his heart, that's why he gets breathless. You notice he's not coughing as much now." I nodded. "I don't know if that's a good sign or not. He could keel over any minute."

"God Almighty," I breathed, holding my head in my hands. I could not come to terms with the situation. I had never been in such close proximity with imminent death. It still seemed incredible for Mario was always cheerful, always full of his caustic wit, always ready to stand his watch. "It would be nice to think that he'd make it back to Wales," I said, "What do they call it? Land of My Fathers?"

Neil stubbed out his cigarette, "That's right," he smiled, "only thing is the land of *his* fathers is over there," he nodded towards the unseen coast.

We kept to the same routine of sailing by day and anchoring at night for the next few days as we proceeded westward always within sight of the northern coast of Sicily. Mario's condition did not worsen appreciably and we sometimes had difficulty in getting him to agree to do shorter stints on watch. "All I've got to do is bloody sit here," he said once, "this boat practically steers itself, it's no sweat." However, Neil insisted that Mario stood down after a maximum of one and a half hours when he would help him to his cabin where usually he would be asleep within minutes.

Eventually we dropped anchor off Palermo, it was late afternoon and we were all tired. Neil had prepared a special meal for us, a three course affair with onion soup and garlic bread followed by spaghetti Bolognese with fruit salad for dessert. That evening we saw off two bottles of red between us followed by a few brandies. Next morning we slept late.

The next leg of our homeward journey would be a long one, probably three or four days and nights of continuous sailing to get us to Sardinia. I wasn't looking forward to it, neither was Mario which was why, I suspect, he used the excuse of a last visit to Italy to give us an extra day's rest. We launched the Mirror towards lunch time and Neil rowed us ashore.

Mario hailed a cab straight away and we were whisked away from the waterfront into the heart of the city. We were dropped off near the market and found a shady table outside a café in a quiet side street. Mario and Neil had a prolonged discussion in Italian with the waiter before ordering some local delicacy, which they assured me I would enjoy. They were wrong but I ate it anyway.

We spent the rest of the afternoon alternately sauntering about the market and drinking wine or coffee at some pavement bistro or other. Neil could not resist the temptation to buy foodstuffs from the stallholders, however, and by late afternoon we were loaded down with carrier bags.

Mario's suggestion that we eat out in a restaurant that evening was immediately quashed by Neil who insisted that he had bought fresh ingredients for a slap up meal and they were not going to be wasted. "Not only that," he whispered to me, "Mario's about all in. I want to get him back on board as soon as we can. He can have forty winks while I'm preparing the food." We took a cab back to the marina where we had tethered the dinghy and Neil rowed us out to the cutter. Mario slept solidly for a couple of hours and it was dark before we sat down in the saloon.

As usual Neil had prepared an excellent meal. Chicken and bacon with onion, green peppers and mushrooms in a white wine sauce was stirred into boiled pasta, eaten with garlic bread and accompanied by a rich Italian red. We spoke little, each of us tired and lost in our own thoughts. When we had eaten Neil said: "Mind if I turn in? You'll have the washing up of course."

"You go ahead boyo," Mario said, "that was bloody delicious. Full marks. Right Jim?" I nodded as Neil waved the praise aside and went out. "Brandy?" Mario held up a decanter he had conjured up from somewhere together with two glasses in his other hand.

"Why not?"

"You asked me once why I picked on you to come on this trip." Mario passed me a glass charged with a generous measure.

"Well?"

"I suppose I admired you." I glanced at him wondering what I had done to engender admiration. "You remember when we were all living in that apprentice hostel?"

"Will I ever forget it?"

"You were the only bloke I knew who could do his technical college homework and listen to jazz at the same time."

My mind flew back across the years. I saw the room again, the two beds set against opposite walls, the view across open fields. My room mate Eddie practicing on his tenor saxophone, whatever happened to him I wondered. The room was identical to twenty others set in an open quadrangle and converted from the stables of the former country mansion which was the apprentice hostel. "We used to come over and listen every Saturday morning remember?" Mario went on. "Me and a few mates. Eddie'd be blowing away accompanying some jazz record or other, you'd be doing homework and occasionally some brush work on that tatty snare drum you had."

I smiled at the rekindled memories. "I'd forgotten about those Saturday mornings."

"It was the only thing to do. We were usually all skint after a few beers on Friday night."

"Money was in short supply. I do remember that."

Mario sipped at his brandy, staring into space. "Funny how we all have different recollections of the same event. You'd obviously forgotten I used to show up but those Saturday mornings stand out in my memory." He sighed heavily. "Yeah, clear as day."

"Talking of admiration," I said, "I must hand it to you over repatriating this icon. I wouldn't have had the staying power to see that through." And as I said it I knew I was probably wrong. With a death sentence hanging over me and a very limited time frame I daresay I could have found the determination and the energy to do it.

"I've still got to get back and tell Aunty Bronwen I've done it," he said.

"Doesn't she know already?" I asked. "I mean with all this telecomms stuff on board you could have got word to her."

"She's not into emails," he replied, "I suppose I could have contacted someone to tell her but I'd rather tell her myself," he sat deep in thought for a while, eventually he said: "Shame about you and Jean, I would have put money on your marriage lasting as long as Aunty Bronwen's and Uncle Benny."

"She went off with the guy she was crewing for at the sailing club."

"Yes I know. You didn't sail at all?"

"I was a member and did some sailboarding. I wasn't into racing. They were fanatics about that."

He looked sideways at me, the trace of a smile about his lips, "d'you think you'll ever see her again?"

"I doubt it."

"Did she and her fancy man get married?"

"If they did it was bigamous. We're still officially married, only the joint assets were split between us when we separated."

"When I telephoned to try and contact you she just said you were working away."

"She could be quite cagey at times," I said, "did she ever mention her lover boy?"

Mario ignored the question. "She just gave me a list of the various agencies you operated through," he said. "They were the cagey ones, anyone would think I was a hit man trying to locate you."

"They have to be careful, you could have been a jealous husband trying to locate the guy who ran off with his wife, instead it was the other way around. Some bastard had run off with mine," Mario nodded, smiling. "I seem to remember you and she got on well at that reunion," I added wistfully.

Mario swirled his brandy around in his glass and looked me straight in the eyes. "D'you miss her?" I met his gaze for a moment. It was as if he were prying and I had a brief feeling of resentment which delayed my reply long enough for him to add: "Still, it's about four years now isn't it? I expect you're well over her by now."

The lump in my throat returned as I looked at him. "I doubt if I'll ever get over her," I said huskily.

He dropped his eyes to study the brandy glass in minute detail as an embarrassed silence followed my confession. Mario eventually broke it: "Well, if the wind sets fair we'll have a day sail to Trapani tomorrow then it's non-stop to Cagliari in Sardinia."

"And after that?"

"After that a day's rest then non stop to Menorca followed by day sails through the Balearics and along the Spanish coast to Gibraltar. That's the plan anyway."

A plan which would be disrupted as it turned out.

The following day's sail to the western tip of Sicily was a leisurely affair. The wind was light northeasterly and we had to cram on as much canvass as we could in order to make any appreciable speed. Mario did most of the helming shouting instructions to Neil and me as we hauled on ropes and pulled sails of various shapes and sizes out of the forward sail locker. Finally we dropped anchor and enjoyed another of Neil's dishes on deck before sunset. That night we all turned in early and set sail around dawn the next day for the long leg to Sardinia.

Towards dusk on the third day we sighted land and anchored in a small bay south of Cagliari. Neil did us proud once again with the evening meal and we spent the following day lazing unashamedly on deck under a cloudless sky, we even rigged the sun canopy it was so hot and Neil took his customary swim before breakfast and before lunch. Once again I declined his offer to join in. Mario's condition had shown no signs of deterioration during the voyage, the only thing I noticed was his increasing shortage of breath after even the most trivial exertion. His general demeanour remained cheerful.

The following morning we weighed anchor and headed west. The wind remained northeasterly during the first two days but some time during the second night it swung to the south and strengthened. Soon after dawn I was roused by Neil with a mug of hot tea liberally laced with rum. The boat was heeled well over and was bucking and crashing through the waves. Neil held grimly onto the ratline above his head. "We've got to reduce canvass," he said, "get that down you and we'll heave to, rig the trysail, get the foresail down and reef the main."

I sipped at the hot liquid dazed and puzzled. All that stuff was like a foreign language to me as I sat in my bunk holding onto the grab rail with one hand whilst clutching my mug in the other trying to drink without spilling too much. "Nothing wrong is there?" I asked.

"No, Mario's a bit concerned that's all. This southerly wind, it's called a sirocco apparently, it's helping us along well enough, too well actually as you can tell but it might indicate a depression coming which could give us some real trouble." Up to that time, apart from my initial sea-sickness I had enjoyed the sailing, the weather had been fair, the days warm, Mediterranean sailing as I'd always imagined it. What was it

Mario had said? How do you fancy a paid holiday in the sun? Storms at sea in a boat without an engine had not featured in my itinerary.

When I got up on deck the sky was overcast, spray showered along the length of the boat each time the bows dipped into a trough. The wind was very strong, Mario reckoned about force 7. He confirmed this using a hand held contraption like a trumpet which, when pointed into the wind, recorded its strength in knots. Fortunately it was a warm wind, not like the one that came later.

It took us over twenty minutes to rearrange the sails. Mario was at the helm keeping us hove to as we struggled with the ropes and canvass, the boat bucking and yawing like a mad thing. We wore our safety harnesses all the time, they were clipped to the lifelines we had rigged down both sides of the cutter as we worked. Finally we got under way again, our speed did not decrease appreciably as far as I could tell in spite of the reduced canvass and the wind remained around force 7 from the south until around mid morning when it fell away gradually, the sea becoming calmer as our speed dropped. "We'll have to get more sail on her again won't we"? Neil asked.

"Not yet," Mario replied. He sat at the helm gazing up at the overcast sky, sniffing the air like a nervous animal. "I don't like the look of it," he said, "the glass is falling and the wind's changing. We could be in for a tramontana."

"What's that?" I asked.

"Basically it's a northerly gale. Bloody cold and bloody strong. Neil could you make up some sandwiches and a couple of flasks of soup or something?" Neil nodded and went below. Gradually the wind strength lessened and within the hour we were becalmed, rolling drunkenly in the swell, the sails uselessly slatting about. "Give us a hand to get below will you?" Mario said. "I've got some figuring to do." I helped him to his cabin. Later, Neil and I sat in the small saloon eating a cold lunch. The wind had gradually gone around to the northeast and was getting stronger. We lay hove to while Mario did his 'figuring' having presumably fixed our position with the GPS. We had checked all the hatches and portholes, secured the dinghy with some extra lashings and made sure that the liferaft was accessible, its deployment unobstructed. These preparations did not serve to give me confidence in the immediate future.

Finally Mario's voice came through the bulkhead. "Here's our course. Keep to it as close as you can. We've drifted further north than I thought." Neil stuck his head into Mario's cabin and took the slip of paper from him then he went up on deck and I felt the change in the boat's movement as we got under way again.

I collected the mugs and dishes and took them to the galley. When I looked in on Mario he was asleep on his bunk. I slid the weather board in place to prevent him rolling out when it got rough, washed up and placed the crockery in the stowage then I went up on deck. The sea was ugly, a great rolling swell with breaking wave tops, the spume blowing like white smoke. "What is our course exactly?" I shouted.

"West by south a quarter south," Neil shouted back.

I looked down at the mahogany box and the compass inside. The divisions, pointers and arrows were blurred from the moisture on the glass. "What's that in degrees?" I asked.

"I dunno. This blasted compass is so old it hasn't got degrees, I've had to mark it with an indelible pencil." I looked again at the ancient instrument. It was little more than a maritime antique but it was all we had to guide us. We were yawing considerably and I watched as the needle wandered either side of Neil's mark. The best we could hope for was to make good an average which was somewhere near Mario's calculation. We took turn and turn about at the helm every half hour or so as the wind steadily increased from the northeast, the temperature falling as the seas rose.

About the middle of the afternoon I went below to the galley, wedged myself securely between the sink and a locker and grabbed a sandwich before drinking a mug of the soup Neil had put in the vacuum flasks, Mario was still asleep. I was feeling a weariness I had not experienced before, we had sailed non-stop for two days and nights and now, more than halfway through the third day, it was beginning to tell. I tied a fresh strip of dry towelling around my neck to keep out the wind and spray, a useful trick Mario had taught me, and went up on deck. "He still asleep?" Neil asked.

"Yes."

"Did he say where our landfall should be?"

"He's never said anything to me about any landfall."

"All he gave me was this course to steer," Neil said doubtfully, "we could be anywhere. You'd better take over, I'll go and wake him." I sat on the cross bench and took the helm clipping my harness to the anchorage point. Neil made his way gingerly to the hatch and disappeared below. The wind had increased again since I went below and the small trysail, as the storm jib was known, was straining at the sheets as was the double reefed main. I slackened the mainsheet a little to spill some wind and the boat seemed to go a bit easier.

Neil seemed to be a long time below and my tired mind began imagining all sorts of frightening scenarios. What if Mario had died? Could Neil take over and guide us to a safe harbour? What if Neil himself were taken ill and I was alone with this great wooden monster sailing on an erratic course to god knows where, unable to leave the helm because of the rising seas. I could die of exposure sitting there and crash onto some razor sharp reef where my lifeless body would be smashed to pulp by the merciless waves. After what seemed an age Neil reappeared at the hatch and made his way cautiously to my side. "You managed to keep on that course?" he asked.

"About as well as you," I answered. "Each wave pushes us off it then I over correct and she swings the other way."

"It's the best we can do in this weather," Neil replied, "he's checking the GPS again. He was hoping we'd make it to Mahon."

"And will we?"

"No idea. Depends where we are now I suppose. Hey, watch your course." I glanced down to see the needle wavering way off the mark. I adjusted the tiller and it swung slowly back. "Want me to take over for a while?" he asked. I gladly surrendered the tiller and took shelter, crouching behind the spray dodger secured by my harness.

Mahon in Menorca. That was where Jean and I had flown to on our honeymoon before spending two glorious weeks in San Luis. Once again I wondered what she was doing now. Once again I cursed that bloody sailing club and the man who had taken her from me then I cursed myself for thinking about her. We were finished Jean and I, had been for years, yet time and time again something would crop up to remind me of her.

Neither of us spoke much as we ploughed on through that tempestuous sea and I must have dozed at some point for I awoke with a start to the sound of Mario bellowing from the hatchway: "Any sign of land?"

I stood up and grabbed the nearest bit of standing rigging. "Where will it be?" I shouted.

"Should be due south," he replied and Neil looked up from the compass, pointing in that direction as I strained my eyes southwards, shielding them from the spray as best I could. Occasionally as the boat crested a wave I thought I saw the dark shape of a coastline against the sky. The light was fading rapidly in the late afternoon and I knew that we were not in any condition to spend another night at sea. Also, in seas like these and so close to land, we could not just heave to and wait for the dawn. "Well?" Mario's petulant voice rang out above the wind and crashing seas.

"I . . . . I'm not sure," I shouted back. "There's something there. Hold on a minute." I peered into the gathering gloom and as the boat crested a roller I saw the definite grey outline of dry land. "Yes," I yelled, "it's definitely land." The boat dropped into a trough and the view disappeared.

"What did it look like?" Mario shouted, "could you make out any features?"

"No."

"See any lights?"

"No. But . ."

"Yeah?"

"There was a sort of lump sticking up." I peered towards the land trying to make out the shape of the coastline and the thing I had seen. As the boat rose onto a crest I saw it again. The undulating skyline of the distant coast had a geometric stumplike shape sticking up at one point.

"What's it look like?" Mario asked.

"Sort of square block sticking up, I can just make it out against the sky."

"Good. Keep watching, when you see a light to the left of that let me know." And with that Mario went below.

All this time Neil was trying to keep the cutter on the course Mario had set. I glanced across at him as he sat hunched upon the cross bench his salt caked eyes peering down at the ancient compass. He was as exhausted as I was, numbed by the elements and nearing the limit of safe operational efficiency. I sat down behind the spray dodger and grabbed the small bottle he was waving at me. That swallow or two of neat rum was a tremendous boost. When tiredness, cold and incessant exposure to the elements has induced a mental state bordering on apathy a shot or two of rum works wonders. I sat there for several minutes letting the spirit burn into my guts, feeling the warmth spread through my body. "Hadn't you better have another look for that light?" Neil asked and as I stood up Mario's head appeared above the hatch coaming again.

"What's the land look like now?" He shouted. I hung onto the rigging and stood on tiptoe as I scanned the southern horizon.

"It's closer. That stump thing's still visible."

"Any lights?"

"No," I replied and then at that very moment a light appeared to the left of the stump-like shape. "Hang on," I shouted, "yes, there's a light now."

"Tell me when it goes on and off," Mario yelled and I saw that he was clutching a stop watch in his free hand as he held onto the hatch coaming with the other. I turned my head back to the south just as the light went out.

"Off," I shouted straining my eyes towards the distant land. "On, off," a longer pause, "on, off . . . on, . . . off." The light had vanished. Dimly against the fading light from an overcast sky I could just make out the darker shape of the land that had obscured it. "I've lost it," I shouted, "it's gone behind a headland or something."

"Can you still see that stump thing?" Mario asked.

"Yes."

"Where is it ?"

"Just to the right of where the light was."

"Good. Neil come hard over," he ordered, "steer due south. Jim, ease sheets. Quickly now, we're going directly downwind." I let out the main and jib sheets until we were sailing directly downwind before the icy northerly gale they call a tramontana and all the time a distant thunderous pounding roar was getting nearer and nearer. Mario struggled onto the deck, clipped his safety harness onto the lifeline and crawled to the tiller. "Let me have her now boyo," he said hoarsely, "this is the tricky bit."

The land was clearly visible now. A rift in the cloud was letting in the last of the daylight, the white painted villas along the coastline stood out against the grey hinterland. The strange stump-like feature seemed to glow deep orange as the afterglow of the day illuminated it's ancient stonework. Mario pointed towards it. "Martello tower," he explained, "just like the ones on the south coast of England. A leftover from the days when the Brits ruled the roost around here," he began to sing: "Rule Britannia, Britannia rule the waves. Britons never never never shall be slaves, yee hah." He threw back his head for that final rebel yell. "Hold tight boyos," he shouted, "this is where it gets interesting."

The thunderous pounding was growing louder and I peered forward. Beyond the bowsprit, which pointed like a lance as if challenging the very waves, I could make out columns of spray reaching twenty feet or more into the air as mighty rollers collided with the rocks. The narrow gullet, which I later discovered, was the entrance to the sheltered waters of Fornells harbour, was a cauldron of swirling foam.

My stomach turned over with the realisation that we had to run this gauntlet. Mario had both hands on the tiller and Neil was grasping his harness with one hand while holding onto the stern rail with the other. Each successive wave lifted the boat bodily and pushed us towards this maelstrom. I was mesmerised, expecting us to be smashed against the rocks with each forward surge. Fortunately we had sufficient speed to give us effective steerage and we plunged into the entrance channel as straight as an arrow.

The wind increased in strength as it funnelled into the narrow defile, it screamed in the rigging and tore at our clothing. The deck was lashed with spray and visibility was minimal, the air laden with a salty mist. The incoming rollers lifted the stern and propelled the cutter forward like some huge surfboard before they overtook us and hit the rocks that jutted out from the sides of the canyon-like entrance. As they did so huge columns of spume lifted into the air with a noise like gunfire.

To my right, through the silver fog of spray, I caught glimpses of street lights along a road that ran parallel to us and there were bungalow type villas with shuttered windows at intervals. Each time a wave lifted us the boat slewed off course and Mario struggled to correct it before the next one came. For some inane reason I heard myself reciting out loud, shouting in fact to be heard above the noise: "breakers to the right of them, breakers to the left of them, breakers in front of them vollied and thundered. Into the valley of death rode the six hundred."

"What you on about?" Mario shouted to me without turning his head. His eyes were firmly fixed on the ill-defined channel ahead, his hands on the tiller constantly trying to maintain our precarious course through that murderous sea. How he steered us through it I will never know but suddenly we were in open water. The light I had seen before in the distance was there on a small island less than a mile in front of us winking its comforting sequence.

The lagoon which was Fornells harbour opened up before us and the wind dropped appreciably as we came under the shelter of the land. There on the starboard side was a stone breakwater and the twinkling lights of the waterside restaurants. We sailed gently on for a while, no one spoke. I think we were all too numbed by the wind and spray, we were all exhausted for sure. Mario steered us closer to the shore. "Get ready to drop the hook me hearties," he shouted in a mock Devonshire accent and Neil went forward as we rounded up into the wind, and at the command "Let go," the anchor splashed into the water. Neil had the storm jib down even before the chain had run out then Mario and I got the mainsail down with the boom nestled in the cruck of the trestle. I helped him to his cabin while Neil was seeing to the riding light, "I think I'll try a drop of that soup Neil made now boyo," he said but by the time I brought it from the galley he was fast asleep in his bunk.

26

The vicious tramontana wind was frapping the halyards against the mast. Down in the main saloon the small stove I had lit gave out some welcome heat as I sat before it clutching a large whisky and soda. Neil came in drying his face on a towel. "You hungry?" he asked. I nodded over the rim of my glass. "Well", he said, "tramontana or not I'm not missing the chance to eat ashore. Especially here."

"Why especially here?" I asked.

"Fornells," he said pausing in his drying, "some of the best fish restaurants on Menorca."

"Oh."

"Didn't you know?" I shook my head. "Even the Spanish King comes here to eat sometimes."

"Does he have to row ashore in a biting bloody gale?" I asked sarcastically.

"It's not too bad here in the shelter of the harbour. We're only about two hundred metres offshore anyway. Look, you get dressed, I'll get the Mirror launched and we'll have a meal to remember."

"What about Mario?"

"He's fast asleep. I'll leave him a note, if there's a problem he can get us on his mobile. We'll only be a couple of hours or so. You up for it?"

I was as hungry as hell and the sooner I got off that boat for a while the happier I would feel. "I'll get changed," I said.

It seemed odd to be getting into the dinghy wearing a pullover and a fleece with a waterproof anorak on top together with gloves and a woollen bobble hat. This was the Med after all and it was still only October. But with this tramontana wind blowing, its ferocity and icy chill made it seem more like Dartmoor in January. Neil shoved off and rowed us towards the shore. There was a restaurant right at the waters edge its lights, reflected in the ruffled water, looked warm and inviting as we approached. There was a concrete walkway around the edge of the building with iron rings for tying up, Neil came alongside and the keel scraped the shingle as I grabbed a ring and secured the painter, Neil clambered out and helped me out of the dinghy.

The waterside restaurant resembled a rectangular conservatory. Tall windows on three sides overlooked the harbour and the warmth hit us as we entered. We peeled off our outer layers of clothing and hung them up in an inner vestibule then we were shown to a table by a smart young waiter. I couldn't fail to notice the look that passed between him and Neil as we sat down and that should have warned me how the evening would end.

Neil ordered fish soup to start and a mixed seafood platter with salad to follow together with a very expensive white wine, all this in fluent Spanish. "What about you?" he asked me, "I can recommend the soup but please yourself about the main."

"I'll take a chance and go for the same as you," I replied.

He smiled. "You won't regret it." He passed the order on to the waiter and leered after him as he went back to the kitchen. I pretended not to notice. "I don't know about you," he continued, "but that sail in this afternoon was the most frightening thing I've ever been through."

I stared out through the windows. Out there, beyond the reflections of the dining room and the other guests, faintly in the distance I could see the rhythmic flashing light on its little island in the lagoon, the light I had helped Mario to identify while we were still well out to sea.

The afternoon's experience Neil spoke of might just have been a dream so unreal did it seem now in the opulence and warmth of the restaurant. I tried to recall my feelings as we were floundering through that boiling spray filled gullet. "The strange thing," I heard myself saying, "was that I was not afraid as such. The whole thing was too numbing. It was as if I was a spectator, as if it was not happening to me at all." Neil lit a cigarette and gazed quizzically at me through the smoke. He nodded but said nothing.

Just then the waiter brought the wine and poured a little for Neil to taste. He rolled it around inside his mouth for a long time, all the while eyeing up the waiter who met his gaze calmly. I was beginning to feel a little uncomfortable sat there between them but then Neil inclined his head slightly and swallowed. "Si," he said quietly and the waiter filled our glasses.

Presently the soup came accompanied by a plate of the most delicious bread. I am not a lover of fish soup but this was superb. We devoured it in silence and in a little while the waiter collected the dishes. The warmth of the place and of the soup coupled with my weariness after days of sailing made it difficult to keep my eyes open. At one point Neil prodded me, "hey, wake up here comes the main course."

I roused up mumbling an apology. "You've been here before?" I asked.

"Yes, several times. The last time was about eighteen months ago. Holiday," he added.

"Where did you stay? Or were you sailing?"

"No, not sailing. My . . .my friend has an apartment a couple of kilometres from here."

"Do you have access to it?" I asked.

"Yes. Why?"

"I just thought we could all take refuge there until this bloody wind dies down."

"You won't get Mario off that boat. He's set on getting back and he'll not truck any delay. I know him."

"But we can't sail in this can we? Anyway we're all knackered, what about some shore leave?"

"This wind will die down in a couple of days, by then we'll be well rested," he countered. I shrugged. At that point I could easily have jumped ship and headed for the nearest airport. "There's only one thing bothering me," he went on.

"What's that?"

"Getting out through that narrow entrance without an engine and with the wind against us. We'll need a tow." I remembered the last tow we had at Brindisi, Mario wasn't very impressed with that as I recalled. Still, if that was what had to be done Neil or someone else would have to organise it, I was past caring.

The main course came and that was really something. A bewildering variety of seafood accompanied by an exotic salad and all helped along with the crisp dry wine. "Mario's missing a treat here tonight," I ventured.

"Mario's not too keen on seafood," Neil said, "he's much more of a carnivore."

"How's he doing anyway?"

"About the same. I've increased his medication as much as I dare. We'll just have to hope he can hang on," he smiled to himself, "he was brilliant today though wasn't he? He conned us through that entrance like Grace Darling"

"Who?"

"Never mind," he said smiling patronisingly, "just enjoy your meal." We ate on in silence amid the general hubbub of the partly filled restaurant. There was a noisy party of Germans in a corner over to my right, somewhere behind us two Belgian couples sat together speaking 'Belgian French' as Neil described it, snatches of Italian and Spanish could be heard from the other end of the room but no English at all. Neil finished before me and excused himself to go to the toilet, or so I assumed, and I struggled on with the meal which was absolutely delicious but too much for me. Eventually I pushed the plate aside and finished off the wine. Neil returned and lit another cigarette. "Couldn't finish it?" he asked indicating my plate.

"It was delicious but I'm stuffed,"

"Brandy?"

"That would be nice." Neil signalled the waiter who came mincing across all smiles, Neil ordered two large brandies unable to keep his eyes off the boy. "I'm really sleepy now," I said, "I'm not looking forward to the trip back to the boat, your mate's accommodation would have suited me very well tonight."

Neil looked away, a vaguely guilty look on his face, "can't be helped," he said.

The German party were preparing to leave, chairs scraped on the marble floor, coats were brought from the vestibule, waiters scurried around. One of the men, the largest, came over to us. "I see you sail in tonight," he boomed, his face serious as if reprimanding us, "good verk I think, ver' good verk," the hint of a smile creased his face. "Guten nacht," he said and turned away with a wave of his hand. They all filed out, their loud voices fading in the distance as the restaurant returned to quiet murmurings and discreet laughter.

"D'you know him?" I asked.

Neil shook his head. "I did see a big motor cruiser with a German ensign tied up in the little harbour as we dropped anchor," he replied, "I bet that's his. He looks a bit of a seafarer." We lapsed into silence, I could barely keep my eyes open. Eventually the waiter brought the bill and Neil paid, leaving a very large tip. "You ready?" Neil asked presently. I nodded and drained my glass then we went out to the vestibule where we were helped into our warm clothing by our charming waiter.

We made our way around the concrete walkway to the dinghy. The wind had dropped slightly but there was still an icy feel to the sporadic gusts that swept around the restaurant building ruffling the waters of the inlet. I stepped down into the boat and untied the painter from the mooring ring. Neil followed and took up the oars as I shoved off.

The cutter stood out against the starry sky, its reflection shattered from time to time as the wind snatched at the surface of the anchorage producing angry wavelets while the riding light swayed above the deck guiding us back. Neil looked over his shoulder from time to time to check he was on course and eventually we bumped alongside. I grabbed the iron ladder and was about to tie the painter to it when Neil said: "Don't tie up. I'm not coming aboard tonight."

I paused standing near the bow, the rope in my hand. "I don't understand," I said, "what about Mario?"

"He'll be fine, I've left all his medication, he knows what to take and when. He's probably still asleep anyway."

"So where are you . . . . .?" Then it dawned on me, that poncy waiter. That and Neil's reluctance for us to take refuge in his friend's apartment. "Well, I'll see you tomorrow then," I said off-handedly. Neil grunted something as I clambered up the ladder then he pushed off, head down, bent to his rowing. I stood on the deck watching as the dinghy was swallowed up by the darkness not knowing what I felt about the situation.

Mario was still asleep as Neil had predicted. I gently closed his cabin door and went into the saloon. The stove was still alight but only just, I put some more fuel on and peeled off the winter clothing to sit beside it for a while listening to the wind, feeling the movement of the boat. Eventually I made my way to our cabin and lay on my bunk.

I lay awake for some time trying to accept Neil's assignation with the waiter, for that was obviously his reason for staying ashore. In all our relationship since my arrival in Corfu, the sailing, the search for the icon, the meals we had enjoyed on board, I had completely forgotten about his homosexuality. Mario had told me about that on the first day I boarded the cutter but since then I had not given it a single thought. I lay for some time wishing he had gone off with some busty waitress, at least that way I could have accepted his absence. I resolved that the next time I saw him I would try very hard indeed to hide the revulsion I felt at the thought of him in bed with that blasted waiter. Presently I slept.

I awoke with the sun streaming through the porthole and Mario standing in the doorway with a steaming mug of tea in his fist. "Morning boyo," he beamed, "some bastard's pinched the bloody dinghy."

"No," I began, "Neil's gone ashore, he's . . ."

"Don't tell me boyo, I know the score, he's gone off whoring with some bloody Spanish nancy boy. Am I right?" I smiled sheepishly as he handed me the mug. "I bet it's the same one he met here on the way out. He'll shag anything in trousers."

"You sleep OK?" I asked anxious to change the subject.

"Like a log, you?"

"Once I got off. You had any breakfast?"

"Just cereal," he yawned, "we've got another day stuck here I reckon before this tramontana wind blows itself out, I'm waiting for a weather report on the net. I'll be in my cabin if you want me," and with that he shuffled off. I followed suit on the cereal and spent the rest of the morning lying in my bunk or sitting in the saloon reading and drinking tea, the wind gradually abating as Mario had said it would. Around midday Neil rowed up alongside and hailed us. Mario was on deck at the time. "What you got there boyo?" I heard him shout.

"Some fresh stores and an English takeaway," Neil replied. I struggled into my fleece and climbed the companionway onto the deck. Neil was handing up bags of supplies from the dinghy and I lent a hand.

"What the hell is an English takeaway?" Mario asked.

Neil handed up the last bag. "In there," he said, "fish and chips." We all went below and sat in the saloon to eat them and they were as good as anything Harry Ramsden could produce.

Neil and I spent the rest of the day sorting stores and generally tidying ship as he called it after the long sail from Sardinia. Mario was sat in front of his computer plotting routes and scanning weather reports. We shared a light meal at tea time before Neil announced that he was going to row ashore and would not be back till late. Mario and I glanced at each other but said nothing.

After he had gone we sat together in the saloon with a large gin and tonic each, the wind had gone around to the northeast and had eased considerably. "You looking forward to getting home?" Mario asked.

"Back to that dreary office? Not much."

Mario smiled. "You've come on well as a crewman, you could sail this thing single handed now."

"In your dreams!"

"No, I mean it. A bit more experience with sail changes and that and you could easily pass muster as competent crew. Have you enjoyed it?"

"Most of it. That sail in yesterday was a bit terrifying."

"The secret is to keep your speed up, you've got to have steerage. The boat must be travelling fast enough so the rudder works. With the current behind you the boat must go faster for that to happen. If the current's against you it can go slower. See What I mean?" I nodded, trying to equate the theory with head and tail winds in aircraft. "Anyway, sailing is not for everyone, you either like it or you don't. You seem to like it. Am I right?"

"It's certainly exhilarating at times and then at night with the stars and the phosphorescence on the water, it's sort of . . . well, sort of magical."

"You've got it boyo, you've got it in one. Magical." His face became serious, "pity you and Jean didn't share the hobby then perhaps . . . ." his voice trailed away.

"That wouldn't have worked Mario," I said, "she was into dinghy racing not this kind of sailing. There's a big difference I reckon."

"Yeah you're probably right, mind you she might have moved on from that kind of sailing by now." He cast a knowing look in my direction which puzzled me slightly before draining his glass. "Well," he said, "I'm for an early night. Nosta."

When I awoke the dawn light was just beginning to filter in through the porthole. Neil was still asleep in his bunk, I hadn't heard him return. The boat was strangely silent, the wind having dropped during the night. I lay there for a while savouring the comfort and the quietness wondering what the day had in store. I knew Mario was anxious to continue the homeward journey and I wondered absently how much longer he could go on. His medical condition did not appear to have worsened but Neil's assessment of its inevitable outcome did not fill me with confidence. There was still a long way to go. I must have drifted off to sleep again for the next thing I remembered was waking up to the smell of coffee brewing and bacon cooking, Neil's bunk was empty. I got up and dressed.

Nothing much was said at breakfast, we all sat quietly eating, wrapped up in our own thoughts. Suddenly Neil said: "D'you want the good news or the bad news first?"

Mario drained his coffee cup noisily, "better be the bad news boyo."

"You two are doing the washing up."

Mario grimaced, "Christ is that all? What's the good news then?"

"I have arranged for a tow out of this landlocked harbour and it won't cost a thing. The wind is set fair and if we have a good a run we could be anchored off Majorca tonight."

"Who's doing the towing?" I asked.

"A genial German gent with a big flash motor cruiser," Neil grinned, "I've arranged for him to rendezvous with us at ten o'clock."

27

Mario was at the helm and Neil stood near the bows holding onto the forestay as the cutter bucked its way through the narrow gullet towards the sea. I stood on the companionway steps my head and shoulders above the coaming. The towing line was secured to a timber post in the foredeck near the base of the bowsprit, I watched as it slackened and tightened as both vessels rose and fell, first dipping into the sea then emerging bar tight with the water being wrung out of it as the tow took the strain. Neil watched it anxiously.

There was still a heavy swell marching into the harbour, it burst into spray as it encountered the rocky outcrops on each side of the channel only this time it rose only a few feet into the air not the twenty or so like before. This time the air was clear and not filled with a salty mist, the road and the villas along it were clearly visible only a stone's throw away to my left while in front of us the comforting throaty roar of the German's engines could be heard above the pounding waves.

The motor cruiser had come alongside on the stroke of ten as arranged. I recognised the two women and the other man from the restaurant two nights before and we exchanged greetings while Neil and the big German attached the tow. Soon we were under way, being towed gently past the little harbour into the entrance channel. Some people up on the breakwater waved as we passed.

Before long we cleared the narrow entrance and were in the open sea, on my left the massive bulk of the Martello tower dominated the coastline. "Stand by to hoist the jib," Mario shouted and I scrambled out of the hatchway ready to haul on the jib halyard. "Are you ready to slip the tow?" he called to Neil who gave the thumbs up sign.

The big German waved from the flying bridge of his vessel and made a sign with his hand like cutting his throat as the sound of his powerful engines died. "Slipping the tow," shouted Neil and as the rope slackened he detached the loop and dropped it over the side. I watched as one of the women operated the winch to pull the towing hawser in over the cruiser's stern

"Hoist the jib," Mario called and as I hauled on the rope Neil was already hoisting the mainsail. The boat heeled over slightly and gathered speed. Once again we were under way under our own power.

The big German brought his craft alongside keeping downwind of us so as not to cause a wind shadow. "We head for South of France now," he shouted, "good luck to you and bon voyage."

Mario waved, "Feilen danke," he shouted back, "bon voyage to you too." Neil dipped the red ensign at the stern in salute and the other woman on the motor cruiser dipped their colours in return then the cruiser's engines roared and the water beneath her stern boiled, the bows lifted and she sheered away leaving a creamy wake upon the grey whitecapped sea.

All that day we sailed west under an overcast sky. The wind was still cold but lacked the icy chill of the tramontana. Mario went below after about an hour and Neil and I shared the helming for most of the day. We ate the sandwiches he had prepared and drank tea or coffee as the mood took us. We sighted Majorca before nightfall and called Mario on deck, after some discussion it was decided to sail on through the night and by mid morning the next day we dropped anchor off the island of Dragonera on Majorca's western tip.

The overcast had broken up around dawn and the sun was shining, "if the wind would only die down a bit it would actually be quite warm," Neil said as the three of us sat upon the cabin skylight, our backs sheltered by the inverted dinghy lashed there.

"Only thing is," Mario said, "we need the bloody wind to get us home."

"It doesn't need to be a cold wind though," I ventured.

"Once we get past Gib we should be okay shouldn't we?" Neil asked.

"The Med can be quite cold in places this time of year," Mario answered. "Once we're into the Bay we should only get westerlies, they're much warmer." We were not to know then that Mario would not see Biscay and looking back on my experience of it, he was lucky.

We rested for most of that day, Neil had his customary nude swim around the boat, he didn't bother to ask me now, he knew what the answer would be. He prepared an excellent meal later which we ate on deck sitting wrapped in our fleeces on deckchairs in the lee of the lashed dinghy. Neil took the plates below when we had all finished and returned with the gin and the whisky, we had two or three nightcaps as the dusk fell. "We should make Ibiza tomorrow if we start early," Mario said.

"I'll make a Greek salad for tomorrow's lunch," Neil said, "and how about hard boiled eggs for breakfast?" Mario and I looked at each other without enthusiasm. "Okay," said Neil reluctantly, "full English it is."

We turned in early that night and weighed anchor the next day just as dawn streaked the eastern sky. Mario took the helm as Neil and I hoisted all the sail we could muster for the dawn breeze was light, even so, according to Mario, we were making only about four knots. Then I sat below in the saloon with Neil enjoying the breakfast he had prepared and when I had finished I went up on deck and took over the helm. "I've marked the compass," Mario said, "Keep her there." He indicated the indelible pencil mark on the glass face of the antique compass at his feet. "What's his breakfast like?"

I belched discreetly, "great as usual," I replied, "ask him to pass me up a mug of tea when he's got a minute will you?" Mario grunted and nodded and went below. The sun was just coming up and the breeze was strengthening, I eased the sheets a little and she heeled a little less without any drop in speed. I estimated it to be about eight knots, an estimate which proved to be quite close when Mario checked it later.

We anchored that night off the west coast of Formentera and that was the first indication we had of Mario's worsening condition. Neil's evening meal was as appetising as usual but Mario just picked at it, excused himself and took to his bunk, his snores resounding throughout the boat within minutes. Neil and I cleared the things away and washed up then sat with a gin and tonic each, listening. "He's very short of breath," I observed.

Neil sat with folded arms his chin resting on his chest. "It's the tumour," he explained, "pressure on the aorta probably. I think we'll have the oxygen bottle up on deck when he's helming. Always assuming he can still do that."

"What about tomorrow?" I asked.

"He's got the route drawn in on the chart," Neil replied, "if he's not up at dawn we'll weigh anchor ourselves and carry on. Is that okay with you?"

I was tired from the day's sailing and just wanted to get to my bunk. Tomorrow was another day as far as I was concerned. I drained my glass, "okay by me," I said.

Mario was still asleep as dawn broke, Neil woke me with a cup of tea in the grey twilight and sat opposite me on his bunk. "The wind sets fair," he said.

"Good."

"How do you feel?"

"Tired."

"We'll get under way in a minute, I've marked face of the compass with the course to steer. If you helm I'll get some breakfast. Toast and coffee okay?" I nodded, "then I'll see to Mario." His face clouded. "I want to get him to Gib. I reckon he'll have to be hospitalised."

"So you don't think he'll make it back then."

Neil shrugged. "There's a hospital there, he could get some emergency treatment," he glanced across at me, "it might mean some day and night sailing to get there as quickly as we can." I already had some experience of the near exhaustion that comes from lack of sleep. Sailing a boat requires a degree of alertness and reserves of energy to deal with unexpected situations or emergencies especially in rough weather. I looked doubtful. "It might not be too bad," he continued, "we'll sail west and make landfall on the Spanish mainland near Alicante then follow the coast to Gib. We'll be in sight of land all the way and, hopefully, within reach of emergency services."

"Let's hoist the sails and get the anchor up," I said. I wanted to put some miles on the log, Gibraltar seemed oceans away, England almost another planet.

For five days and nights we followed the Spanish coast. Sometimes, when the wind direction was right, we lashed the tiller and slept, trusting to Mario's anti-collision gismo to rouse us. Sometimes Mario kept watch for us but the slightest exertion made him breathless. We did anchor once when the wind fell light and we were making no headway and I slept solidly for six hours. Our diet, usually so varied and appetising, became mundane in the extreme. Cereal with reconstituted milk was a regular standby, bread and jam an occasional treat, fresh fruit a daily indulgence. Sometimes we drank just plain water to avoid the chore of making tea or coffee. Neil kept Mario going with tinned soup or pasta mixed with diced corned beef and canned tomatoes. He ate very little anyway and slept a lot.

The day we sighted Gibraltar the sea had a lazy oily swell and the breeze was fitful, there was a hazy mist along the coast and the boat moved with a sluggish reluctance. Neil hailed me from the foredeck, "I can just see The Rock," he shouted, "fine on the starboard bow."

"How far?" I asked.

"The rest of the day I'm afraid. At this speed we'll be lucky to make it before dusk. Unless the wind picks up that is."

Mario appeared then. It was the first time he had shown himself on deck for days. He stuck his head out from the companionway. "Did you say Gib's in sight?" he asked and I gave him a thumbs up sign. "Neil," he said, "come below, I've got things to plan." Then to me: "You okay on the helm for a while?" I waved and nodded. I had been steering the cutter most of the morning anyway, keeping the compass needle as close as I could to the indelible pencil mark of the day. They disappeared below.

The sun was quite warm, it shone faintly, diffused through a thin overcast which gave the sea an uncomfortable glare. I sat drowsily at the tiller, almost unconsciously keeping an eye on the compass needle as my thoughts drifted aimlessly.

Gibraltar. A place I had never visited but seemed to have known intimately since childhood through innumerable films and photographs. Seeing it rising out of the mist in the far distance gave me a feeling of comfort as if I was somehow closer to England and home. That train of thought led automatically to Jean yet again and I tried unsuccessfully to rid my mind of her memory. Amid the monotony of that restless sea I moved the tiller slightly to keep us on course without even realising it.

The memory of that holiday on Corfu was suddenly very vivid, the way we had raised our glasses and looked into each other's eyes across the table at Kassiopi, the wine, the music, the motorcycle ride back to Sidari. No, that was when I was with Neil. Memories old and new became entwined in the dazed stupor that comes with prolonged lack of sleep. As I sat there holding the tiller, watching for changes in the wind whilst keeping half an eye on the compass, her face seemed to appear before me, smiling.

The Rock grew imperceptibly while we made our painfully slow approach. Like a distant mirage it hung above the sea mist as the time dragged by. Neil was still closeted below with Mario and I wondered absently what they were discussing. It looked as if Mario would not make it after all and that was sad. He had fulfilled his uncle's pipe dream, brought us all this way. He deserved to get back.

It was well into the afternoon before Neil's head appeared above the companionway hatch. "Change course," he said, "steer nor'west, that *is* marked on the compass face. I'll ease sheets, the breeze is still southerly." He scrambled out and made the necessary adjustments to the ropes that controlled the sails, the sheets that is, a term I still found confusing, as I pulled the tiller towards me and watched the compass needle swing onto the new heading.

"Where we going then? I asked.

"Closer inshore. Mario wants to anchor for the night. The wind should be stronger tomorrow, we can make Gibraltar by midday."

I glanced down and adjusted the tiller so we were on course. We were somewhere west of Marbella, the traffic on the coast road just discernible through the haze, the high sierras inland standing out against the sky. Mario's condition could not have worsened if he was still giving orders regarding our progress for I knew Neil wanted to get to Gib as soon as possible. "The shore still seems a long way off," I observed.

"We should be able to drop anchor in less than an hour I think, I'll just have a look at the chart," and with that Neil disappeared below again.

In fact it took over an hour and a half before the anchor splashed into the clear blue water of a secluded bay not far from Estepona. By then the breeze had died to almost nothing and the sails hung limply, flapping feebly now and again as the sun went down. I rigged the anchor light as Neil dowsed the sails and tied them loosely to the boom and the bowsprit. "Chicken Tenereife okay tonight?" he asked.

There it was again. A word, a place, a song. Something always led back to her. "That's fine," I replied. The dish was Jean's favourite. An occasional Friday night treat used to be a trip to our local restaurant, she would invariably order Chicken Tenereife while I usually went for poached salmon. I smiled to myself at the memory. "You were a long time with Mario." I said, "is he okay?"

Neil came and sat upon the cross bench, lit a cigarette and leaned against the tiller. "I've arranged an emergency admission for him at the hospital in Gib tomorrow."

"How on earth did you manage that?"

"I've got a . . . a friend. He was a high ranking medical officer in the military, he's a civvy consultant now. We've always been . . . . very close, I've known him for years. This was a special favour. We were chatting on the satellite phone for ages."

"Mario's agreed?"

"Mario was asleep when I was arranging it but I have told him. He just shrugged, you know Mario. Then he spent a good half hour talking me through all the hazards from Gib to Porthcawl, reminded me how to operate the GPS and then what d'you think?" I raised an eyebrow. "He got me to witness and date his signature on his last will and testament."

"What was in that then?"

"I don't know, he didn't show me, it was all folded up, I just watched him sign and date it then did the same under his signature."

"Is it legal? I mean I thought you needed a lawyer or something."

"Dunno. Soldiers often write a will before a battle don't they? No lawyers present then is there?" I shook my head. "Anyway that's for someone else to decide. By the way, I've given him some tinned soup, he should finish it soon. He said he'd like a word with you so go in and fetch his plate in ten minutes or so while I get our food ready."

Mario was sat before his computer when I entered his little cabin some time later. The soup dish was empty on the table near his bunk. "Come in boyo," he beamed, "sit down for a minute."

"How are you?"

"I feel like shit boyo. Hey, you've done well to get us this far. The wind was piss poor so I thought, bugger it, we'll anchor and sail into Gib tomorrow. You ever been to Gib?" I shook my head. "Great place man, great place."

"Neil tells me he's got you admitted to the hospital. What will they do?"

"Do? What the fuck can they do? Only the same as before in the UK. Whack another load of radiation into the tumour. Zap the bloody thing and hope it'll shrink a bit. Enough to give me the breath to get home." His flippancy, in the face of his complaint as he called it, almost fooled me. I thought, if anyone could make it back, surely Mario would but then I looked into his eyes, saw the despair, felt the hopelessness. In spite of all that I could not have anticipated his actions the following day.

After a while he asked: "You know what hiraeth means?" I shook my head. "It's a Welsh word," he said, "there's no exact English equivalent. The nearest thing would be sadness I suppose."

"Oh, sadness," I repeated as I sat down on his bunk.

"But it's much more than that", he said quietly, staring at the floor, "it's a desperate aching sadness, a deep insatiable longing for things that can never be." He sighed deeply before seeming to rouse himself from his reverie. "Neil will be accompanying me to the hospital tomorrow," he said with forced brightness, "that means you'll be looking after the boat. I've sent for another crewman, well, a qualified coastal skipper actually," he smiled at me with a mischievous wink, "that person will be flying out and I want someone to be aboard as a welcoming party." With that he dismissed me with a wave of his hand and turned to the computer. I collected the empty soup dish and took it to the galley.

The next morning we weighed anchor soon after sunrise as the breeze was favourable. By early afternoon we were less than three miles from the Rock. I was below washing up the breakfast things and Mario was still in his bunk when Neil called from the helm: "Motor boat approaching." I hurried up on deck as a Naval patrol boat approached.

"D'you have a Mario Franzoni aboard?" A smartly rigged out rating called through a loud hailer as two others near the stern were preparing a towing hawser.

"He's still in his bunk," Neil shouted back.

"We're ordered to tow you in," came the reply.

"What's all this about," I asked, "have we done something wrong? What's the Navy doing, arresting us?"

Neil turned to me, "It's nothing like that," he explained, "I arranged it with my friend, here take the helm, I'll get the sails down and attach the tow." I took hold of the tiller and hove to as I watched Neil lower the main and then the staysail and the jib. I couldn't help admire the lithe agility of the man, envy him his youthful vigour. Since leaving Menorca his escapade with the waiter had not been mentioned, I think both Mario and I had forgotten all about it. Sailing a boat seems to drive all other distractions from your mind. Neil attached the tow and the motor boat took the strain. Slowly we gathered speed and I steered the cutter to follow in the centre of its wake.

We were towed into the commercial harbour and tied up alongside a jetty just behind a large trawler, the patrol boat slipped the tow and backed off before drawing alongside. An officer leaned out of the wheelhouse. "There'll be an ambulance along soon," he shouted, "you'd better get him ready." Neil waved an acknowledgement. "Then we'll have to tow you around to the civvy marina okay?"

Neil waved again before turning to me. "You'll have to steer her around there, there's a berth reserved. Just tie her up, I'll be back as soon as I can. D'you want to go and wake him up?"

I went below, knocked on Mario's cabin door and entered. The sight that greeted me stopped me in my tracks and I stood frozen to the spot. Mario was sitting on his bunk fully dressed. His left hand was clenched tight holding a crumpled sheet of paper. In his right hand the menacing black shape of the German luger rested upon his knee. He turned and looked up at me, his tear streaked face a mask of despair.

"Mario," I gasped, "what's going on?"

His lips twitched into a smile. "I had a bad night," he replied, "decided to finish it. I thought: I've got the gun, I've got the bullets. What's the point of dragging it out. I'll not see Wales again so . . . sod it I'll do it."

I just stood there not knowing what to do. In the end all I said was: "Bloody hell Mario."

He held up the crumpled paper. "I even wrote the suicide note. My best handwriting too, got dressed all tidy like and then," he paused and tossed the paper into a basket under the computer table, "and then the gun went 'click'. The ammo's fucked see. Damp I suppose. All those years buried, even in the oil and the wrappings." He struggled to his feet and gripped my arm. "Jim," he begged me, "don't breathe a word of this. This is just between you and me. Promise?"

I nodded slowly. "Okay I Promise," I said, "but look Mario, it's on condition you give me the gun."

"It's alright I won't do this again. As soon as the thing didn't go off I knew I shouldn't have done it." I watched as Mario operated the cocking mechanism and the dud round went spinning to the floor, I stooped and picked it up slipping it into my pocket. Mario clicked the safety catch on and handed me the pistol avoiding my eyes.

I breathed a sigh of relief and tossed the weapon onto his bunk, "you ready for this hospital trip?" I asked quietly.

"As ready as I'll ever be boyo," he replied, "help me up on deck."

28

The Naval ambulance came in less than fifteen minutes accompanied by a team of paramedics. They strapped a reluctant Mario onto a stretcher and manhandled him into the vehicle with Neil in close attendance and drove off. The patrol boat came alongside then and two ratings jumped aboard. One attached the tow while the other cast off the mooring ropes and stood by the tiller, and in no time at all we were under way and heading for the nearby marina.

All this time I just watched, sitting near the cabin roof light by the upturned dinghy. They manoeuvred the cutter expertly between the lines of expensive yachts and cruisers finally berthing her stern on to a floating pontoon. "Got to slot you in arse end on," shouted a rating, "that bloody bowsprit blocks the walkway." They secured the mooring ropes, slipped the tow and then they were gone. I stood upon the foredeck watching the patrol boat as it turned away, heading for the Naval dockyard, a final wave from a smart as paint rating as they rounded the breakwater was the last I saw of them.

Suddenly I was alone. No one came to check on me, presumably all the berthing arrangements had been made by Neil. I paced about the deck in the warm sun feeling at a loose end. That episode with Mario and the luger had upset me, I remembered the bullet in my pocket and surreptitiously dropped it over the side before going below and retrieving the pistol from Mario's cabin. I sat on my bunk for some time just holding it, feeling its cold weight in my hand and thinking of the SS officer whose life it had taken all those years ago in Italy and the life it almost snuffed out here. Eventually I put it in my drawer and covered it over with some papers then I got a can of lager from the fridge and sat on the cross bench by the tiller drinking. It was late afternoon before Neil returned.

"How is he?" I asked.

"A bit depressed I think. The civvy hospital medical team has taken over now, X-rays, scans and tests I expect. I'll phone in the morning."

"How come the Navy turned up like that?"

"My consultant friend is ex RN. he's still got connections." He smiled. "I remember something Mario said to me once, *Neil*, he said, *All you need in this life is money or the right connections. If you've got both you're laughing.*"

"So with you're connections and Mario's cash you make a good team eh?"

"Well, my consultant friend arranged all this, the tow in, the ambulance. This berth is his, fortunately his own boat is out on loan or hire or something so there's no cost there. Mario will have to pay for the hospital treatment of course," he lit a cigarette, "our new skipper hasn't turned up then?"

"When was he due?"

"Sometime today. Mario arranged it by email through the agency."

I wasn't much concerned about those arrangements, being more interested in exploring as it was my first visit to Gibraltar. "I fancy having a look around the place while we're here," I said, "d'you fancy coming along?"

"No. You go ahead, I'll stay and mind the boat. Here, you'd better have this," and he passed me a slip of paper with the security code for unlocking the iron gates to the floating pontoons of the marina. I walked towards the quayside past the maritime gin palaces moored on each side of the pontoon, there were four or five pontoons jutting out from the quay each one housing yachts and cruisers, all of them polished and pristine and expensive. Mario's salt encrusted relic looked totally out of place in their company.

I strolled out through the gates as a taxi pulled up. A woman got out and reported into the marina office and I watched as she went in. She was carrying a grip and had a headscarf which she wore like an arab sheikh, it covered her head and the lower half of her face for there was a dusty wind blowing and the style seemed appropriate for the conditions. From the back she reminded me of Jean, I sighed as the memory of her once again gave me a pang and mentally I kicked myself for being a sentimental old fool. I headed up through the town.

All the films, all the pictures of Gibraltar I had ever seen could not have prepared me for the real thing. Everywhere was dominated by the Rock. It towered above the whole place dwarfing everything. I wandered along the pedestrianised Main Street as far as Casemates Square before walking back along the narrow street they call Irish Town. I spotted a pub up an alleyway so I went in and sampled a pint of beer, cool and refreshing, I lingered over it as the sun dipped towards the horizon.

Resisting the temptation to have another I resumed my leisurely stroll through the town. I was unsteady on my feet and stumbled occasionally, the constant movement of the cutter now no longer needing to be compensated for. I must have explored the place for a couple of hours or more before stopping off at a pavement café in the Piazza to have a coffee and a rest before making may way back to the boat. Neil was below in the galley cooking when I got back. We had eaten little all day and the smell made my mouth water. "Risotto okay?" he asked.

"I could eat a horse."

"We can stop off at Saint Rochelle on the way home, you can eat a bit of one there if you like. Go and sit down, I'll bring the food in."

I went into the small saloon and saw that the table was laid for two. There was a bottle of red already breathing on the table, I poured two glasses and sat down. "Any sign of our new skipper?" I shouted.

Neil came in carrying two plates of steaming risotto. "You'll never believe it," he smiled, "our new skipper is a woman. I was a bit rude I'm afraid, said there was probably a mistake, I mean, whoever heard of a woman skipper? Then she showed me the agency's copy of Mario's email. Anyway she took umbrage at my male chauvinism and stalked off to book into a hotel for the night. You okay?" I was thinking of the woman by the marina office, the one that reminded me of Jean. I stared into space, thinking of her again of course. "Hey, wake up," he said nudging me, "take your plate."

We ate in silence, in the gathering dusk. The wine was excellent, full bodied and rich in flavour, it and the food combining to send me into a drowsy stupor following the days and nights of sailing. After the meal Neil went up on deck for a cigarette and I sat slumped in my chair finishing off the wine. I was wondering how Mario was getting on, whether they could do anything for him which would enable him to see his beloved Wales again. Presently I went into our cabin, lay on my bunk fully clothed and fell asleep.

I did not wake until well after sunrise the following morning. Neil was fast asleep in his bunk so I got up and helped myself to some cereal followed by a cup of strong coffee. I went up on deck, I was still tired and felt scruffy and unkempt from sleeping in my clothes. Farther down the pontoon I saw a man emerge from a yacht, towel and sponge bag in hand. On impulse I went below and grabbed my own stuff then followed him to the shower block. He punched in the security code glancing at me over his shoulder. I smiled sweetly and said something about the weather then followed him in. That shower was luxurious after all the cat licks we had endured at sea and I emerged feeling totally refreshed, it was only when I glanced in a mirror that I discovered I had grown quite an impressive beard!

Neil was up when I got back, he was dressed in fashionable casual gear, the sort of clothes more suited for a jaunt ashore, I thought he looked rather sheepish. "Wish me luck," he said.

"Where are you going all tarted up?" I asked.

"I've arranged a working breakfast with our new skipper. Hope to mend things a bit. Mario wants you to come along too."

"You're the one who broke things in the first place," I said, "I'll leave it to you."

"Thanks a bunch, I could have used some moral support."

"She'll feel outnumbered if there's two of us," I countered, "anyway I've already had my breakfast."

"See you later then," he said climbing over the side rails, "keep an ear to your mobile, Mario might ring."

I had forgotten all about the mobile. It seemed like another existence when Spiro had handed the thing to me high on the New Fort when Mario first sailed into Corfu. Neil must have checked it for charge because, when I went below, it was on the table in the saloon switched on. I was half way through a cup of coffee when it bleeped. It was Mario. "'Morning boyo," he said, "sleep okay?"

"Fine. You?"

"Not too bad considering. Is Neil with you?"

"No. He's gone to have breakfast with our lady skipper."

"You didn't go with them?"

"No."

"Pity."

"I was out exploring the town when she turned up. I just hope she's more competent than the last skipper we had."

"You cheeky bastard. Well give me a call when you meet her, I want your reaction. Now, about getting home. Get under way as soon as you can, you'll need enough provisions for at least a fortnight, I'll give Neil a bell, he'll see to that I expect. I've got a date with the radiologist this afternoon and I'll be emailing you about a rendezvous in a few days."

"A rendezvous?"

"Too bloody right. You don't get rid of me that easy. I want to sail her into Porthcawl myself." He rang off and I went up on deck again to finish my coffee. Mario was certainly a fighter, apart from that moment of utter despair with the luger he seemed to have returned to his usual determined self but we were still a long way from home and he was very much on borrowed time. I found myself wishing, no praying, that he would make it back to Wales. After all he had achieved thus far, it would be a cruel fate for that final goal to elude him.

The sun climbed higher and the day warmed up and there was still no sign of Neil or the new skipper, a couple of hours or more must have gone by before I saw him trundling a four wheeled trolley down the pontoon. It was stacked high with provisions and we spent the next hour unloading and storing the stuff. "Where is she then?" I asked as the last of the stores were put away.

"She's spending another night ashore in her hotel. I've arranged for a tow out of the marina at dawn. She'll be aboard for that."

"What's she like?" I asked and Neil looked sideways at me, a half smile on his lips. He said nothing. "Well is she good looking? A battleaxe or what?"

"Can I really be a judge of that?"

"No I suppose not," I replied remembering his sexual orientation.

"She suggested we all ate out tonight to get acquainted."

"Great."

"But I turned her down. Said we've got too much preparation to do what with the long haul up through Biscay and everything."

I looked at him in disbelief. We had not eaten out since Menorca and the luxury of a decent restaurant would have been a nice memory of the Rock to take home. "What preparation for goodness sake?" I asked.

"Look, there are meals to prepare for micro waving in case the weather turns foul, the batteries need checking over, water to take on, Mario's bog to empty. She'll be sleeping in his cabin. There's a rip in the foresail I want to fix and the boat needs a good clean all round, haven't you noticed?" I hadn't but when I looked I could see he was right. We spent the rest of the day doing all the things he had mentioned, and a few more beside, before having a grilled steak with Greek salad for our evening meal. We washed up and stowed everything ready for the morning before turning in.

I awoke before sunrise the next day to the sound of a motor boat and water sluicing alongside, we were under way and I wondered vaguely why Neil hadn't roused me to help. The gentle movement of the cutter through the water and the soporific sound of the towing vessel transmitted through the timbers did not give me any incentive to get up so I just lay there, listening.

After a while footsteps on the deck and the sound of pulley blocks told me that someone was hoisting sail. This was followed by shouted farewells and the sound of an engine fading into the distance, there was also more movement as the cutter breasted the swell of the open sea. Still I lay there, unwilling to leave the warm comfort of my bunk, then I heard footsteps coming down the companionway. "You going to lie there all day?" It was Neil.

"The skipperess steering?"

"Of course. Look, I'm going to fix us some breakfast. The wind's heading us we'll have to tack soon," and with that he withdrew to the galley. Reluctantly I got up and dressed and made my way to the forward hatch, I opened it and stuck my head out. We were close hauled and under full sail, The Rock was still close on our starboard side, I couldn't see the skipper. When I turned to look aft, the saloon rooflight with the dinghy lashed on top, hid her from view. "How long before we go about?" I heard Neil shout to her.

"Half an hour," she replied.

"I'll give Jim his breakfast then I'll relieve you," he shouted.

"Fine," she answered.

I closed the hatch and went back to the saloon. Neil came in presently with two plates of 'full English' which we both did justice to, he glanced at his watch. "We're due to go about soon," he said, "could you wash up and fix her breakfast? No eggs though, she wants tomatoes instead, the sausage and bacon just need finishing off," I nodded. "When we go about we'll probably be less than an hour on the starboard tack, then it's the port tack again and so on until we get out of Gibraltar Bay. Once we turn north it should be plain sailing." I nodded again, this sailing lingo was still a bit foreign to me although I had learned quite a lot since leaving Corfu.

"Ready to go about!" Her shrill voice came down from the helm.

Neil got to his feet, "you get her breakfast, I'll do the sails." He went up on deck and I cleared the table and went into the small galley. There were two partly cooked sausages in the frying pan and three rashers of bacon under the grill. I lit the appropriate burners and emptied the contents of a half full can of tomatoes into another saucepan. Cooking was never my strongpoint, I usually burned something or forgot something or undercooked something. However, I did remember to put a plate to warm under the grill as hot food on cold plates is a pet hate of mine, then I cut a generous slice of bread ready to fry in the sausage fat and gave the tomatoes a stir now and again. As I was turning the bacon rashers I felt the boat heel slightly when it went onto the other tack before it settled down.

I was turning the fried bread over when I heard footsteps on the companionway ladder and out of the corner of my eye I saw the new skipper as she passed by to go into the saloon. I don't know why I felt so nervous about getting her food because we would probably all be taking turns at cooking in the days ahead depending on the watchkeeping schedule. In the end I just arranged the food in as attractive way as I could, took a deep breath, then carried the plate into the saloon.

She sat facing me as I entered and how I managed not to drop the plate I will never know. "Jean!" I gasped, "what on earth are you doing here?"

She just sat there looking at me wide eyed, the colour rising in her cheeks. I put the plate down in front of her and stood back open mouthed and totally speechless. She was just as I remembered her, a few more lines around the eyes which some people call crows feet but kindlier folk call laughter lines. Her hair, streaked with grey now, was cut in a shorter style than I remembered but she was as alluring as ever and I felt my blood rise at the sight of her. It was she who broke the silence. "Your beard suits you," she murmured self consciously, then added "would you like some coffee?" I sat down opposite her as she dispensed the beverage into a mug from the tall pot in the middle of the table, "still two sugars?" she asked, avoiding my eyes.

"No, er I don't take sugar any more," I stammered, "not in coffee or tea. Haven't done for . . . . some time now." There was an awkward pause as I struggled to think of something to say. What do you say to an ex-partner who betrayed you, who ran off with an older man but still makes shivers run up your spine when she appears before you in the flesh and out of the blue?

"D'you mind if I eat?" she asked eventually.

"No. No of course," I said apologetically, "I'll leave you to it." I picked up the coffee and beat a hasty retreat from the saloon, grabbed my coat from the cabin and joined Neil at the helm. "Did you know about her?" I demanded.

He gave me a guilty look. "Not all along," he admitted.

"What do you mean *not all along*?"

"Look, Mario told me he had already arranged with the agency for a coastal skipper to help on the long haul from Gib. When a woman turned up I genuinely believed there had been a mistake, so I phoned Mario as soon as she flounced off. He told me who she was and asked me not to say anything. So I didn't."

"The scheming bastard."

"Don't be too hard on him. He used to go on about what a shame it was about you two, how he wished he could do something about it. He'd kept in touch with her over the years you see, she even crewed for him sometimes. Then she and this chap of hers split up. He must have known about it, so maybe he thought here's my chance, who knows?"

"So she was as much in the dark as I was then?"

"It seems so. Anyway, one thing's for sure."

"What's that?"

"You can't ignore each other on this trip, there's not enough room. Not only that, she's the skipper, you'll have to do as you're told."

"Bollocks," I said.

"D'you fancy taking the helm for a while?" he asked, "seeing as you didn't bring me any coffee I'll fetch it myself."

"I forgot," I replied. "What's the course anyway? I can't see the indelible pencil mark of the day on this bloody antique," I glanced down at the compass.

"Don't worry about a course. Our new skipper just said to keep as close to the wind as you can. Watch the foresail for luffing, you know the routine," and with that he went below.

The breeze freshened and I concentrated on keeping the boat as near to the wind as possible. We went about several times as we beat our way out of Gibraltar Bay, Neil had already rigged the staysail and tightened up all the canvass so she was well and truly close hauled. I found myself in a constant battle with the tiller as I watched the leading edge of the foresail for the trembling shivers they called luffing which would slow us down.

Eventually Neil relieved me. "There's a sandwich on the saloon table," he said.

"Where is she?"

"On the computer."

Mario's cabin door was shut and there was the sound of someone tapping away on a computer keyboard. I went into the saloon and sat down. Now that I was relieved of the concentration of keeping the cutter going in the right direction I relaxed over my coffee, my mind drifting over this turn of events. Jean was obviously as shocked as I was, coming face to face like that. Neil had said that the relationship with her sailing partner was over but so what? She might have someone else in tow for all Mario knew. The trouble was I still had feelings for her. I knew those feelings must remain secret at least until I knew if she still harboured any for me. I had just finished my sandwich when the saloon door opened. "May I join you?" she asked.

"You're the skipper," I replied.

She moved across the floor with the same sensuous grace that I remembered and sat opposite me clasping her mug of coffee in both hands, I noticed that she was not wearing any rings. Her hair was tied back with a red chiffon scarf knotted at the side and she wore a

Guernsey sweater which, although slightly too large, still failed to hide the soft curve of her breasts. "This is all a bit awkward," she said.

"Blame Mario," I retorted.

"Did you know about me?" she asked.

"No I did not. When I saw you sitting there this morning I nearly had a fit. I realise now why Neil let me lie in. He knew who you were last night, Mario told him."

"Is all this going to be a problem? My being here I mean?"

"Not to me. I'm the only landlubber it would seem, so with Mario unavailable we need your expertise to get us home."

"There's still a long way to go. We could put back to Gib if you like. Mario would pay for your flight home."

"I've become rather fond of sailing," I said flippantly, "unless my presence gives you a problem I'll stick with it." She inclined her head with the hint of a smile. "Do I give *you* a problem?" I asked.

She sat staring into her coffee for several seconds. "No," she said at last.

"That took some thinking about."

"Not really. I was just thinking about before. Before we separated that's all."

"You and him. How long since . . . ?"

"Since we split up? Over a year now and no, there was, there is, nobody else. What about you?"

"No. No one." She was still staring into her drink and I found myself wanting to take hold of her hands and draw her towards me, to kiss her full on the mouth, feel her body pressed against me.

"Look," she said at last, "we've got to get this boat back to the UK and it's not going to be a picnic. I'm drawing a line from La Coruna to Brest and that's slap bang across the Bay of Biscay. We could be out of sight of land for a week or more depending on the weather. I've got to know that we can work together, no snide comments, no backbiting, a professional working relationship. You okay with that?" I looked at her, the grey green eyes, the slightly pouting lips, the finely chiselled chin and cheek bones. "Well?"

"Yes. Yes of course."

She smiled. "Okay. Now would you relieve Neil for a while and send him down. He's got to have the same pep talk." I got up and opened the saloon door, "James," she said and it stopped me in my tracks because that was what she always used to call me, "let's try and make the best of this. For Mario's sake?" I nodded slowly and went up on deck to relieve Neil and so we sailed on throughout the day.

The wind had shifted slightly as dusk approached so we altered course towards the northwest, which enabled us to lash the tiller and let her sail herself. I was sitting on the cross bench by the tiller keeping a general lookout, Neil was below preparing the evening meal and Jean had her head and shoulders above the hatchway scanning the coast through binoculars in the fading light. "That's Cape Trafalgar over there," she said.

"Really?" I turned to look at the distant coastline imagining that epic battle of long ago, trying to picture the conditions aboard the ships, the cramped gundecks, the noise and the smoke, the smell and the awful, the terrible carnage.

Jean clambered out of the hatch, "mind if I sit here?" She sat on the crossbench on the other side of the tiller.

"You're the skip . . ." I stopped myself. "No of course not," I said. "Do you do this sort of thing often?"

"This sort of thing?"

"Crewing or acting as skipper on other peoples' boats."

"The agency contacts me from time to time with delivery jobs. If it's convenient I do them."

"And this job?"

"Mario told the agency he particularly wanted me for this one," she paused glancing sideways at me, "for obvious reasons it appears."

"How did you get in touch with Mario after that reunion then?"

"We exchanged phone numbers that evening, he said he sometimes needed crew. I forgot all about it, then after we . . . after I . . . left, I found his number in a handbag and phoned him on impulse. We went down to Porthcawl a few times, that's what got me into bigger boats and away from dinghy racing."

"You said we ?"

"Yes. We."

"So Mario knew your . . . your bloke then."

"Yes, he knew my bloke. Disliked him at first sight. Very intuitive is Mario as I eventually found out."

"You know about his condition?"

"Yes. He told me a few months back. It's such a shame."

"Did he tell you about this expedition we've just been on?"

"He asked me to go along but I said that it was a job for men only. I guess that was when he thought of you and this little scheme of his."

"Getting us to meet up again you mean?" She nodded but said nothing, staring out across the sea, the wind ruffling her hair. "D'you think that was another example of Mario's intuition?" I asked.

She turned and looked me in the eyes for the first time, a faint smile on her lips making my heart beat faster. "Time will tell," she replied.

Just then Neil stuck his head above the hatchway. "Dinner is served," he shouted, "stew and dumplings, who's coming down?"

"You go," I said, "I'll stand watch," she made her way to the companionway. "Oh Jean," I called after her, "better switch the navigation lights on. It'll be dark soon." She waved an acknowledgement before disappearing below and I was left alone with my thoughts in the gathering dusk, the faint smell of her perfume still in my nose.

30

We sailed all through the night, the lights of Cadiz always visible on our starboard side. Then all the next day and the following night across the Gulf of Cadiz each of us doing two hours on and four off, we were averaging ten knots in a stiff breeze across a rolling swell. The corkscrewing motion would have had my stomach contents over the side at one time but now it felt totally natural. After rounding Cape Sao Vicente we turned north for Lisbon which we sighted at dusk on the third day.

That watchkeeping regime was a killer, all sense of time in relation to day and night became blurred, we became like zombies moving about the boat in dazed semi consciousness, taking turns to brew tea or coffee, make sandwiches or heat the plated meals Neil had prepared earlier. Conversation became stilted with only communication essential to sailing the boat being attempted. We became tetchy and irritable, I remember Neil and I nearly came to blows over some trivial thing or other down in the saloon. Jean was on deck at the time and our raised voices brought her down where she put us firmly in our place.

The day after that incident she told Neil to heave-to then called us both into Mario's cabin. "We're going to have a rest day tomorrow," she announced, "there's a convenient anchorage near the town of Nazare, just there," she pointed to the chart, "we'll stock up on a few things, fresh fruit maybe. Okay?"

We looked at each other like recalcitrant schoolboys and just nodded, "I'll get under way again then shall I?" Neil asked.

"No," she replied, "James can do that. Why don't you prepare one of your delicious Greek salads with a meat meze, ready for when we drop anchor. I'll choose a suitable red from Mario's cellar."

"Sounds good to me," Neil said and I went up on deck, unlashed the tiller and got us under way again heading north. The prospect of a full night's sleep followed by a jaunt ashore and then maybe another night's sleep was certainly inviting.

We anchored just after sunset and I rigged the riding light before going below and sprucing myself up. Neil's food was superb as usual, the Greek salad sprinkled with freshly ground pepper and liberally dressed with olive oil, the meat meze a mixture of pork, chicken and goats meat all accompanied by freshly baked bread. "How do you do this?" Jean asked him as she spread butter on a thick slice of it.

"Mix the dough," he replied, "let it rise in the microwave on very low power then put it in the proper oven till the outside just browns."

"It's very nice anyway," she said as she poured the wine, "you certainly are a very good cook." I glanced across at Neil who shot a glance in my direction, a self-conscious smile on his lips, I couldn't be absolutely sure but it looked like he was blushing slightly. Jean turned to me. "What do you think of the wine James?"

"A good choice."

"It wasn't difficult. Mario has impeccable taste in wine, I could have shut my eyes and picked at random but as we're anchored off Portugal I chose this Bairrada," she took a large sip, "mm, it *is* good."

The conversation around the saloon table that evening was not very stimulating, we were too tired I think. The meal was excellent and we all tucked into it. Neil finished first and excused himself, going up on deck for a smoke before going to bed. Jean and I sat on after finishing our food to finish off the wine. We spoke little, partly through fatigue and partly I think because we were still uncomfortable in each other's presence. I found myself covertly admiring her hair, her eyes. Those breasts so tantalisingly disguised under that shapeless Guernsey.

Neil came clumping down the companionway and called 'goodnight' as he made his way to our cabin. "I'll take a look up top," she said, "then I'm turning in. It's been a hard few days."

"You can say that again," I replied. "D'you want the last of this wine?" I held up the almost empty bottle but she shook her head, drained her glass and went out. I sat there for a while feeling the gentle rocking of the boat at anchor, wondering how Mario was faring and becoming more drowsy by the minute. Eventually I drained my glass, paid a visit to the heads and went to bed.

The following morning we slept late and had a light breakfast of cereal and toast followed by coffee then Jean checked on the stores while I tidied ship. Neil telephoned the hospital at Gib on the satellite phone to be told that Mario was stable and recovering from the radio therapy then we unlashed the Mirror and launched it over the side. Neil stepped the mast in its forward position and set the mainsail only, catboat fashion, and thus the three of us sailed into the harbour at Nazare.

"I need to find a hairdresser," Jean announced, "Can we all meet back here, say, late afternoon?"

"Are we dining out tonight?" I asked.

"If you like," she said, "d'you fancy that Neil?" He nodded agreement so she went on, "I know a good place on the Boulevard, I can recommend it."

Neil and I exchanged glances, "that sounds good," I said.

"See you later then," she said. I watched her as she walked away.

"You still fancy her I take it?" Neil asked.

"Well," I said, "she is still my wife. We only separated and split the chattels, there was never a divorce."

"Time you demanded a continuation of conjugal rights then eh?"

"Somehow I think that would be premature," I replied with sarcasm. Even so, such a prospect certainly fired my loins.

We spent the rest of the day exploring the town, stopping occasionally to sit in the shade with a cold drink. At one point we wandered down onto the beach, I had a paddle in the sea while Neil sat smiling on the sand. "All you need is a knotted handkerchief on your head. You look like a wakes weeker at Blackpool," he shouted.

We sat outside a café overlooking the harbour in the late afternoon when Jean appeared. She was carrying a large bag full of fresh fruit of various kinds. Neil was on his feet in an instant to relieve her of the load. "Thanks Neil," she said, "that was breaking my arm. We all set to eat?" Without waiting for a reply she hailed a passing taxi and we piled in. She told the driver the name of the restaurant and within five minutes we were seated at our table.

The meal that night was a much more convivial affair, we polished off three bottles of wine between us before finishing with a large brandy apiece. Neil practiced his Portuguese on a charming young waiter, the chemistry between them not going unnoticed by Jean. At one point, when Neil had gone to the toilet, she turned to me, "About Neil," she said furtively, "is he er . . . ?"

"Gay? Yes. Didn't Mario tell you?"

"No. Why should he?"

"Well, no. No reason for him to say anything. He only told me by accident so to speak," and I thought back to that first day on the boat with Neil spreadeagled naked on the raft in Sidari Bay. I almost told her about Neil's assignation in Fornells but thought better of it. Such gossip was pointless.

When it was time to leave Jean paid in cash and got a receipt. "Mario is generous to a fault," she explained, "but he has to have proof of expenditure. It comes from years of family business influence."

We got a taxi back to the harbour and clambered aboard the Mirror. There was very little wind so Neil, having had the foresight to take the oars along, rowed us out. When we got clear of the harbour the breeze picked up and we hoisted the sail.

I lay upon the foredeck and Neil sat on the thwart while Jean was probably in her element at the helm of a dinghy again. We should have had some difficulty finding the cutter as we had not rigged the anchor light but Jean had noted the coastal features as we sailed in, she steered us straight to it and we tied up alongside. Neil made straight for his bunk with a slurred g'night for we were all slightly drunk and looking back that probably explains what happened next.

Jean asked me if I fancied a nightcap and I readily accepted. She went into Mario's cabin, her cabin now, and fetched a bottle and two glasses which she brought into the saloon. She poured two whiskies and handed me one, "cheers," she said raising her glass. I walked or rather stumbled towards her intending to touch glasses, all the time looking into her eyes. She was returning my gaze, that half smile which I remembered so well playing around her mouth. The saloon table was on my right and on impulse I put my glass down and embraced her, clumsily groping her breast as I did so. She drew back in alarm. "D'you mind?" she exclaimed as some of her drink spilled from her glass.

In an instant I was sober. "I . . . I'm terribly sorry," I stammered, "I don't know what I was thinking about, I didn't mean . . . I hadn't . . I'm so sorry!" I turned and fled the saloon.

I stood in my cabin unable to believe what a fool I had made of myself. Neil was fast asleep snoring gently in his bunk, dead to the world and probably dreaming of that Portuguese waiter. I waited until I heard Jean return to her cabin before retrieving my drink from the saloon then sitting on the edge of my bunk and taking a long time to finish it.

The next day the wind was fair and the sky flecked with cloud, the barometer was high and steady. Neil cooked a full English and we sat around the saloon table enjoying it. "We'll get under way after breakfast," Jean announced, "I've marked that excuse for a compass with the course. James you take first watch, I'll help Neil clear away as soon as we've set sail."

"Okay," I said not looking at her.

For the rest of the day I confined myself to doing whatever job was needed at the time, saying very little and avoiding Jean as much as possible. My reticence was noticed by Neil who asked me if I was alright more than once. In the end he came and sat beside me on the cross bench by the tiller. "What's up with you today? You've hardly said a word to anybody."

"I made a fool of myself last night when we got back aboard."

"With her?"

"Who else?"

"Oh." He lit a cigarette and sat in silence for some time, eventually he said: "Look, do you want to get back with her?"

"I don't know. All I know is I fancy her like hell, physically I mean."

"That's a start."

"A start maybe. Not the basis for an enduring relationship."

"Some people manage it. Anyway it's not just physical surely?"

"Well no, not entirely but the attraction is so strong . . ." I paused, "I can't be sure that's not all it is."

"Can you cope with the fact she went off with this other guy?"

"I think I forgave her for that a long time ago."

"Well then," he smiled, "no problem." He flicked his half smoked cigarette over the side. "Coffee?" he asked and without waiting for an answer he went off to make it.

We put in at Viana do Costello north of Porto for another twenty four hour rest period even though our watchkeeping regime was now not so rigid. We were within sight of land at all times and very often, with the tiller lashed and relying on Mario's anti-collision gismo, we all slept. At La Coruna we took on stores and checked all the survival gear before sailing out and anchoring near Cape Ortegal. It would be our last sight of land before the Cotes du Nord.

That last night before setting out to cross the Bay of Biscay, Neil prepared Jean's favourite meal - chicken Tenereife with salad. It was preceded by canned asparagus soup and followed by cheese and biscuits and, of course, port wine. We ate the meal in a somewhat strained atmosphere, the conversation desultory. Ever since my faux pas at Nazare I had treated Jean with complete probity. She had retained her usual efficient management style, not too remote, not too familiar. I even thought I detected a tendency on her part to become less formal towards me, however, I dared not respond in case I was wrong. Neil finished his port. "Well," he said, "I'm off to bed, we sail at sunrise yes?"

"The forecast's good," Jean replied, "we're fully provisioned, so yes."

"Goodnight then." Neil gave me a surreptitious wink and left.

"Some more port?" I passed the bottle to Jean in the awkward silence that followed.

"Thanks." She took it and poured a token quantity into her glass. "About the other night," she said, "at Nazare." I opened my mouth to apologise again but she waved me into silence. "You took me by surprise you know James. I'd forgotten what an impetuous bastard you are."

"I'd had too much to drink," I offered weakly.

"We all had. Anyway, I've been thinking. Mario's motive for this surprise reunion was, presumably, that we should get back together yes?"

"I suppose so."

"So how do you feel about that?" She eyed me over the rim of her glass and I felt my blood rise again. Was it love or lust? Only time would reveal that.

"I was gutted when you went off with that ponce from the sailing club," I said. "Then I began to miss you, then to hate you, then to want you. Want you more than anything." I felt my colour rising, angry at my openness. "There I've said it," I snapped, standing up and draining my glass, "Sorry, it must be baring my soul week. G'night." I slammed out of the saloon and went into our cabin where Neil was lying in his bunk still awake.

"Another tiff?" he asked.

"Piss off," I retorted.

31

We weighed anchor at sunrise and set off on the long leg across the Bay of Biscay. The wind direction often allowed us to sail with the tiller lashed so the cutter could practically sail herself. This meant more rest all round and less fatigue. As long as Mario's anti-collision system worked we were okay. "Only trouble is," Jean said over breakfast, "we haven't been able to test it."

That test came on the second day out. The sea at that time was relatively calm according to Jean, although to me it seemed incredibly rough, we were all below in the saloon drinking tea when Jean pricked up her ears. "Did you hear that?" she asked. Neil and I looked at each other and shook our heads. "There it is again!" she exclaimed and rushed into Mario's cabin with us close on her heels. There was a bleep from some equipment on a side rack and an amber light blinked, a small screen indicated a compass bearing. Jean grabbed a pair of binoculars and hurried up on deck.

The sky was overcast but visibility was good, she made her way gingerly to the dinghy, which was lashed securely over the saloon rooflight, resting her elbows on it as she trained the binoculars towards the north. "Neil," she shouted, "stand by the tiller. James come and look at this." I clawed my way to where she was crouched and took the binoculars pointing them in the direction she indicated.

At first I could see nothing except the undulating horizon but then something caught my eye. There was a dark grey smudge which came and went above the irregular line of constantly shifting waves. "What the hell is it?" I asked.

"Let me have another look," she replied and took the glasses back. After a moment or so she said: "Well it's a ship obviously. A big one too. Probably a merchantman, possibly a container ship? No wait a minute, I think it's a . . . it is . . . it's an aircraft carrier." She turned and shouted: "Neil, unlash the tiller and bear away about five degrees. We've got an aircraft carrier bearing down on us," and then to me, "well at least we know now that Mario's anti-collision thingy works."

The French carrier passed us on our port side about half a mile away, one of its escorts to starboard of us by about a mile, The sea was too rough for their wakes to cause any problem so we lashed the tiller again and went below. The receiver which picked up the radar pulses from the warships was obviously doing its job as was the software which recognised the constancy of direction and warned of possible collision. We went to our bunks that night much reassured of our safety.

The further north we progressed the more mountainous the sea became. It was almost impossible to sleep. First there was the sensation of being pressed down into my bunk as the boat lifted like a rocket as it was borne up towards the crest of a wave. Then the downward swoop into the wave's trough, like being in a lift when the cable breaks, your stomach comes up to your throat, you breathe out quickly to stop the muscles tensing but it doesn't work and by dawn they ache like they've been punched all night.

After only a few days I found it impossible to stay up on deck, the sea was just too frightening to look at. The waves were over forty feet high, huge towering walls of grey green water which threatened to engulf the boat then, as we were lifted up the sides of these monstrous things, we would look down into a deep watery chasm. In my brief periods of fitful sleep I had nightmares in which I truly believed we would never see land again and a giant hole would appear in the deepest trough to swallow us all.

It was during such a nightmare that I awoke in a panic to find Jean holding me in her arms with Neil standing behind her, a glass of rum in his hand. I took it from him and swallowed the lot before clutching Jean again until my trembling subsided. "You okay now?" she asked and I nodded. "I'm going up on deck for a while," she said, "It's almost two in the morning, I can't sleep either."

After she had gone Neil said: "I've never been in seas like this either, most of our sailing was in the Bristol Channel, a far cry from this lot. If you like, I've got something better than rum which might help."

"What's that?"

"This." He held up a syringe.

"Drugs?"

"Vallium. Administered intravenously it would calm you down."

"Is that what's been calming you down?"

"I haven't needed it, but then I haven't been affected like you."

"Lucky you then," I said churlishly.

"Look, we're all different. This seascape's given you the heeby-jeebies, I've heard of such things, nothing to be ashamed of. If you prefer it I've got some pills."

I sat on the edge of my bunk holding on tightly as the boat swooped and plunged its way northeastwards, my stomach an aching knot. "I'll try the pills," I said.

I lost track of the days and nights during that interminable journey. I remained below, preparing food, making tea, anything to avoid the awesome sight of those mountainous seas. Jean often sat with me, holding my hand, passing me the occasional, no, the frequent glass of rum and gradually the seas diminished as we approached Brest.

The GPS gave our position 150 miles west of Lorient when Jean decided to anchor for a day or two. By then I was able to do a stint at the tiller for the sea was slightly calmer and I seemed to have shaken off the dreadful fear it had engendered. Some time before dawn we saw the loom of a lighthouse which she identified from the chart and soon after sunrise we sighted land for the first time since leaving Portugal.

Jean steered us into a sheltered anchorage near Audierne and I stood at the bow ready to kick the retaining pin which held the anchor chain. From below came the mouth watering smell of Neil's cheesy-hammy-eggy, the first time he had prepared that delicacy since the Med. We all sat in the saloon, the boat unnaturally still, eating our breakfast. "We'll give ourselves twenty four hours rest here," Jean announced, "then it's practically due north to Lands End and up the Bristol Channel to Porthcawl."

"And d'you think Mario will be there to greet us?" I asked.

Neil opened his mouth to say something but at that moment the satellite phone sounded in Mario's cabin and Jean went to answer it. "How long is it since we left Gib?" I asked Neil.

"God knows," he answered, "it seems like months."

"How d'you think Mario got on?"

"I've been wondering about that. If anything serious had gone wrong we would have been told. My friend at the hospital would have got in touch."

"Maybe this call is from him."

"Could be."

Just then Jean came back in and sat down. "Well," she said, "it's plan B I'm afraid." We both looked at her quizzically. "We've got to divert to Alderney."

"Alderney?" we both echoed.

"That was Mario, he's recovered from his radio therapy and he's chartered a private plane to fly him to Alderney. He wants to join ship there."

"Why Alderney for goodness sake?" I asked.

"I think I know," Neil said thoughtfully, "we sailed there once, Mario persuaded me to crew for him the first summer I met him. Another hospice nurse came along too. He was a very good friend of mine," he added rather sheepishly and Jean and I exchanged knowing glances, "he was also an experienced sailor which was just as well as I was quite a novice then. Mario was enthralled by the island, I expect that's why he wants to go there again," his voice dropped, "for the last time you see."

We all looked at each other, no one said anything. Diverting to Alderney would put extra distance and time onto our homeward journey but still, if it was what Mario wanted, none of us begrudged him that.

That evening we launched the Mirror and sailed round to Audierne. The place was still busy with surfers even this late in the season and the usual youthful rowdiness was everywhere, however, we managed to find a small restaurant tucked away and had a pleasant meal. The patron hit it off with Neil straight away and I thought Jean and I would be sailing back to the cutter alone. Instead we just drank his wine late into the night and somehow managed to find the dinghy and then the cutter and finally our bunks. The following day we rested.

To get to Alderney we had some hazardous sailing to do requiring skilful navigation around Pointe du Raz and various rocky islands to the north. Tidal streams and various currents had to be allowed for before setting a course and that was usually held for only a short time before a change was ordered. The ancient compass face had many different indelible pencil lines marked upon it and much use was made of the hand bearing compass to distinguish our relationship to various landmarks on the coast. All this being totally unnecessary according to Neil who would have relied entirely on our GPS.

"I need the practice," Jean retorted, "anyway what if the GPS goes on the blink? I just use it to check up on my chart dead reckoning. I feel safer that way." Neil just shrugged but I felt reassured by her caution and her competence with the calculations while at the same time admiring the curve of her breasts as she leaned over the chart table. We sailed into the harbour at Braye three days later just as the sun was setting and tied up near an iron ladder which allowed access to the quay. "Someone'll have to be on watch all the time here," Jean announced, "the tide rises and falls so much we've got to adjust the warps every so often."

"We'll have to draw lots then," I suggested.

"No," she said calmly, "I've drawn up a roster, it'll be two hours on and four off except near slack water when there's a good four hours they can be left alone. You boys get up to St. Anne now, you'll probably find Mario propping up the bar."

The island of Alderney is less than four miles long and only one and a half miles wide with the main town of St. Anne perched on high ground somewhere near the centre. Neil knew the guest house Mario would be staying at, they had visited it on their previous visit, so we set off from the harbour in the gathering twilight along the road that crossed the lowland greensward. The evening was quiet with only the occasional cry of a gull, the grasses either side made a hissing noise as the salty wind buffeted them, the sound of our feet upon the road surface inordinately loud.

Jean was right about the bar. Mario had flown in two days previously and booked into the small hotel near the centre. The owner was a Swansea woman and had taken Mario under her wing immediately. He was well into his fifth pint of the evening when we found him. He was apparently about to demonstrate his skill in the wheelchair, a bar stool slalom had been set up across the cramped lounge and the owner was taking bets from customers, a stop watch in her hand. Mario's face lit up as we entered. "Ah hah," he beamed, "my motley crew have arrived. Place your bets boyos, how long will it take me to get round these stools and back to the bar?"

The woman handed us a slip of paper each. "Write your names on the top and the time underneath," she instructed, "the one who comes within ten seconds either way of the actual time he takes wins the pot. Are you ready Mario?" We handed the chits back as she counted down to the start. There were about a dozen or so people in the room all keeping well back all expecting, as we were, a race against the clock. "Three, two, one, go!" She started the watch and Mario set off, not at some frantic pace but slowly, carefully, skilfully avoiding contact with the bar stools. When he got to the end of the line he paused, "never touched one did I boys?" he said before weaving his way back along the course without haste. He reached the bar and the woman clicked the stopwatch with a flourish.

Needless to say every estimate was way too low, none was within ten seconds of the time Mario took to dawdle around the course. Someone near the bar chirped up that he was the closest. The woman put him right: "Are you within ten seconds either way?"

"No."

"Sorry."

"No worries boys," Mario smiled, "all your money goes into the Cancer Research box on the bar. Neil, mine's a gin and tonic."

Neil walked up to the bar shaking his head and smiling, "you crafty sod Mario. If only we'd been five minutes later coming in." He paid for a round of drinks for the three of us.

We helped to get Mario to bed later and the following day Neil borrowed the proprietor's car and took him around the island on a sightseeing tour which left Jean and me together on the boat. All I had in prospect was a day of constantly adjusting the warps that tied the cutter to the quay, or so I thought, until she suggested we go for a sail.

"Go for a sail?" I said incredulously, "you cannot be serious!"

"What's wrong with that?" she answered, "there's a decent breeze, and it's better than sitting around here surely. How much helming experience have you had?"

"Not much."

"Well then."

We spent the rest of the day sailing up and down the coast, going about, gybing, heaving to, every manoeuvre she could think up. I learned more about sailing a keel boat that day than all the time we had been at sea and by the time we tied up in Braye harbour late that afternoon I was exhausted.

Just as the sun was going down Neil and Mario turned up with a crowd of well wishers including the Swansea woman and the guests from the hotel. They all lent a hand to get Mario aboard before waving their farewells as we got him down to the saloon. Arrangements had to be made then in order that Mario could move back into his cabin. There was a small berth just aft of the chain locker but it was extremely cramped. In the end it was decided that I would move in there while Neil and Jean shared our old cabin. The prospect of a female sharing with a homosexual apparently acceptable all round. As I was transferring my things to the forward berth Neil asked: "Have you eaten?"

"No and I'm starving. We've been out all day sailing."

"I know we watched you for a time. Look, we had a slap up dinner ashore in the hotel. I'll prepare something for you both when we get under way."

"Get under way? We're not sailing tonight surely?"

"No but Mario wants to anchor off, he says It'll be awkward getting out from here in the morning, something to do with tidal currents and the wind. You cast off and I'll get the sails up, Jean's at the helm."

So in the gathering twilight we crept out of Braye harbour and made for a nearby bay. The sky was overcast and the wind light as Jean steered us into the sheltered anchorage, at her signal I kicked the retaining pin and the anchor splashed into the dark waters, the chain rattling out after it. I lit the riding light, the smell of Neil's cheesy-hammy-eggy wafting up from below.

My new berth although cramped was cosy. So cosy in fact that I did not wake the following morning until we had been under way for over an hour. I dressed as quickly as I could in the confined space and made my way to the galley looking in on Mario on the way. He was still asleep. There was hot coffee in the pot so I poured myself a cup and returned to the saloon. Thrown on the back of a chair was Jean's red headscarf and I thought of yesterday's sailing lesson. It had been an enjoyable experience, just the two of us, the boat and the open sea. The wind in our hair, the sun on our faces the white-capped waves. I sighed deeply. The saloon door swung open. "You finally got up then you lazy sod." It was Neil.

"You could have called me," I said defensively.

"Couldn't find you," he joked, "stuck in that little cupboard up front. You had breakfast?"

"No."

"I'll rustle something up. Go and relieve Jean at the helm." I drained my cup and struggled into my coat then went up on deck. Jean was sat on the cross bench one hand on the tiller, the sky had a hazy glare which reflected off the sea, accounting for the sun glasses she was wearing.

"You obviously slept well," she said.

"Obviously," I replied. "You want to go below for a while? Neil's getting breakfast."

"Mario awake?"

"No."

"I don't think we'll be getting much help from Mario for the rest of this trip," she said, "he's very weak now."

"He always said he wanted to sail her into Porthcawl harbour. D'you think he'll be able to?"

"We'll make sure of it won't we?"

"Definitely."

"Well, the course is northwest," she relinquished the tiller and as we brushed past each other I felt again that strong physical desire her close proximity always provoked. I sat on the cross bench forcing myself to concentrate on the face of that ancient compass.

Jean was right. Mario spent almost all his time in his cabin either in his bunk or at his computer. He was emailing or on the satellite phone every time I looked in on him and he would send me away with an impatient wave of his hand. Not that we had much time for socialising, we were sailing day and night, two hours on and four off living off tinned food mainly. A severe gale warning was issued not long after we rounded Cape Cornwall and we were forced to anchor in the lee of Lundy Island for two days while it blew itself out. It was a welcome respite from the rigorous watchkeeping schedule and I slept a full eight hours in my cubby hole aft of the chain locker.

The night before we set off on the final leg up the Bristol Channel Neil treated us once again to Chicken Tenereife with freshly baked garlic bread, the meal accompanied by one of Mario's delicious red wines. Mario sat with us in the saloon but he didn't do justice to the meal, he had a high colour and was not his old convivial self. "I think I'll get off to my pit now boys and girls if you'll excuse me," he said, his food only half eaten. Neil helped him to his cabin as Jean and I finished our meal in silence.

Presently Neil came back and sat down, he drained his glass then topped it up again and did the same for ours. "You know," he said quietly, "I'm a hospice nurse. I'm supposed to be hardened to death. Supposed to give my patients cheerful care right to the last. Mario's outlived the best estimates of the specialists by nearly four months. At one stage I almost believed they'd got the diagnosis wrong. Stupid really."

"You think he's nearing the end?" I asked.

"Like I said before, he could keel over any time. You know what he's just told me?" We both shook our head. "That last will and testament he got me to witness, he's put me down as executor!"

"What does that entail?" Jean asked.

"I would have to ensure that his wishes as expressed in the will were properly carried out, that his estate was disposed of as he wanted. His solicitor is the other executor, we'd have to work together."

"How big is his estate?" I asked.

"I don't know. I think he's disposed of many of his various inheritances over the years, salted money away offshore, left some to charity, his solicitor might know about that. Of course this expedition must have cost quite a bit but if he can afford to charter planes and all that he must be fairly well loaded. And now there's the party."

"Party?" Jean said.

"He's booked us all into some swank hotel for a few days and they're putting on a party to celebrate his return. I hope to God he makes it."

"Well," Jean said, "the glass is rising slowly and the wind's died down how about we make an early start tomorrow?"

"We could sail tonight couldn't we?" I asked, "we've been cooped up here for two days, I feel well rested I don't know about you."

"Better let me do some calculations," she replied, "we want to time our arrival to be late morning or early afternoon if possible. If we arrive off Porthcawl in the middle of the night we don't want to be stooging around for hours."

"Couldn't we could just heave to in that case?" I suggested.

"Not in those waters, James. Too many currents and too many rocks. Look let's all get some shuteye, I'll do some figuring and call you, okay?" And so Neil and I turned in while Jean crept into Mario's cabin to check up on the charts and the forecast and the tidal currents.

We set sail a couple of hours before dawn creeping along the eastern side of Lundy and as we cleared its northern tip and came out of its shelter the wind strengthened and we began to make some knots. Neil provided a cheesy-hammy-eggy breakfast before sunrise and we settled into the usual watch keeping routine of two hours on and four off, even Mario did a stint at the tiller around midday. As the day progressed the wind gradually decreased and even though we crammed on every stitch of canvass our speed fell away. We were more at the mercy of the tidal currents then and it was almost dusk when we dropped anchor in Port Eynon Bay off the Gower Peninsular.

"Almost there now boyo!" Mario beamed as we sat in the saloon finishing the evening meal Neil had prepared. Jean was in Mario's cabin getting a weather forecast and wrestling with tide tables ready for the morrow, Neil was up on deck smoking.

"You finally did it Mario," I said.

"Can't wait to see their faces man. Aunty Bron, the lifeboat crew, Mr. Wang."

"Who?"

"Oh, I never told you about him did I?" I shook my head. "It's just history repeating itself boyo," he smiled, "My people coming over here selling ice cream and opening cafes and all that. Now it's the Chinks or the Thais or the Indians selling chow mein or curry or whatever. Mr. Wang bought the restaurant I had inherited, subject to providing me with a penthouse flat for as long as I need it."

"And no doubt you're getting used to Chinese food by now eh?"

"No fear, I never touch it. They understand mind, they're nice people the Wangs. He was worried about setting up business here at first, being foreign and all that. I told him if he looked back a generation or two the place was all bloody foreigners, Tiger Bay even had an Arab quarter."

"Tiger Bay?"

"Cardiff's old dockland boyo, Bute Town to give it its proper name. Now remember, just make sure I'm at the helm when we sail into Porthcawl. I'm off to my bunk." Mario struggled to his feet, waving aside my offer of help and made his way to his cabin. Soon afterwards Jean came in carrying a tray with three glasses and a whisky bottle, she put it down on the saloon table.

"Well," she smiled, "that's a stroke of luck."

"What?"

"There's a fresh southerly forecast for tomorrow which means a starboard reach all the way," at last I knew what she was talking about, "not only that I reckon we should be off Sker Point soon after the ebb begins to run. We should be in harbour about noon, that's well before low water."

"That's good?" I asked, puzzled.

"Yes because the inner harbour dries out."

"I see." I didn't really. There were still things about this sailing lingo that remained a mystery. "So what time do we set off?"

"About six o'clock, that gives us some margin for error." She poured three stiff whiskies reaching into a wall locker for the soda. "Yes?" She held my glass under the siphon.

"Half as much again," I replied. She passed me my glass and charged hers with about the same amount.

"Cheers." She stood smiling down at me, her glass raised. My heart seemed to miss a beat at the sight of her, so close yet even now so remote. I remained seated as I raised my glass and drank, once bitten twice shy I thought, as I recalled my earlier faux pas. Just then Neil came in and we all sat around the table with our drinks. "We'll all muck in with the washing up in a few minutes," she went on, "then how about a light breakfast, just cereal and coffee? We can have that delicious soup Neil's made as we go along, then we'll be all set for Mario's welcome home party."

We set sail soon after six the following morning, the sky was flecked with cloud and there was a fresh southerly breeze as forecast. We were in no hurry to cover the twenty five or so miles so we 'sauntered along', as Jean put it, under main and jib doing around five knots. We passed Mumbles Head and hove to for a while in Swansea Bay and I studied the coast through binoculars.

This was the sight that had greeted Mario's Uncle Benny from the deck of that battered old collier all those years ago except that there would have been more industry then. Now there were fewer smoking chimneys, less industrial haze from the multitude of smaller factories that once cluttered the coastal plain. The distant oil refinery still exuded flames while the storage tank complex adjacent to Swansea Docks looked deceptively close. The chemical plant at Baglan Bay shimmered in the sun and further down the coast the docks and steelworks at Port Talbot could be seen.

"Come on James," Jean called from the stern, "time to go, put those bins away I'm unlashing the tiller," and so we resumed our course eastwards gradually leaving the docks and industry behind. The treacherous rocks at Sker Point were abeam when I spotted a boat approaching at speed, it was an inshore lifeboat and it circled once before coming close on the leeward side.

"You got Mario aboard?" the helmeted steersman called out.

Neil was helming at the time, "down below," he replied.

"Well get the old bastard up on deck, he's supposed to be steering her in." With that the lifeboat sheered away and continued its patrol along the coast.

Mario's head appeared through the hatch, "you going to be alright helming?" Neil asked anxiously.

"Yeah, I'll be OK," Mario replied as Neil relinquished the tiller to him. He had a quick look all around, he was in familiar waters now. The breakwater and light were up ahead and Mario pushed the tiller over. "Stand by to harden up," he commanded and Neil and I prepared to tighten up the main and foresail. "Now," he shouted as we swung into the wind. He was sailing away from the coast now but we assumed he knew what he was doing. After a while he steered off the wind and the cutter heeled over. "Ease sheets a bit," he called, "spill a bit of this wind." We did as he asked. Up ahead I could see some broken water, Mario pointed towards it, "Tusker Rock," he shouted, "just under the surface at this state of the tide. Ready to go about?"

"Ready!" Neil and I shouted out together. Mario swung the cutter round and we were heading for the harbour the wind almost directly behind us, the ebbing tide helping us along. About a quarter of a mile out he came up into the wind again and Neil and I got the mainsail down and lashed it to the boom. Then he resumed our course under foresail alone and we rounded the breakwater into the outer harbour. Mario put the tiller hard over and we swung round and came to a stop. The lifeboat reappeared then and towed us into the inner harbour.

"There's Aunty Bronwen," Mario shouted pointing up at a white haired lady wrapped in a black shawl. There were at least twenty other people including the off duty lifeboat crew all waving and cheering.

"Shouldn't she be wearing that witches hat thing?" I asked.

"Don't take the piss boyo," he replied, "they went out of fashion a bit back." They hoisted Mario up onto the quayside using a mobile crane as he sat in his wheelchair, the rest of us having to climb the iron ladder set in the stonework. We watched as Mario was welcomed back into the bosom of his family and friends and then we were all introduced and there were handshakes all round. "Meet my trusty crew," crowed Mario, "they deserve a bloody medal getting us back here in one piece. Three cheers for my crew, hip hip." And the cheers rang out around the tiny harbour as we stood smiling self consciously. "Alright boys," Mario shouted, "let's go." A burly lifeboatman wheeled him up to the road where a fleet of taxis and minibuses waited.

"Excuse please," I felt someone touch my elbow and turned to face a man of small stature with a distinctly oriental appearance, "I am Mr. Wang." We shook hands. "Mr. Mario ask me to take care of you."

I beckoned Neil and Jean over. "Mario mentioned you," I said and introduced the others.

"Mr. Mario ask me to take you to hotel. We make boat secure then bring all luggage ashore, okay?" We all looked at each other slightly bewildered, clambered back down to the cutter and packed our things into cases and grips. We locked all the hatches and watched as the mobile crane lifted our luggage up to the quay. The tide had already dropped a couple of feet and the bottom rungs of the iron ladder were slimy as we climbed back up to the quay. "Please to follow me," Mr. Wang smiled, "my car up near lifeboat shed." We followed, carrying our stuff.

33

No one spoke during the short drive along the Esplanade to the Seabank Hotel, Mr Wang pulled up at the entrance and ushered us into reception. "You all sign in," he commanded, "I arrange to get your luggage up to rooms."

We walked over to the desk to where the receptionist smiled brightly, "Mr. Armitage?" Neil stepped forward and she passed him a pen to sign in. She turned to Jean and me. "You must be Mr. and Mrs. Grayson," we exchanged embarrassed glances. "Mr. Franzoni has asked that you all have rooms overlooking the sea," she handed Neil a key, "room 59 Mr. Armitage." Neil took the key and headed for the elevator giving me a nudge and a wink as he passed. "Now Mr. Grayson would you sign here?"

I took the pen and stared at the sheet. It was years since I had visited a hotel with Jean. The girl looked quizzically at me as I just stood there with the pen poised. Jean must have sensed my hesitation for she stepped forward and said: "What room are we in? I'd like to freshen up."

"I'm so sorry," the girl produced a key, "it's Room 60, top floor." Jean took the key and walked towards the lift, I half turned and watched her go. "You alright Mr. Grayson?" the receptionist asked, "you haven't signed."

"Mm? Sorry I was miles away."

"That's okay," she said admiringly, "it must have been quite an adventure, sailing all that way and Mr. Franzoni . . ." she paused, "Mr. Franzoni so ill."

"Yes. Yes quite an adventure," I stared down at the blank sheet. Eventually I wrote *Mr and Mrs. J. Grayson, 76, Railway Terrace, Coventry, West Midlands.* I put the pen down and turned away making for the stairs.

I was in no hurry to climb to the third floor and by the time I arrived at room 60 our luggage had been delivered. The door stood ajar so I pushed it open and went in, Jean was looking out of the window. I stood there for several seconds just watching her sillouetted against the light, taking in every curve of her body, wanting her so and yet unsure of her feelings towards me. I closed the door and she turned. "Hello," I said.

"Well," she smiled, "Mario can certainly spring surprises."

"He's just a scheming bastard," I said defensively.

"As I see it," she said coolly, "we can only play this one way."

"How do you mean?"

"Well, Mario obviously thought he could maybe bring us together again, yes?" I nodded. "So he's got us this far already. Now, we could just treat this as a one night stand, plenty of people do that these days I'm told, no strings and all that. Then, if afterwards we both feel, well, more committed we take it from there."

I shrugged, "It all sounds a bit cold blooded doesn't it?"

"I'm just trying to be practical," she replied, "If you think it's not a good idea well, there's the bed and there's the settee. We could toss for it."

"Well, we'll just see how it goes then shall we?" I said lamely. The whole situation was too contrived, too artificial and here she was trying to turn it into some sordid one night stand. In the silence of the room the surf breaking on the rocks far below was the only sound.

After some moments she said: "Mind if I take a shower first?" and without waiting for an answer she picked up her grip from near the dressing table and went into the bathroom. I wandered over to the windows and stood looking out across the sea, the Devonshire hills were just visible as grey shapes on the far horizon, and the sea was flecked with whitecaps as the onshore wind fought with the ebbing tide. I was thinking of our approach to Menorca then, of the fearful surf filled entrance to Fornells harbour with Mario guiding us through.

I turned and surveyed the hotel room the result, once again, of Mario's generosity. It was a welcome change from the cramped quarters of the cutter and yet somehow I missed its cosy intimacy. The bedside phone rang and I picked it up. "Hello?"

"It's Mario. How do you like your room?"

"You crafty sod," I replied, "fancy dropping this on us."

"I thought you were both getting along fine," he said, "that day out on the briny when we were at Alderney and all that. When are you coming down? There's champagne and a buffet. Neil's already here. Still, if you want to stay in bed that's fine by me."

"We're not in bloody bed. She's having a shower and I'm just trying to come to terms with the situation."

"Just give her one boyo. You'll feel much better for it."

"Crude bastard. I'll be down soon." I hung up and looked in the mirror. I judged myself presentable enough for Mario's 'do' and I certainly did not want a shower, I much preferred a proper bath where I could lie and soak for a while. I knocked on the door of the bathroom, "Jean," I shouted, "I'm going down to the party. See you down there."

The party was in one of the large banqueting suites. Mr Wang and Neil were both looking after Mario, wheeling him around meeting people or getting him food and drink from the buffet. He certainly was a popular fellow judging by the many people attending his homecoming. Taped music could just be heard above the general hubbub as hotel staff mingled with relatives and friends. Several lifeboatmen stood about chatting in twos and threes and I spotted Aunty Bronwen sitting by a table deep in conversation with a sombre looking individual whom I later discovered was a Methodist preacher.

I helped myself to a glass of champagne from the tray a waitress offered and fell into conversation with someone. It was mainly small talk, the sort of generalised empty chit chat undertaken out of politeness and avoiding anything that might be in any way considered controversial. We were just making our second foray into discussing the weather when Jean appeared. She was dressed in a dark grey trouser suit and wore a bright red neckerchief, her hair arranged in the sort of pageboy style I remembered with the grey streaks at the temples adding to her mature beauty. She always did know how to dress and that outfit certainly turned a few heads. I excused myself from my companion and made my way towards her. Before I got halfway she was intercepted by two burly lifeboatmen offering drinks, I surreptitiously altered course and made for the tuna sandwiches.

"You were a bit too slow there, Jim." It was Neil at my elbow. "I'm just getting a sandwich for Mario. He's holding up well but he's really knackered, Mr. Wang and I are going to get him to bed in his flat soon."

"Will he be okay?" I asked, "I mean you've been on hand with his medication all the time up till now."

"Mr. and Mrs. Wang can cope with all that tonight. I've got to see about getting him into the hospice, that is if the stubborn old sod agrees. How are you getting on with your wife by the way? I see she's taken to the lifeboats. Some gorgeous hunks among them too." With that he grinned and went off.

I couldn't let the day pass without having a word with Mario's Aunty Bronwen so I muscled in on her part Welsh, part English conversation with the minister. It was hard to reconcile this white haired old lady with the bubbly young girl who had taken Mario's Uncle Benny under her wing all those years ago. We talked together for a while and just before I excused myself she asked about Spiro. "Lovely boy Spiro mind," she smiled, "proper gentleman too considering he's Greek but can he drink?" and so she prattled on the way she must have done with Benny when she guided him to his brother-in-law's cafe in Duffryn.

Soon after Mario left, the party began to break up. Jean still seemed to be getting along well with her lifeboatmen, they were laughing and joking together and I felt a sullen jealousy which bothered me, as did the feelings of animosity towards the gorgeous hunks as Neil described them. I decided to take a walk along the seafront, at least I would be out of sight of them fawning over her. As I passed reception the girl called me over. "Oh Mr. Grayson, Mr. Franzoni has booked you and your wife in for dinner this evening. It's at eight."

"And Mr. Armitage?"

"Mr. Armitage will be checking out. He has to go to Cardiff. Some arrangements for Mr. Franzoni I believe."

"Oh I see. Just the three of us then."

"Three?" The girl looked puzzled for a moment. "Oh no Mr. Grayson. Mr Armitage said Mr. Franzoni was all done in and will be having an early night at his flat."

"Right. Well, just the two of us." I walked out of the hotel and crossed the road, the tide had receded quite a way by then, the sound of the surf much fainter. I walked on the lower level of the promenade which gave some shelter from the wind which was still fairly strong, I stepped it out a bit because the afternoon was chilly and I had not brought my fleece. By the time I had covered less than half the distance to the harbour I was thoroughly chilled so I turned back. A figure approaching in the distance looked familiar and as we drew closer I realised it was Jean walking towards me and carrying my fleece and sailing jacket. "Fancy meeting you here," I said.

"Saw you leaving and realised you'd be perished."

"Cheers," I struggled into the garments and immediately felt warmer.

"Were you going back anyway?"

"Only because I was cold."

"So shall we carry on down to the breakwater? Maybe have a look at the harbour?"

"Why not?" And so began a magic afternoon. We walked to end of the breakwater and back, climbed down onto the deck of the cutter and discussed the items of care and maintenance it was in need of after its long voyage, and then explored the rock pools all the way back to the hotel.

Our conversation was unforced, totally natural, the way it had been on that Corfu holiday all those years back. I found myself telling her about finding the icon, describing the ghostly emptiness of Ano Perithea, telling her of Mario's angry outburst at Brindisi over the icon's authenticity and in no time at all it seemed we were back at the hotel and it was getting dark.

The receptionist handed me the key to our room then turned to Jean. "The maitre d'hotel would like a word madam. Would you come this way?" Jean shot me a puzzled glance before going off with her.

"Mr. Grayson?" I turned to face a tall thin man dressed like a pall bearer. He looked me up and down with a practised eye. "Would you just turn around for me sir?" I did as he asked. "Ah, just as I thought sir. I think you'll find the clothes suitable. If not just telephone reception."

"What clothes?"

"Well sir, Mr. Franzoni left instructions that you and your wife might like to dress for dinner. He realised you had not brought suitable attire with you because of the nature of your um, holiday. So he has asked us to furnish an evening suit for you. There is a black double breasted one or you may prefer the white tuxedo?"

"So where are these clothes?" I asked in surprise.

"In your room sir, laid out on the bed. Your wife is at this moment choosing from a selection of evening dresses."

"I see. Well, thank you. This is all quite a surprise."

"Mr. Franzoni wanted to, how did he put it? Create the appropriate ambience? I can also recommend the table d'hote menu tonight sir and we have a modern jazz quartet to entertain."

"Wonderful."

"So Mr. Grayson, bon appetit and er, bon chance." Maybe it was just my imagination but I could have sworn that the old swine had a lecherous grin on his face. Still, this was all part of Mario's master plan so I was ready to play along with it. I just hoped it wasn't too contrived for Jean but then it was she, after all, who had suggested the one night stand scenario. I tried to put that out of my mind, went upstairs and, just for once, had a shower for quickness. After some hesitation I chose the white tuxedo, left a note for Jean and made it to the bar in record time.

The dinner was superb, the wine excellent, the music suitably seductive. We sat together in a shadowy corner at an intimate table for two. The dress she had chosen flattered her shape of course but also her taste. "Suits you," I said. "Thank you kind sir," she replied with a fluttering of eyelashes that got me right in the loins.

No need to go into the details of that night. We stayed until well after midnight and then took the lift to conserve our energy. Moonlight cast its faint shadows across the room as we undressed in silence. There was no frantic tearing of clothes from each others back, no grasping and clawing for each other, just a warm and tender conjoining of our bodies. It was as if our long separation had engendered a built in patience which each of us exploited in full in order to extract the maximum pleasure from our renewed intimacy.

I wished that night could have lasted forever. But at 6am the phone rang.

"What time was this?" I asked.

"My wife she think 'bout four o'clock this morning."

Jean rolled over. "Who is it?" she asked.

I covered the mouth piece and whispered to her: "Mr. Wang." Then I spoke into the instrument, "tell me again," I said, "from the beginning."

Mario's penthouse flat was connected to the ground floor by a small lift. It had a dual role, being used as a dumb waiter linking the basement kitchen to Mr. Wang's ground and first floor restaurants and also to give Mario easy access to the outside world. Apparently Mrs. Wang had been awakened by the sound of the lift about 4am. She was tired having had a busy evening in the restaurant and was roused only to semi consciousness by the noise. She went back to sleep.

The human subconscious is a powerful and tenacious thing. It would not let Mrs. Wang sleep easily, it knew that there was no reason for the lift to have been operated at four in the morning. It caused her to toss and turn for almost two hours before waking her with a start telling her that something was amiss. She roused her husband.

Mr. Wang got up and went out of the bedroom along the corridor to the lift, he pressed the call button but nothing happened. He used the stairs and found the lift on the ground floor, its doors still open. It was a strict house rule that the lift doors should always be closed after use to enable it to respond to the next user on whichever floor it was needed. If the doors were not closed it must have been a deliberate omission. Mr. Wang got into the lift closed the doors and pressed the penthouse button.

The room looked the same as it had done the previous day when he and Neil had put Mario to bed after the welcome home party, a little tidier perhaps, correspondence and documents set out neatly on the dressing table. A little too neatly Mr. Wang thought. It was then he decided to call me at the Seabank.

"Could he have gone down to the boat?" I asked.

"Is possible I think. But why?"

"No idea," I said, "look, we'll go and check. What's your number?" I scribbled it down on the hotel notepaper and got dressed.

Jean had already grabbed her things and gone to the bathroom, she emerged fully dressed. "It's Mario isn't it?" she asked.

"He's gone walkabout somewhere by the sound of it," I told her, "I said I'd check the boat, you coming?"

"Too right."

The morning was cold and damp. A grey sea mist shrouded everything, muffling the sound of the waves upon the unseen rocks beyond the limit of visibility as we hurried along the promenade towards the harbour. We peered down at the cutter. It looked sad and forlorn in the early light and there was no sign of life aboard. Suddenly Jean said: "It'gone!" I glanced at her. "The dinghy," she gasped, "it's not there."

The saloon skylight, usually hidden by the upturned Mirror dinghy, reflected the grey overcast, the green tarpaulin cover lay crumpled upon the deck where it had been hurriedly cast aside. We turned away without a word and made for the end of the breakwater with its small white painted lighthouse. There was nothing to be seen from there except the grey sea, calm and sullen in the mist as the tide came in. "The wind should get up a bit with the flood tide," Jean said quietly, "hopefully clear this fog away."

"You think Mario's gone off in the dinghy?" I asked.

"Too much of a coincidence don't you think?" she answered, "Mario gone from his room, the dinghy gone from here. Who else would have taken it?" I said nothing. She was right of course and I just stood there staring out into the murk feeling totally helpless. "You'd better phone Mr. Wang," she said.

Less than fifteen minutes later the inshore lifeboat crew had launched and vanished into the mist which was already thinning, dispersed by the breeze that Jean had predicted would arrive with the incoming tide. Over towards Southerndown on the other side of the bay a watery sun picked out the fields and the white painted bungalows and houses as the mist rolled away and suddenly I saw it. I grabbed Jean's arm. "Look," I exclaimed, "over there. What's that on Tusker Rock?"

Behind me a voice cried: "I see it!" Mr. Wang had arrived, he was looking through his binoculars, "it got red sail. It floating I think. Here." He handed me the glasses and I focussed them on the distant rock. The unmistakeable red sail of the Mirror dinghy stood out against the grey rock and the foaming surf, the wreck of the actual craft was less discernible. That was being buffeted about by the incoming waves, I could see that it had been holed in several places, its mast was no longer in place, it floated nearby, still attached to the hull by a single piece of standing rigging. There was no sign of Mario.

Breakfast back at the hotel was a quiet affair. Word of Mario's disappearance had spread and the staff were subdued though still efficient. The delicious memory of our lovemaking last night was lost in a curious feeling of guilt as I contemplated Mario's furtive voyage. As we both slept he must have been struggling to launch the dinghy in the pre-dawn darkness, fighting for every breath that he took.

Jean and I watched from our room as the half submerged dinghy was towed back to the harbour then the inshore lifeboat swept the coast from Nash Point to Baglan Bay without result. About midday Neil arrived back from the hospice and the three of us sat in the hotel bar gloomily sipping our drinks while awaiting news.

The call when it came was not unexpected. I was summoned to Reception where they had Mr. Wang on the line. Mario's body had been washed up on Coney Beach, he said and he was just leaving for the mortuary in Bridgend for formal identification. I suggested that Neil, as Mario's nurse, should accompany him also. He readily agreed and Jean and I waved from the hotel entrance as they drove off together. "D'you think it was suicide?" she asked.

"The inquest verdict will be misadventure I expect," I replied. "Mr. Wang said nothing about a note and Mario would know that suicide would negate any life insurance. It may have been deliberate but Mario was canny enough to make it look like a sailing accident."

"Is that what you think?"

"I'd bet on it."

"So where does this leave us?" she asked.

"Has Mario achieved his objective you mean? Getting us back together?" She looked across at me but said nothing. "I love you Jean," I said softly, "I always have in spite of everything. We've got a lot of catching up to do. Will you come back to Coventry with me as a first step?"

She slid her arm through mine. "As a first step," she agreed.

35

Three weeks later, at about the same time that Jean and I were boarding the train at Coventry and heading for Wales, Neil was picking up Spiro at Cardiff airport. We all met up at the pub in Duffryn.

Things had moved fast since that fateful day at Porthcawl. The inquest was over, the verdict as I had predicted was indeed 'misadventure', the cause of death heart failure brought about by exposure and the cancer of course. Mario's will was all but executed thanks to Neil and Mario's solicitor. The Royal National Lifeboat Institute, the RNLI, was the beneficiary of the bulk of Mario's estate while various friends and relatives received bequests, some in cash some in property. Neil, Jean and I received generous cheques and the residue paid for all the hotel expenses, Spiro's air fare plus the funeral costs and legal expenses.

Mario was laid to rest alongside his Uncle Benny in the chapel cemetery overlooking the valley, there was a light westerly breeze laden with a fine drizzle as we all stood hatless around the grave. Mr. Wang stood with an umbrella protecting Aunty Bronwen from the damp as the coffin, draped in the Italian Tricolour and the Welsh Dragon, was lowered into the ground and out of the corner of my eye I saw Spiro cross himself as he fiddled with a rosary, his lips moving in some silent Greek chant.

"First time I've noticed that," Neil said to me softly.

"What?"

"Red white and green."

"What are you on about?" I whispered.

"The flags," he said, "Italy and Wales. They've got the same colours, red white and green."

We four, myself, Jean, Neil and Spiro were the last to file past the grave and throw some soil onto the coffin, Spiro held back and I saw him take something from the pocket of his overcoat. He looked at me, his tear streaked face gypsy dark from the Mediterranean sun, "I bring him something," he said hoarsely, "a little bit of Kerkyra." And there in his hand was a small Greek flag, the sort any tourist shop might sell, he unfolded it to show me the generous handful of loamy soil he had brought from Corfu. He shook the soil into the grave, the flag fluttering down after it. Once again he crossed himself, "God bless you Mario my friend," he breathed.

Needless to say Spiro got very drunk at the wake later, he taught Aunty Bronwen a Greek dance and a few choice Greek swear words and eventually Neil managed to calm him down and get him to eat some food to absorb the drink. Some time during the afternoon Neil took Jean and me on one side. "What are your plans?" he asked.

"We just bought a day return ticket from Coventry" I replied, "so we'll be heading back. Why?"

"Just wondered if you fancied a sail in the pilot cutter."

I looked across at Jean. "Well, as for me," I said, "I'd rather not right now. We've not come prepared at all." Jean nodded her agreement.

"The thing is," Neil went on, "Mario's donated the thing to the Maritime Museum at Swansea. I just thought it might be good for us all to sail it there together. Spiro as well. Sort of grand finale to the whole expedition as it were."

The prospect had a certain dramatic appeal. Jean and I thought it over for at least ten seconds before agreeing then Neil made all the arrangements. So the following morning the four of us, including Spiro with one hell of a hangover, sailed out of Porthcawl harbour escorted by the inshore lifeboat and watched by Mr. Wang and the staff of the Seabank Hotel all waving from the breakwater.

We must have looked a strange bunch, Spiro in his funeral clothes, Jean and me the same. The only one looking remotely like a sailor in oilskins and lifejacket was Neil as he stood at the tiller.

Halfway across Swansea Bay the lifeboat sheered away with waved farewells from the crew and that was when I remembered the luger. I went down to my tiny berth aft of the chain locker and retrieved it. I stood there for several moments feeling the deadly weight of the weapon in my hand. Presently I went back up on deck. Spiro was standing beside Neil who was at the helm, I walked over to them, "remember this?" I said.

Spiro flung his latest cigarette end over the side. "That what we get from Ano Perithea?" he asked, "Let me see."

I passed the pistol over to him and watched as he examined it, he released the safety catch and aimed it at a seagull which had alighted some distance away. "It's no good," I said, remembering that awful occasion in Mario's cabin, "the ammo's got damp. Buried too long in that spooky ruined town up in the mountains."

"Pity," he said still pointing it at the seagull. Suddenly there was a loud crack and a little spurt of water shot up alongside the bird which flew off unconcerned. "What you say about ammo?" he asked.

I just stood there totally speechless as he continued firing. To my stunned amazement he emptied the entire magazine into the sea.

By general consent, the pistol was ceremoniously consigned to the deep there and then and no one was any the wiser about Mario's abortive suicide attempt. The bullet that had thwarted it lies at the bottom of a swanky marina in Gibraltar.

All that happened some weeks ago.

There is talk of Porthcawl having a brand new state of the art inshore lifeboat. It is rumoured that it may be called the Mario Franzoni.

The Bristol Channel pilot cutter, the one we sailed all the way back from Corfu, lies afloat in the harbour at the National Maritime Museum in Swansea now. Jean and I plan to visit there soon and maybe meet up with Neil if his work at the hospice allows. There is a standing invitation from Aunty Bronwen to call on her at Duffryn any time and maybe sample some of the apple tart or rhubarb crumble so enjoyed by Mario in the past. Also we received a letter from Mr. Wang at Porthcawl offering us a free Chinese meal any time we are in South Wales and we may have time to fit that in also.

Number 76 Railway Terrace in Coventry is up for sale. The place will be too small for us soon as Jean has told me she is pregnant. The timing seems to fit in with that night at the Seabank Hotel. It is early days yet but we have discussed names together. If it is a girl we are both agreed on Marion Bronwen. If a boy I would like Benjamin Neil. Jean is not quite sure about *Neil*. She sometimes accuses me of fancying him, I'm sure she's only joking.

Spiro telephoned his congratulations and best wishes the other day and invited us over to stay with him for a few weeks in *the bloody building site in Kerkyra*. I assume he meant Sidari. I'm sure we'll take him up on it because in the spring we plan to take a train to Italy and visit Monte Cassino Abbey. I want to show Jean that icon. We could then carry on to Brindisi and get a ferry to Corfu Town where Spiro could pick us up in his battered old Fiat.

We'll see.

THE END